Beyond Kidding

LYNDA CLARK

First published by Fairlight Books 2019

Fairlight Books
Summertown Pavilion, 18-24 Middle Way, Oxford, OX2 7LG

Copyright © Lynda Clark 2019

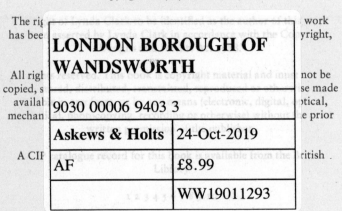

ISBN 978-1-912054-84-8

www.fairlightbooks.com

Printed and bound in Great Britain

Designed by kid-ethic

For Graham.

Here's mine.

PART ONE
THEN & NOW

1

Rob gazed out of the police car window. In the pre-morning light everything looked grey.

Was he really going to claim someone else's child? Because that was really wrong. Wronger than all the other stuff by far.

He drummed out a little ditty on the passenger door with his fingertips.

And what if it wasn't over there? What if they did DNA tests and found out the child wasn't his? Or what if they took his word for it, and he had to have a funeral for someone else's kid? Because surely the only explanation for them having *found* the kid was that they'd unearthed a body too disfigured for them to be certain. It was the only possibility.

No, better to say it isn't him. Better to just view the odd dead kiddy every now and then than face all the other possible consequences. His stomach unknotted a little and he knew that was the right thing to do. Well, the rightest he could do at present.

'Mr Buckland? Mr Buckland?'

He raised his head, realising they'd come to a stop and he'd been staring aimlessly into the footwell for a good long while. The policewoman beside him patted his hand.

'You've really got nothing to worry about,' she said, unclicking her seatbelt. 'I'm sure you'll feel much better once you've seen him.' Rob watched as she walked round to the passenger door, tall and skinny-looking.

'I know this is a big moment,' she said, and it seemed opening the car door was a struggle for those stringy arms. 'But there's really no cause for concern. I'm sure he'll be glad to see you, even if he can't say it.'

She stood expectantly holding the door open, a gentle smile on her face. He returned her smile grimly and followed her into the police station. Her shoes squeaked on the plastic floor tiles. His didn't.

Maybe this is a dream.

She greeted a colleague at the front desk, explained Rob's presence, and then led him down the corridor to an interview room. Rob's stomach flipped. He was suddenly gripped with a terrible, irrational fear. Something bad was on the other side of that door, and after he'd seen it there would be no going back. He didn't want her to open the door, but her hand was already on the handle, turning it.

It isn't him, remember. Even if whatever corpse they've found resembles him somehow, it can't be him, because it isn't possible.

Detective Bellamy, big and hale and hearty as ever, rose from his seat and pumped Rob's hand. Bellamy's large, thick palm was greasy with sweat, and he seemed unsure of when to stop, or what he'd do when the handshaking ended.

Rob allowed the handshaking to continue. He didn't want it to stop either, because when it did, he'd have to react. He'd have to figure out a whole series of things to do and say to the figure in the chair beside Bellamy. The living, breathing figure. Rob's arm became a piston, independent of his body. Bellamy spoke, but he may as well have been clicking and grunting, pouring out a bevy of alien noises, because all Rob could do was stare and stare at the impossible, alive child on the chair.

Everything about him was terribly, uncannily perfect. Huge dark eyes, russet hair, a dusting of freckles. Rob didn't need to pull back the lips to check for the gap in the teeth because he knew it was there. The kid was Brodie. Statue-still and silent; the only difference between him and Rob's photo was the lack of a smile.

Finally, Detective Bellamy let go of Rob's hand. He sat down and indicated the chair opposite. For a second there was a fleeting moment of doubt in his kind, hard eyes and he glanced from Rob to Brodie and back again.

Of course. Most parents would've sprinted to their child and wrapped their arms round him, sobbing with joy.

Rob thought he should probably do something like that. Anything other than staring with his mouth open. He approached the kid cautiously, tentatively. Glanced back at Bellamy. Bellamy smiled, looking relieved Rob was finally behaving as expected.

Rob was scared to touch the kid.

If he did, it meant he was actually doing it. Claiming someone else's child as his own. Someone's living child. That was worse than claiming a dead one, surely?

Rob knelt down in front of the boy and peered into his face.

The boy looked back, eyes blank and trusting as a seaside donkey. Slowly, slowly Rob leaned forward and put his arms round the boy.

He rested his chin on the boy's shoulder, convinced the kid would let out a banshee pod-person wail, splitting the eardrums of everyone in a hundred-mile radius. But the kid stayed quiet. Didn't react at all, in fact. Sat rigid and unyielding as if he was carved out of wood. But he was a real boy. Rob could hear his quiet breaths, feel his back slowly rising and falling. He had a slightly odd smell, almost like the upholstery in a brand new car, a scent evincing durability and precision engineering. Other than that, he was exactly as Rob would have expected Brodie to look in the flesh.

Rob pulled away and looked to Detective Bellamy again.

'Where...?' he asked. 'I mean, how...?'

'Darndest thing,' said Bellamy, waving a teacup at an officer standing just outside the door. 'PC Cornwell found him wandering down the high street at 2am. Alone. A little confused and frightened, but otherwise fine. Cornwell brought him here and I recognised him right away. Even wearing the clothes he disappeared in. Couldn't believe my eyes!'

You couldn't. How do you think I feel?

*

'That must have been incredible.' Jules's eyes are shining. She's already got the wrong impression, seems to think I'm telling her some heart-warming story of how I was reunited with my son all those months ago. I thought she was smarter than me. I mean, if this was that kind of story, I'd tell it in a restaurant, on a proper date for once, or in the work canteen with a shared slice of cheesecake. I'd tell it freely, anywhere. I wouldn't be telling her in the confines of my mildewed bathroom. I wouldn't have ushered her in here and locked the door to keep my 'son' out. I wouldn't be petrified he had his head against the door right now, listening in.

I can't decide if she's purposefully ignored the bits where I said I was confused and afraid to see a real live child, or if she's just latched on to the good parts. Good parts to her mind, anyway. And why would she think anything else? I made her think that. I made her believe getting Brodie back was the most important thing in all the universe to me. She's only reacting based on the information I've given her.

Unless...

What if she's the same as Bummer? What if she can't grasp what I'm telling her because of whatever's affecting him? I consider stopping right there. I don't know if I can put myself through that again. But what else am I going to do? Mum's in Malta, and the sad fact is, I don't have anyone else. Jules and Bummer are all I've got.

She's staring at me, expectant, waiting for me to continue.

*

By the time the paperwork was complete the sun was coming up. A different police driver took them home in an unmarked car. He gave Rob some cards with contact information on them and said someone would be in touch soon. Rob watched him drive off up the main road until the car was a distant speck. The kid had already wandered inside, up to the flat like he knew where Rob lived.

Rob let him in, avoiding touching him even in passing. He didn't want to touch the kid, not at all. Not without witnesses. He told himself this was because when the kid's real parents finally showed up, he didn't want them to say he was a molester or anything, but really it was because being in close proximity to Brodie made him feel strange. Like staring at an optical illusion. He went to make the bed for Brodie and then fetched Bummer's sleeping bag from the airing cupboard for himself.

Is he a pod person? Rob wondered, smoothing the sheets and straightening the duvet cover. *Made of me when I was a child?* That might explain why looking at him made Rob feel so sick and wrong. *They say if you meet your doppelgänger, you die.*

Clean bedding would probably have been nice for the kid, but Rob was damn tired and even used sheets had to be better than bunking down in a crack house or wherever this kid had come from. He went to tell the kid his bed was ready and found him in the kitchen, studying the finger-paintings on the fridge intently.

'Are you a pod person?' Rob blurted, immediately feeling foolish. The kid stared at him. If he understood the question, he gave no indication, swiftly returning his attention to the paintings.

Is that... recognition? Does he remember those? The kid pressed his fingertip onto one of the painted fingermarks as if comparing the size. They almost matched, almost as if he did paint it, as if he did remember. *Well he can't, because that's Bummer's little finger. May look too small to be his, but it's—*

Rob's stomach went cold. The painting. It was back there.

It had gone when Bellamy came round to investigate the burglary, hadn't it? He'd asked about the Blu-tack and the painting that wasn't there.

It was definitely the same picture. A splodgy fish in green, with big blue eyes and pouty red lips. The kid traced the lumps in the paint with his index finger, taking time over the blobs that made up the googly eyes, before turning back to Rob. A curtain dropped down behind his eyes as he did so, returning them to their blank, expressionless state. Rob had to master his roiling bowels and be a father.

'C'mon then,' he said, leading the way to the bedroom.

The kid followed, treading softly and staring down at his feet like he'd never walked on carpets before.

Maybe he hasn't. Are crack dens usually carpeted? Are spaceships?

Rob pulled back the duvet, gestured to the bed. The kid looked at him vacantly.

'You can sleep here.' No response. 'Sleep?' Rob mimed sleeping, making a pillow of his hands and laying his head against it. Still those black eyes, tunnelling into Rob's soul. 'Oh, you want pyjamas?' Rob had no idea what the kid wanted. He had no idea what any kid wanted. He'd never had one and he hadn't been one for a long time. He rooted around in the wardrobe anyway, because at least then he only had to feel those eyes drilling into his back rather than actually look at them. A bit of digging turned up the horrendous red-striped flannel pyjamas his mum had given him one Christmas.

'Here, how about these?' As he turned to offer them to the kid, he thought he caught the fleeting tail-end of a smile disappearing, but the kid looked blank as ever now.

The kid wouldn't take the pyjamas. Rob tried putting them in the kid's hands, but he kept his arms locked down at his sides.

Well, I'm not about to strip him.

'Come on, Brodie, into bed.' A weird thing happened when he said the kid's name. He blinked and looked at Rob as if he was looking at him for the first time. Then, slowly, like petals unfurling, opened his arms.

This is it, any second now it's pod-person wail and my brains bleeding out my ears.

But the kid just waited, patient as a tree, and Rob realised he wanted to be picked up.

'You can't get into bed yourself? Big boy like you, I'm sure you can.' Still the kid waited, forcing Rob to bend and pick him up, and the moment his arms were round Brodie's waist, the kid wrapped his arms round Rob's neck and held on tight. Rob froze, waiting for tendrils to come snaking out of the boy's fingertips and force their way down his nose and throat, extracting DNA to make a plant replica. But the kid just rested his chin on Rob's shoulder. *Ridiculous. Too many movies.* So Rob lowered him onto the mattress, pulled the duvet over his legs and stood at the side of the bed.

The kid sat bolt upright, never taking those deep, dark eyes off Rob's face for one second. Not even another blink. Rob had never paid much attention to people's blinking behaviour, but he was pretty sure that wasn't normal.

'I'll just be through there if you need anything. You like bacon? Sure you do. We'll have a nice big fry-up, for breakfast, huh? And maybe ring Uncle Bummer and get him round.' *See if he knows what the hell's going on.* He moved to step back, but the kid's arm shot out, lightning fast, grabbing his wrist.

The fingers were small and thin, but they gripped tight, turning white.

'What?'

Rob watched the kid's fingernails closely, still mindful of those tendrils however ridiculous an idea they might be, heart hammering. The kid's hand became moist, but remained cold, so Rob guessed the sweat was his own. They stayed like that a while, regarding each other, but the kid didn't let go until Rob sat on the edge of the bed to ease his aching calves.

'You want me to stay?'

Brodie shuffled down in the bed and closed his eyes.

This is some fucked-up shit.

*

'They've remade that movie again, you know,' Jules pipes up.

'What?' I can't believe she's being like this. Flippant. Is that the word?

'The one with the plant replica people. We should go see it.'

For a brief moment, I allow myself a glimpse into that imagined world. A world where I leave Brodie at Bummer's for the evening and go to the cinema with Jules to watch some soulless Hollywood remake of a sci-fi classic. We'd eat nachos even though they're a rip-off, but not popcorn, because why does anyone eat popcorn? It's like foam packing peanuts. We'd almost be a normal couple. I smile at the thought. But we don't live in that world, we live in this one, the one where I've fucked up every significant life choice I ever made.

Well, except befriending Jules. That one was good. She's probably regretting it now, but at least she's here.

'Maybe,' I say. Then, trying to get her back on track: 'But don't you see how frightened I was? Of him?'

She laughs. 'Of course you were! You hadn't seen him in weeks. You felt like he could be taken away again at any second, right?' *Wrong.* 'And you watch a load of sci-fi and so your overactive imagination took over...' She raises her wine glass like she's about to make a toast. 'Your overactive imagination and love of sci-fi are ninety per cent of the reason we're friends.'

'What's the other ten per cent?' I ask in spite of myself.

'You buy me cheesecake.'

*

Time didn't matter with Bummer. He operated outside the usual circadian rhythms, so calling him straight after breakfast wasn't an issue. He answered the phone after a couple of rings. In the background Rob could hear money-off announcements over a PA system, the clashing of trolleys and whichever kid he was with saying: 'I wanna *Blight Brigade* comic. I WANNA *BLIGHT BRIGADE* COMIC!'

'All right, Kidder?'

'Yeah,' said Rob, automatically, then: 'No. Not really.'

'What's up?' Bummer's words crunched. He was eating something on the way round the supermarket.

'The kid's here. They brought him back last night.'

'What?'

Rob felt a tiny thrill of relief at the shock in Bummer's voice. This was what he needed. Someone who knew the impossibility of Brodie's existence.

'I know, right?'

'Kidder, that's fantastic! I can't believe it! I'm coming right over!' And he hung up.

'What? No!' Rob gasped into the dead phone.

That's not what you're supposed to say. You're doing this all wrong.

He looked back at the sleeping boy. He was motionless, deeply asleep, unaware of the fact he didn't exist.

2

'I meant to ask, actually, why do you call him Bummer?'

I stare at her, incredulous. She's sitting on the edge of the bath, her glass of wine casually tilted as if we're chatting in a cosy bistro. My voice is hushed so the kid can't hear what I'm saying, and she copies my low volume, but the room is small and echoing, so whispers fill every corner.

'That's what you took from that? I tell you all that, and that's what you fixate on?'

'Oh, I mean sure, the other stuff is pretty interesting.' Her eyes dance with that mischievous fire I adore and despise in equal amounts. 'But c'mon! You call the guy Bummer!'

I put my wine glass down on the edge of the sink. This isn't going how I thought it would. I thought Jules would come through for me where Bummer had failed. I thought she'd look into my eyes and know I wasn't a crazy liar. Well, of course I'm a liar. I invented Brodie and Karen and that stuff on my CV about lacrosse... And my mental state isn't exactly the best right now, what with the broken sleep and no one else remembering things how I remember them, but... not where this is concerned. No lies and no craziness here, I know it.

She sees the hurt in my eyes and the mockery drains from her expression.

'Sorry Rob,' she says. 'This is heavy stuff. You know I don't deal well with heavy stuff. I make stupid jokes instead.'

Normally I love that about her, but nothing has been normal this last month or so. I drain my glass. The white wine's so cheap it burns my sinuses. That's what happens when you get it free from a Chinese takeaway, I guess. I wince at the pain and pinch the bridge of my nose.

'Maybe I didn't go back far enough,' I say, more to myself than to her. 'I guess there was lots of weird stuff that happened even before Brodie showed up. The Empornium alone had so much weirdness...'

'But Bummer!'

'He likes to bum things, okay?!'

She nods, looking guilty.

Eyes closed against the pain in my head, I try to come up with a suitable starting point, a time before Brodie, that might help explain things. 'Yeah, that was it. It all started because of that bloody woman. The bloody woman with the vibrator.'

*

'It didn't work from the moment I took it out of the packet,' the woman said to me.

Women rarely came into the Empornium, but when they did, they fell into two categories: giggling hen parties and this woman. Good-looking once, now a little faded round the edges.

Puckered mouth and crinkled eyes hidden behind expensive lipstick and the latest anti-crease make-up. Probably a doctor or a lawyer. Maybe a local councillor. Some pillar of the community.

'Hasn't been used, I assure you.'

Rob ran a practised eye along the shaft. The Birthday Every Day model had a gloss finish. This one's coating was dull. He flicked the switch. On unused examples, even faulty ones, the Birthday Every Day's switch had a firm, satisfying click. This switch was loose. He put the Birthday Every Day back on the counter and looked at the woman. She hitched her handbag higher on her shoulder and pursed her lips, braced for confrontation. Any moment now, she'd get hostile.

Rob knew she was lying. He could see it in the tightening of her top lip, in the minute narrowing of her eyes. He imagined saying to her: 'Madam, if you've never used this product, would you be so good as to allow me one small test? One tiny thing by way of proof. I'd like to lick it, right now. Here in front of you, just run my tongue along it. One. Good. Long. Lick. Because it wouldn't taste of anything, right? Just plastic?' To see that moment's hesitation, that second of recognition that she'd been caught out. That's how Bummer would have handled it. But Bummer had an iron backbone, whereas Rob was a bigger pussy than the latex XLs in the window display.

So instead, he said: 'Exchange or refund?' and slung it in the used bin with the others.

'Refund please,' she said chirpily. 'Cash. I have my receipt right here.'

Course she did. They always did.

Rob took it. It had that dried-out look receipts sometimes

got when they were really old. Text faded to nothing. He didn't bother trying to make out the date, because he knew he probably sold her the thing when they were new in last year. He opened the till drawer. *Dammit Bummer.* No pound coins. He tutted to himself under his breath.

'Do you have the penny?' he asked. 'So I can give you thirty-five, rather than thirty-four ninety-nine?'

'No,' she said without consulting her handbag, 'I don't.'

Just have a look for Christ's sake. Everyone has a few pence stashed somewhere, you just can't be bothered to look, you lazy cow.

'For Christ's sake,' he muttered, then loudly, over his shoulder: 'Bummer!' The woman frowned, exposing wrinkles beneath the layers of concealer, as crumpled and dusty as her receipt. He corrected himself. 'VIC!'

'I'm on the bog!'

Rob rolled his eyes and took a deep breath.

Fucking Bummer.

Bummer's default setting was 'on the bog'. It was his hobby. The windowsill of the toilet was like a newsagent's, piled high with books, magazines and newspapers, enabling Bummer to remain in there for hours at a time.

'You all right to wait while I nip and get some change?' asked Rob, keeping his tone as polite as he could manage. She made a show of checking her watch and peering at her car parked at the kerb outside. The protesters hurried to get into her eyeline, waving their signs with renewed vigour.

'Well, all right then,' she answered with a sigh. 'If it can't be helped.'

Rob took a twenty-pound note out of the till and locked

the drawer behind him. Someone who'd return a used sex aid as faulty would probably think nothing of helping themselves to a few quid.

Outside the shop door his path was immediately barred by two elderly men and a tall, prim-looking woman. Their numbers just kept growing, like bacteria. About fifteen in total, although he didn't want to stand around and count. They pressed their placards into his face, bellowing scripture.

'You are poisoning the city's youth!' said the woman before launching into a lengthy biblical quote. He let her do the whole passage, imagining taking a lighter from his pocket and setting her sign ablaze. He never would, of course. He didn't own a lighter, for starters. The closest he came to rebellion was trying to step around them, but they closed in, using their placards to block his escape route.

'Your products devalue the act of love!' said one of the old men. Rob glanced at them briefly, sizing them up. The only one directly blocking him was the old fella who'd just spoken.

Knocking him out of the way, would that be assault? Can't weigh more than a sheet of paper.

A woman with a pushchair stepped in, looking up at Rob for a moment before saying to the others: 'Remember, this poor man is without a moral compass. He needs our pity, not our scorn.' Rob wondered about smiling at her. She seemed almost sympathetic. 'He'll be out of a job soon anyway,' the woman continued, wiping the drool from her toddler's chin with a tissue. 'When he's on the streets he'll see the error of his ways.'

The error of my ways is not owning a lighter.

The toddler had a placard that read 'MY EYES ARE

NOT YOUR CESSPOOL', although its woolly hat was pulled down so far over its eyes, the only cesspool it was privy to was shitty knitting. Thankfully the baby dropped its dummy, and when the old man stooped to pick it up, Rob made use of the distraction to scoot through the picket line and into Baby World, knowing they wouldn't follow him there.

Out of the corner of his eye he noticed the petition, pinned to the window with the suckered foot of a fluffy orange cat. A further reminder of the Empornium's precarious position. And Rob's. Just inside the door, he steeled himself, praying he got Heather and not the other one.

Oh, thank you Jebus.

Heather stood behind the counter tall and solid as a beef cow, gazing off into the middle distance. The shop was quiet, just one young couple drifting along the aisle, fingers loosely linked. Rob watched them stop in front of a row of cots, comparing the various inoffensive pastel designs. Lemon-coloured ducklings or beige towelling lambs.

'Do we want our child to be mundane, or generic?'

'All right, Heather?' Rob called out, trying to sound cheerful and matey, but not too friendly, because she always looked like she was waiting for him to ask her out. She turned those big bovine eyes on him and smiled.

'Rob!' she beamed, square jaw working gum.

'Look, I'm in a bit of a rush, out of pounds and Bummer's in the bog, can you change this for me?' He waved the twenty at her. She gawped at it.

'Why's he always in the bog?'

'He lives off Frubes and curry, look, quickly Heather, please, I've got a customer waiting.'

For a moment there was a stab of hurt in those big deep eyes and then she took the twenty and disappeared into the back of the shop, leaving Rob to feel like a complete shit. He knew he should be nicer to her, but there was always the risk she'd try to kiss him or something. Completely unrequested, an image of himself and Heather, naked and slick with sweat, popped into his head. It made him feel sick and weird, worse than when he'd pictured himself with that sexy cartoon rabbit from the chocolate adverts. Needing a distraction, he watched the young couple giggle at the breast pumps.

The woman didn't even look pregnant yet, but she must've been, because she put the breast pump back on the shelf and pulled her partner along by the elbow to look at playpens.

Imagine being that organised. Imagine actually planning to have a kid, rather than just getting them by accident like Bummer did.

While watching the couple, Rob had strayed in among the cuddly animals. They freaked him out, and not just because some of them were rabbits in dresses. All those staring glassy eyes and fixed grinning mouths just weren't right. One step away from the vacant expressions of the sex dolls. The fluffy toys smelled weird, too, like they'd been disinfected and bleached and starched so their fur couldn't house one single germ. He picked up a pristine white bear and sniffed its fluffy head. Nothing. His own childhood bear had a wonderful, warm, slightly singed smell from being left in front of the electric bar fire.

He sniffed the hypoallergenic non-smell again.

'What are you doing here?'

Rob jumped, banging his hip on the shelving unit and dropping the bear on the floor.

How does she do that, the creepy old bag!

The Poo Witch advanced on him from behind a display of cut-price prams and pushchairs and picked up the bear. Her hair and clothes were all the same dull shade of brown. Her eyeshadow and lipstick were brown, too, with a glossy, slightly sticky look to them, like she fell face first into a mud puddle and didn't wipe it away properly. The only thing not brown was her skin, which was flaky white with red patches. She was like a stain on the otherwise sanitised, child-friendly surroundings, patient zero to the protesting multitudes outside.

'Change,' he stammered, rubbing his hip.

Where the hell is Heather? Going to the bank in town would have been quicker.

'Poor organisation, yet another of your shop's deficiencies.' She emphasised her point with the bear, jabbing it at Rob on 'poor' and 'deficiencies'.

'Not my shop.'

'Well, it won't be Mr Harris's shop much longer either if we have our way.'

'I know.'

'You know? You know and still you came here? Well, I never did!' Bright red spots of rage formed on her sharp cheekbones. Spittle flew from her slick brown lips. 'Are you morally bereft, Mr Buckland? Are y—'

'Here you go, Rob.' Heather lobbed the bag of pound coins across the shop. It hit him in the head and a couple rolled out onto the floor. He scrambled to pick them up as the Poo Witch circled him, working herself into a religious fervour.

'Thus were they defiled with their own works, and went a whoring with their own inventions,' she said, eyes fever-bright.

'Whoso loveth wisdom rejoiceth his father: but he that keepeth company with harlots spendeth his substance.' A strange smile quirked the corners of her mouth.

Rob suppressed a shudder, fumbled the coins into the bag and then struggled to his feet. She yelled after him into the street: 'For this is the will of God, even your sanctification, that ye should abstain from fornication!'

God may well have said that to you to do everyone else a favour.

The protesters surged forward again as he left the shop.

'No sex – Know Jesus!' chanted an old lady, echoing the sentiment of her sign.

Rob made the most of a jogger, dodging through the Poo Witch's protesting minions as they parted in his wake.

*

'Poo Witch?!' If Jules had found Bummer's nickname amusing, she was beside herself over this one.

I suppose from the outside it seems like a stupid babyish name for two grown men to choose for their neighbour. Why not Shit Witch, or Turd Witch? With hindsight, Shit Witch has a better ring to it. But think of it this way. When she first moved in, she was just a minor annoyance. We thought it was funny, a batty old lady who always wore brown trying to sell baby goods next to a sex shop. We figured she'd see the error of her ways soon enough, like the others who didn't do their research before signing the lease – the fairy cake guys and the prom dress lady.

Poo Witch was a light-hearted, trivial name, because that's

how we felt about her. We used to watch her going off to church in her dollop of a hat and we'd elbow each other and snigger.

One day she came back and she'd got several of the other fogies with her, and they stood and pressed their faces to the glass, trying to see in. It's darkened stuff to make it hard to see what we sell from the street, in compliance with the local council, I might add. Apart from the few bits and pieces on the display stand, and they're carefully chosen. We absolutely pissed ourselves. These old farts, hanging their noses longingly over the fleshlights, puzzling over their use. Bummer went out and asked if they'd like to come in and see the full range.

Well, that backfired. A week later, there was the first load of placard-bearers, although we still didn't think too much of it. We hid below the bottom of the window display and did puppet shows for them with the rubber fannies.

Then I forgot to double-bag Half-Chub John's arab strap, and they called the police. Only got off with a caution because the copper could barely keep a straight face. That's when we knew the protesters were serious.

But it still didn't really affect Bummer. His kids were his escape route, one that was denied to me. He'd go off for the whole of half-term, taking them to the beach, the zoo, the pizza place. If one of them was spending half-term with their mum, one of the others was sure to want to see Bummer. So it was muggins who got the daily lectures on morality, the scathing assessments of my career choice, the constant looks and jeers of disdain and disgust from people who could recognise an arab strap through a plastic bag at forty paces.

'Bummer tries not to swear,' I add, remembering suddenly why Shit Witch was rejected. 'Doesn't want his kids picking up any bad habits.'

Jules nods, but her eyes are narrowed, and I don't think it has to do with Poo Witch.

3

Back in the Empornium, Birthday Every Day lady was examining the edible underwear, oblivious to the commotion outside. She hastily returned the pair of jellied panties to the shelf and inspected her fingernails instead. Rob wanted to roll the notes of her refund up and tuck them into her cleavage. *There you go love, why not treat yourself? They come in raspberry, too; we've got them in your size.* Even Bummer wouldn't have done that. Instead Rob laid it all out on the counter, getting some small satisfaction from the fact she couldn't pick up the coins with her manicured talons.

As she left, he heard her say to the protesters: 'I know, I know, it's terrible! Don't worry, I'm from the council. We'll put a stop to this!'

When she'd gone, Bummer shuffled out onto the shop floor scratching his arse and reading a scientific journal.

'Shouldn't give refunds so easily mate,' he said sagely. 'You should sniff it to check it's unused, or something.'

Rob stared at Bummer for a long moment, trying to

determine whether or not he was joking, but he remained absorbed in his article. Rob shook his head.

'Had another run-in with Poo Witch. You spoken to Chloe about her yet?'

'Nah.'

'Why not?' Rob asked. Bummer shrugged, still staring intently into his magazine. 'For God's sake, Bummer!'

Bummer threw his magazine onto the counter. It fell open on a page about evidence of alien life. Rob reckoned he was looking right at it. 'Let her do what she likes, Kidder. Half-term next week.' He retreated to the back of the shop again.

'Aww, what!' Rob followed him. There was only one guy in the shop and he was too busy frotting himself against a mannequin in a latex suit to nick anything. 'Leaving me again? Which one is it this time?'

The shop kitchen barely accommodated both of them. It was more of a pantry with a microwave, so Rob was forced to hover in the open doorway. Bummer bent over to rummage in the fridge, treating Rob to a view of his expansive arse-crack.

'Tenike.' Bummer emerged with a packet of salami and a block of old cheese and carried them back out to the shop counter. 'Sandwich?'

Rob declined.

'Oi, mate,' said Bummer, assembling his sandwich with one hand and hitching his jeans up with the other. 'You're going to have to buy that now.'

The frotter turned towards them, eyes wide. A sweaty little man with a strawberry blond comb-over, red-faced and rapidly growing redder.

'But... I...'

'Practically second-hand now you've rubbed your nuts all over it.'

'I...'

Bummer took a bite from the sandwich and chewed it calmly, watching. Waiting.

The man buckled under that steady, non-judgemental gaze, reaching into the pocket of his tweed jacket and producing a bulky leather billfold wallet.

'Can I get the mannequin, too?'

'For an extra fifty.'

'Okay.' The man meekly pulled out the notes. Fifties, naturally. A surprising number of customers paid with the elusive red note. Elusive for Rob at least. Loads more left in that guy's wallet. 'Can I get it in a box?'

Bummer glanced at Rob, and Rob knew what he was thinking. He was considering claiming he didn't have a box and watching the poor git struggle down the high street with a dummy in a gimp suit under his arm.

It would be fucking funny. Might distract the protesters for a bit.

Bummer made the guy wait a little longer. Rob could see the guy eyeing the dummy, clearly wondering if there was any way he could get it out of the shop *sans* box without everyone recognising it for what it was. Fresh beads of sweat broke out across his already moist top lip.

'Rob,' Bummer said, just as the guy looked like he was about to start begging. 'See if we've got any boxes out back.'

There were loads of boxes out back.

*

'He calls you Kidder?'

I don't remember mentioning it, but then I have been struggling with details lately, what with so many new ones to keep track of.

'Yeah,' I say, holding out the wine bottle to offer a top-up. It's almost empty. I don't fancy going back out to get another one, so I hope she'll shake her head, but this is Jules we're talking about. She nods eagerly. I stash the empty bottle under the sink between the bog brush and the plunger. 'Sometimes Our Kid. I think he developed Kidder out of that. Or maybe Kiddo. Not sure. Never asked.'

'Oh, okay. Fuck, this wine's disgusting,' she says, taking another big mouthful regardless. 'I thought it was because you're a big kidder.' She wiggles her eyebrows. So that's how it is. She thinks I'm joking around, telling tall tales. 'Wait, I thought you were an only child? I thought he was just your mate?'

'Yeah, he is. It's just our friendship, we're so close, y'know? It's as if he's my brother from another mother.' I feel daft saying it, but it's kind of true. Maybe. If that other mother was a giant sloth.

*

Rob held onto the end of the receipt roll as it spooled out the day's sales. Bummer sidled up to him eating a caramel-filled chocolate bar, the rabbit's large, eyelashed eyes peeping out from the wrapper. It was like Rob couldn't escape from that damn rabbit.

'Need you in early tomorrow.' Bummer's lips were sticky with the chocolate bar's gooey filling, reminding Rob of the Poo Witch and the rabbit simultaneously. Made him feel sick. And hungry. 'About seven.'

'Seven! Fuck's sake, Bummer! We don't open till nine!'

'Yeah, but I get in at seven to do the tills and tidy up before we open.'

'You do not "get in" at seven, Bummer. You roll out of bed and take money from petty cash to buy Frubes.'

'Look, I wouldn't ask, but something's gone off at Joel and Jacob's school. Donna needs me.'

'Unless one of the kids has gone on a shooting rampage, that's no excuse.'

'Joel's teacher's had a nervous breakdown actually, not that it's any of your business.'

For a moment, Rob felt terrible.

Maybe there was *a shooting there in the past. Not as if I watch the news.*

Bummer continued: 'One of the little bleeders really got under her skin and she went loopy. Completely off her rocker. They've sent her to the nuthouse for now, but there's talk of letting her carry on teaching after, 'cause she's not got long till retirement and losing out on her pension is the last thing the old dear needs.'

Rob's sympathy died. *The only nutty old woman I care about is my mum. And even then not if it means an early start.*

'Anyway, they're closing the school. Some kind of emergency counselling session with the other teachers to make sure no one else goes over the edge. So it's not like Donna can do anything about it. She needs to get off to work.'

'You need to get off to work. Let her sort it.'

Bummer screwed up the wrapper and sighed. Rob knew what was coming.

'I know you don't always think of me as your manager, Kidder, but I am your manager. And I'm telling you to get in, get the banking done and clean the dead flies out of the window. At seven.'

Pulling rank. What a dick.

'Fine. Whatever.'

Bummer said when he opened this place it'd be fun. All the latest porn and plenty of time to look at it.

Rob got a cloth from the kitchen and climbed into the window to deal with the dead flies. The protesters banged on the glass and pointed him out to passers-by as a promoter of immorality. Rob turned his back on them and tried to pretend they weren't there.

*

'This wine glass isn't getting any fuller.'

'Will you give me a minute? This is important.'

*

When Rob got home from the corner shop with his half-bottle of vodka-flavoured spirit drink, the phone was ringing. He contemplated leaving it in case Bummer wanted some last-minute stocktaking or similar bollocks, but then recognised the number on the caller ID and picked up.

'Hello Mum.'

'It's Gordon.'

Rob thumbed the pseudo-vodka's shiny red cap, contemplating opening it and knocking it back in one. 'Oh, right.' *Hello Stepdaddy. Hello not-my-real-daddy.*

'You still there?'

'Yeah. Sorry. What's up?' *Perfect end to a perfect day.*

'Your mother cooked all this food because Colin and Helen were coming round, and now Helen's got diarrhoea, so...'

'You've got stuff that needs eating.'

Gordon paused as if to consider saying something else, probably some platitude about how it was always nice to see family. But if Gordon had one thing going for him, it was that he always said exactly what he was thinking. Honest to the core. Even when the truth hurt or was gross.

'Pretty much.'

Rob contemplated an evening of that honesty. An evening of honest appraisals of his career, relationships, life choices.

'Can I bring some vodka?'

*

'Ooh, vodka, now there's an idea!'

'Will you give it a rest? I'm trying to give you vital backstory here.'

*

Rob's mum and Gordon lived in a nicer part of town than Rob would ever be able to afford. Ex-council houses and ex-council tenants; it was rough when Rob was a kid. But Mum stuck it out and made it through the era of burnt-out cars and moped gangs and now she lived in a period of urban gentrification.

Until she dies and leaves it to me, at least. But until that day, Rob had to take two buses to stroll around drinking in an atmosphere of amateur topiary, wrought iron gates and twitching net curtains.

When he reached the front door of the red-brick terrace, Rob didn't bother knocking. He tried the handle. Open as usual. He rolled his eyes.

Why do people get burgled all the time round my way? We lock our doors and don't have anything worth nicking.

As he stepped into the porch, his mum's cats materialised to wind round his legs. Louise and Finella were soon shedding all over his jeans, but Queenie, an arthritic old Persian with a rattly chest and permanently snotty nose, took longer to get there, for some reason choosing to hobble over the shoe rack rather than taking a direct route.

'Hello,' he called into the house, trying not to let Queenie's nose touch him anywhere. 'It's me.'

Mum and Gordon were in the conservatory playing a game of darts. Rob put his bag down on the threadbare old sunlounger and joined them. Mum won by a mile. After the game they ate cold roast chicken and bowls of couscous salad. Mum never cooked stuff like that when it was just for Rob. He got given fish and chips or roast dinner. She'd only cook things like this for guests, because she had to show her friends she could do Mediterranean even though she never went abroad because Gordon wouldn't fly. Food was nice, though.

Usually when Rob went round, conversation degenerated into his mum pleading for him to 'give her a grandchild' while Gordon chuckled and chipped in that a 'child couldn't raise a child.' So far that hadn't happened. They were all keeping it light.

'Almost had you at darts, didn't I Mum?' he grinned, stacking the empty plates and handing them to her.

'Course you did, love,' said Mum with a wink, heading into the kitchen. This had been their little joke since the pre-Gordon days, when Rob was about seven. Even at that age, he'd known Mum was unbeatable. She could place a dart anywhere on the board. They didn't have the conservatory back then. They played in the garden with the board nailed to the fence, eating bags of unbranded crisps that tasted of salted nothing, and Rob never won a single game, but he didn't mind. He enjoyed playing just to see her skill and imagine her as a young woman in an old man's pub wowing everyone with her precision. Unfortunately she met Gordon at a darts tournament, and their games and lives became less fun. Although they didn't have to have unbranded crisps any more, which was good.

Mum returned from the kitchen with the dessert bowls and set the table with them, positioning each bowl on a place mat reverently. She must have put the gateau in the special cut-glass bowls in advance, when she still thought their neighbours Colin and Helen were coming. Last time Rob remembered seeing them was about four Christmases ago, when his ex, Lisa, came round for Christmas dinner. That was a real boon for Mum. Fussed and fretted round Lisa like she was royalty.

Folded the napkins into lilies for Christ's sake.

Rob put his fork down. He wasn't hungry any more. Why did Gordon have to mention Helen's diarrhoea? How could he be expected to eat soft brown food with that on his mind?

'Eat the gateau, love, I need the room in the fridge. When

are you going to meet a nice girl and settle down?' Smoothly linking the two as if they were somehow related.

'Don't keep asking the boy that,' said Gordon, smiling.

Thank you, Gordon.

'He's not forced to settle down with a girl.'

Fuck you, Gordon.

'I'm not gay, Gordon.' Rob sighed.

'It's fine if you are.'

'I know. But I'm not.' It would be great if Gordon said that out of a genuine sense of acceptance, but he didn't, he said it because he thought 'woofters' were funny, the gross old homophobe. Rob cast around for a subject-changer, something to distract them from this line of questioning, but just ended up looking at the carefully selected pictures on the mantelpiece. Nothing with Bummer, or Lisa, or Bodie, the dog he used to have that got hit by a car. Nothing that even hinted at conflict, or loss, or sex shops.

Like if they don't have a photo of it, it never happened.

'Victor's a nice enough lad.'

'Victor? Even his mum doesn't call him Victor!' Rob's gaze fell on a picture of himself at the seaside age eight, their first beach holiday. He loved digging on the beach as a kid. Not to build a sandcastle or anything. Just for the simple pleasure of seeing a hole get bigger. Gordon said it wasn't normal, digging without a purpose. 'And yes, he is, but I have no interest in—'

'You're not getting any younger, you know,' Mum chimed in.

'Thanks, Mum.'

The gateau turned to clods of freshly dug sand in his mouth.

'You're our only chance at grandchildren.'

If Rob had had a spade, he would've sprinted to the back garden and started digging right there and then.

'Vic's got plenty to go round. I'm sure he'd let you take a couple of his to feed the ducks.'

'It's not about that, son,' said Gordon. 'It's about family. Leaving a little piece of yourself in the world to continue after you're gone.'

'Wouldn't be a piece of you, though, would it Gordon?' Rob shocked himself by saying it aloud. He immediately wanted to take the words back, but he couldn't, so he just said: 'Sorry,' weakly instead.

Gordon forced a smile, but Mum took the rest of the gateau away and said pointedly: 'I'll put it in a Tupperware. You can eat the rest at home.'

Rob glared at the ostentatious glass bowls with their stupid swan and cygnets design.

Stupid smug swans.

He wanted to smash them.

*

'Parents, eh?' says Jules, but she says it like she's understanding some deep truths about me and it's infuriating. Like I'm freaking out because I never had a father, and not because my son is... not my son. And not in the way I'm not Gordon's son, either. I'm not 100 per cent certain why I'm telling her all this. I have that odd sensation again, like I'm in the passenger seat and someone else is driving.

Or maybe I'm just working it out for myself. Brodie is a mystery to be solved, and there are clues from the sex shop days, I'm sure of it.

4

Next morning on reaching the pedestrian crossing, Rob contemplated turning round and heading straight back home.

That'd show Bummer.

Instead, he pressed the button and waited for the green man, head inclined to avoid making eye contact with the protesters. For once he was glad the lights took ages to change. He concentrated on the lit panel over the button, telling him to WAIT.

The day was grey and dull and a tentative rain spattered his face. He looked up to see if there were clouds overhead, but there was nothing, just monotonous sky. The lights changed and he crossed quickly. Turned out it was too early even for the protesters. He was almost disappointed.

Even people willing to stand outside a sex shop for hours at a time have better things to do at seven in the morning.

The sooner he could get a brew on, the better. He needed to forget about being stuck selling vulcanised rubber cocks and hairless latex vaginas day in, day out. To forget protesters and petitions and Bummer and stupid fucking glass bowls with arsehole swans on them. He raised the shutter and unlocked the front door.

Devaluing the act of love.

The protesters just wouldn't leave him alone, even when they weren't there. Maybe they were right. Maybe people like him were the root of all the evil in the world. Rob stepped inside, leaned back against the closed door and took a deep breath.

How can Bummer just ignore it? How does he deal with it every day?

At least among the nipple clamps and butt plugs there was familiarity, comfort, safety. The blow-up dolls wouldn't judge him or ask him why he hadn't been out with a girl in two years. The cardboard cut-out of Sharon Silk wouldn't flirt with Bummer even though Rob was standing right there with a clean shirt and no beer belly and a desperate ache in his balls.

'YAAAAARRRRRGGGHHHH!' The bondage chains shook and a masked figure dropped from in among the expensive imported porn on the top shelves. Rob jerked backward, cracking his head on the toughened glass of the door. He'd always imagined that in this kind of scenario he'd somehow become an impromptu mega-ninja, throwing out perfectly choreographed kung fu moves. All that actually happened was his stomach clenched and he needed to fart. The figure crouched, watching him with beady black eyes.

Doesn't seem that big, could probably fight him off.

He swallowed. His collar suddenly felt tight. Breathing became difficult.

Yeah right, be real. He could have a knife. He'll gut you in seconds and you'll do nothing, like you always do.

The figure straightened. Muffled laughter escaped the gimp mask. A small hand reached up to undo the mouth zip.

'Knew you'd shit a brick!'

'Christ! What the hell is wrong with you, you little bi—' He stopped himself and exhaled slowly. Relief overtook anger so swiftly he felt weak. *Weak-er.* 'Tenike! What are you doing here? You shouldn't be,' – he gestured to the trusses and bedroom swing sets – 'with this stuff!'

Tenike pulled the mask up over her head. A few stray hairs had burst out of her tight neat cornrows and there was a sheen of sweat on her top lip.

'Oh please.' She waved her hand dismissively. 'Adults do all kinds of gross things to each other. I don't even worry about it.'

Rob rubbed the back of his head. A lump was rising to go with the bruise on his hip from his Poo Witch encounter.

'And you're here because…'

'Inset day,' she said, twiddling with the knotted ends of a flail.

'But why are you here? Put that down.'

'Dad's at Donna's.' She said this with a curled lip and wrinkled nose. Bummer's family was surprisingly harmonious considering it was actually four families coexisting, but there were clashes.

'Oh, yeah, right, of course. And you're here alone?'

'I'm fourteen. Legally, children can be left alone from the age of twelve, provided their guardian leaves emergency contact numbers and returns within three hours,' she recited.

'That true?'

She shrugged.

'Then save it for your social worker. And make us a cuppa.'

'Don't have a social worker any more,' she said indignantly. 'What did your last slave die of?'

'Had a heart attack when some idiot in a mask jumped on him.'

Rob found himself acting oddly with Tenike around. She was supposed to spend most of her time in the flat above the Empornium, but she was always finding reasons to come down to the shop floor. Her pen had run out, did Rob have one? It was too hot up there, couldn't Rob do something about the central heating? When the DVD delivery arrived, instead of flipping through the box to find a contender for Bummer's Most Obscure Fetish award (current winner: *Loaf Love: Adventures in Yeastiality*), Rob found himself putting them all face down and wrapping the really filthy ones in a thick layer of bubble wrap to hide engorged and dripping bits. He spent most of the morning counting and categorising the flavoured condoms because that display was the closest thing in the shop to being child-friendly. The bright colours and sugary fragrances would have evoked memories of an old-fashioned sweetshop if not for the heavy background scent of latex.

At least they promote protection from sexual disease.

On the packet a sexy lady strawberry was enthusiastically going down on a smug-looking male banana.

Kind of.

*

Early afternoon, Bummer showed up. The protesters were late arriving today, the group relatively small, probably due to the Inset day. Rob watched from his vantage point behind the till as Bummer nodded and smiled like a politician meeting his constituents. He stopped in front of one elderly man, grasped his hand firmly, shaking it and chatting amiably. The protesters collectively stepped back in shock and he gave them all a little wave and left them to it.

'I'll make sure it gets delivered on Wednesday,' he said loudly through the open door. 'In brown paper as usual!'

The man's mouth opened and closed like a fish drowning in air.

'Who the hell's that?' asked Rob.

'No idea,' said Bummer cheerfully, taking off his jacket. 'Twins all right?'

'I think so.' Bummer nodded, immediately rifling through the cardboard box of DVDs on the counter. 'Donna managed to swap shifts so I only had to do a half-day. I'll cover for her again when she makes up the hours.'

Rob nodded back, wincing at the cover of *Teabag Through the Two Lips* even though Tenike was safely upstairs doing her biology homework. He wondered if he should bring up the fact he'd technically minded her all day for free.

'Nah, no contenders,' said Bummer with a sigh. 'Looks like the bread-boffers are still in the lead.' He disappeared off upstairs, presumably to see Tenike.

As Rob prepared to do the bank run, his annoyance rose. He'd been multitasking all day and Bummer hadn't even noticed. Childcare and retail, tidying and childproofing, and now banking and... thinking. Rob stuffed the cash into the Titillator satchel, a cushioned bag covered in rubbery veined protrusions. Bummer's argument was that no one would have the guts to nick it, regardless of how much money it contained.

Maybe Bummer's got this down, Rob thought, looking out of the window. The sun had broken through the clouds, any hint of rain long gone. *Maybe it's just about going with the flow.* He leaned out of the door and offered the protesters a friendly wave. He'd show them, and Bummer, too.

Multitasking.

'Tenike?' he shouted back up the stairs. 'Bring the tea tray down, will you?'

'Want me to dance for you as well?'

'I made the f— flippin' tea earlier, just put the pot on the tray and bring it down!'

Amazingly she did, and with the good cups, too, not Bummer's chipped collection of 'Best Dad in the World' mugs. He thought Bummer might come down with her to see what was going off, but she was on her own, so Rob beckoned her over. He held the door open, then indicated the pot of tea, saying to the protesters: 'Tea, anyone? Tea?'

The old man reached for a cup, only to have his hand slapped away by an old lady. When the lady launched into 'Run from anything that stimulates youthful lust!' Rob felt brave enough to say with a smile: 'I am poisoning the city's youth!' They faltered in their chants. He smiled wider, adding: 'My products devalue the act of love!' The protesters stopped chanting and glanced at one another, unsure of how to proceed. Tenike looked nervous, biting her lip and clutching the tea tray like it was a life raft. She avoided making eye contact with any of the placard-wavers, just like Rob used to. To show her there was nothing to be afraid of, he gave the Titillator satchel an affectionate pat and strode off down the high street, whistling.

Bummer would be proud of us both.

*

The girl behind the bank counter kept staring at his bag. He held it up and said: 'Do you like it? It's designer.'

She smiled and nodded. 'I thought it was – that French guy isn't it?'

She was small and pretty with elfin features and he could've asked her out, but she was obviously kind of dumb to believe something with rubber cocks all over it was the latest thing from the Parisian catwalks. So he just handed over the cash and the bank book and nodded.

When he returned, the protesters were gone. A sign saying 'Prostitutes and Immoral Women are a Deadly Trap' was propped beside the shop door. Rob took it in to show Bummer. The shop was empty, so Rob headed up to the flat. Bummer was sprawled on the sofa beside Tenike. He seemed unimpressed.

'Stick it in the stockroom with the others.'

'You should have seen their faces!' said Rob.

'You shouldn't have gone out there, princess,' Bummer said to Tenike. 'No matter what some idiot tells you.' Rob's annoyance returned as a tightness in his guts. Bummer was stretched out on the sofa eating a bowl of sugar-coated cereal like he thought he was a Roman emperor. When he smiled at Tenike's solemn nod, milk dribbled down his chin.

Pot calling kettle idiot.

Bummer turned his gaze on Rob, eyes stern. His management eyes.

'You don't use my kids that way,' he said. 'I had to rescue her from those people. They scared her. They've got some funny ideas about stuff.'

Rob shrugged. 'They're gone now.'

'No thanks to you,' Bummer said, washing his cereal down with Special Brew.

Came in early, looked after his daughter all day, did the banking without being asked and I still get told off. This is bullshit. I should walk out right now. Rob took off his jacket and threw it over the back of the sofa.

'Customers,' he said, heading back down to the shop.

A policeman was waiting by the till. Not the usual one, a young guy with a shaved head and a less jaded expression. He peered around at the PVC minidresses and bondage board games with polite curiosity.

'Mr Harris?' he asked.

'No, he's—' Rob imagined Tenike sitting primly on the sofa as her dad fielded questions from the Feds. 'He's out.'

'So you're in charge?'

Rob glanced at the new bondage mannequin and the cardboard cut-out of Sharon Silk. Neither offered any suggestions.

'I guess.'

'We've had reports of a minor on the premises?'

'Yeah, that's Bu— Mr Harris's daughter. But she's never in the shop itself. Just the flat above.'

'Witnesses said she came through the shop to serve tea.'

Ungrateful bastards. Maybe custard creams would have kept their mouths shut.

'That was a...' *Bribe? No, don't say that, moron. Unless he's a bent copper. They're all bent coppers on telly. Maybe if you give him...*

'A what?' The policeman didn't look angry, yet, just expectant. His biro hovered over his notebook.

'A peace offering.'

The biro went into an inside pocket; the notebook closed and followed it.

'Look,' said the policeman softly, 'we all know about Mr Harris at the station.'

'You do?' The regular guy had been making his mouth go, it seemed.

'Point is, he's harmless.' He thumbed through the erotic playing cards on the till display, expression unchanged. 'And it's better that all the weirdos come here, buy whatever gets their rocks off and take it home. Mr Harris encourages that kind of culture and we'd like it to stay that way.' He leaned closer, lowering his voice. 'Mr Barclay used to beat off in a parked car outside Newridge's supermarket until this place opened.'

'Yeah, we let him use the staff toilet. Puts the other customers off otherwise.'

'Exactly, that's what I'm talking about. But having Harris's kids hanging around here doesn't look good. Can't turn a blind eye to that, can we?'

5

At half past five he locked himself in and headed for the fridge in the pantry. Pulled out a six-pack and trudged upstairs. Bummer snored softly on the sofa, an open packet of peanuts spilling onto his chest. Tenike's voice, high and animated in the next room as she chatted to a friend on the phone.

Rob sank onto the armchair and cracked open a can.

'I resign,' he told Bummer's sleeping form. Bummer twitched in his sleep.

Definitely telling him that when he wakes up. Definitely.

Rob came round to find someone had wrapped a blanket round him. It was clean and smelled of fabric conditioner, so had to be Tenike's handiwork. She'd cleared up the beer cans and Bummer no longer languished on the sofa, so she must have sent him to bed, too.

Some benefits to having kids, I suppose.

Rob got up and looked around, scratching his head. He winced at the sore spot where he had cracked it on the door when Tenike frightened him. His six-pack had gone, but he wasn't sure if he'd finished it or if Tenike had returned the rest of the cans to the fridge.

His bladder throbbed, hinting at why he'd awoken. He went to pee and considered going home. On the way back to the lounge, he noticed the computer in the alcove by the front door. Tenike had left it on, and when he moved the mouse, it clicked and whirred back to life.

She'd been playing with some editing software, scanning in photos of her school friends and giving them goofy teeth and wild hair. Rob smirked, and closed the program. The internet browser was open behind. Credit Co. He hoped Bummer was the one looking at that. His gaze wandered. Above the computer were two rows of framed photos. One row of Bummer and his friends, one row of his kids. The first row included a school photo. Bummer and Rob, side by side, all outdated haircuts and freckles. Usually they only let brothers have their picture taken together like that, but as they were neighbours and both poor, the school made an exception and let their mums split the cost of the pictures.

Rob smiled at the memory. All the other lads in the first year were well impressed he knew a sixth-former well enough to have his picture taken with him. None of them had brothers that much older than them. Apart from Tom Harvey, and everyone knew his brother was in prison for dealing crack, so there was no way he was coming to do a photo.

Rob ran his eye along Bummer's offspring. Neil, Chloe, Tenike. There was a little bit of Bummer in all of them. In Neil it was the slope of his forehead and the dimple in his chin. Chloe had the eyes, grey and uncompromising, but always ready to smile. Tenike had his nose.

Is that last one the twins, or am I seeing double?

Rob struggled to focus. He must have finished the six-pack. He sat down in the swivel chair, gazing up at Joel and Jacob. Brothers. Twins. He glanced back at the screen, closing the Credit Co window as it flashed a garish advert inviting him to 'JOIN US!' There was a folder on the desktop called simply 'Dad'. Any sense of shame he may have had was dulled by the alcohol. He opened it. Tenike's pictures. She'd been working her way through them, editing them to enhance key elements. Rob was drawn to one in particular. She was standing on Bummer's feet, dancing, looking up at him with shining eyes and white teeth, laughing. It must have been Christmas or New Year, because the nondescript dance hall they were in was decorated with streamers. She'd added a border, a dark grey fade edged in lilac butterflies, putting the focus squarely on herself and Bummer and their happiness. In the border, in neon italics, she'd typed 'Me and my dad' and a big kiss, 'X'.

MWAH! Rob made a kissy face. *No one's ever mwahed me.*

He thought about Lisa and Valentine's Day, when she bought him a huge padded card and a teddy bear wearing gloves and a goalie shirt that said, 'Keeper of my Heart' and he bought her some supermarket flowers that were on discount because they were past their best and a card his mum had spare in her Special Occasions drawer.

I was too young, for Christ's sake.

He looked again at the picture of himself and Bummer as kids and compared it to the one of the twins. Imagined if the twins were little copies of him instead. Red hair and freckles instead of snub noses and chubby cheeks. Would things be different then? Would Mum and Gordon be proud? Would

Bummer treat him as an equal? Would coppers offer grudging respect, would someone edit a photo of him, would he matter? He slowly moved the mouse, drifting the cursor over Tenike's text and imagining a different life.

*

'Are you...' Jules's eyes are large and unnaturally bright. I can't tell if that's because of the bathroom's aggressive lighting or the alcohol. '...are you trying to tell me Brodie isn't yours? That you... passed off one of Bummer's kids as your own or something?'

'You watch too much daytime TV,' I say. And I watch too much science fiction. We're quite the pair.

'Well, then, is there a point to all this? I still don't get why we're hiding in the bathroom.'

I put a finger to my lips and she shushes, but I know it won't last. Also, she's right. I'm stalling. I was stalling back then, too. I knew I couldn't stay at the Empornium for ever. It was eating me from the inside out, but I couldn't tell Bummer.

*

Rob stared at the toilet door. 'You got the paper in there, Bummer?' Bummer claimed he was using the shop toilet because Tenike had taken over the bathroom with all her moisturisers and perfumes and Bummer couldn't have a nice relaxing poo with all that going on. Rob thought Bummer was doing it to keep an eye on him.

He knows something's up. Knows I want the paper for the job section. Well, he shouldn't have taken me for granted all these years, should he?

Finally Bummer emerged, working on a sudoku puzzle as if no one had been waiting outside for forty-five minutes.

'Well?'

'Well, what?'

'Where's the fucking paper?'

'In there.'

'You couldn't just bring it out with you?'

'Why can't you go in and get it? You some kind of invalid or something?'

'No, Bummer, I just don't want your toxic shit gases to melt my face, okay?'

'Whatever.'

He didn't fetch the paper, forcing Rob to go in with his jumper pulled over his nose, holding his breath.

He pored over the job adverts, going back through looking at the stuff he'd circled, and realised there was one he'd circled a few times over now, several days running. Credit Co, that credit card company Bummer had been looking at online. They advertised an awful lot for a company with 'excellent benefits'. Although the only benefit Rob was really interested in was not having to touch anything that had been inside another human being.

'Don't I pay you enough?' Bummer asked. Rob had assumed he'd gone straight back upstairs after his shit, but he'd lingered in the shop.

'It's nothing personal,' said Rob. 'I just need to get out of here. Get a job where there's a chance for progression, y'know?'

'You're leaving?' said Bummer, face hardening into a mask of cold anger. 'I thought you were looking at a credit card or a loan or something.'

Rob was midway through tearing the ad out. He tried to stop, but the paper went on ripping without his input. The sound was deafening. For a moment, Rob thought Bummer was going to punch him, or snatch the paper out of his hand and make him eat it. When he finally spoke, his voice was very soft, so soft Rob couldn't hear it over his own rapid breathing.

'What?' he was forced to ask.

'I said you needn't bother coming back!' Bummer yelled so loud, Rob's shoulders jerked completely of their own volition. Rob thought about saying something more, but the way Bummer was looking at him had changed. It was the way Gordon had looked at Bodie when they went to visit him at the vet for the last time. Annoyed he'd spent so much money on the dog and it had died anyway, but sad it was dead.

*

'Yikes,' says Jules.

'I know.' This reminds me again why I was a complete idiot to ever even consider Amber over Jules. Amber would have fixated on the shitting, and how disgusting it was that I'd tell her about it, but Jules sees straight to the heart of what I'm trying to say.

'Bummer's got a really bad diet, huh?' My head whips round, but she's teasing me again. 'Sorry,' she says. 'Like I said before, I wasn't expecting to go down this dark road with you. I thought we were past this.' For a moment we're both silent.

We. She said we. 'So that put paid to adopt one of Bummer's kids, I guess?' she asks.

I nearly drop my wine glass. She's not getting this. She's really not getting this. She keeps expecting Brodie to pop up in the story, but he's not going to, is he? Not for ages. Because all of this happened before I'd made him up, well before this impossible Brodie imposter showed up. I should have known she'd react like this. She only knew me post-Brodie. If Bummer can't accept that we made up a child, how can I expect her to? I continue because to stop would be to admit I've lost.

*

'This one's nice, love? Isn't it? Isn't it nice?'

Rob sighed deeply. *It's not nice. It's brown. No one wears a brown suit. Except Poo Witch. And maybe paedophiles.*

'And you could put it with this shirt and tie. They are lovely. Looo-ve-ly.'

'Not a fan of paisley, Mum. Can't we get this one?'

He picked up a slate-grey three-piece from the designer rail. A classic cut with broad lapels and slim-leg trousers. The kind of thing a debonair secret agent would wear to charm ladies into giving away intel.

And their hearts.

Three times the price of the off-the-peg piece of shit Mum was holding.

'Grey makes you look washed out, love. You can't get away with grey with your complexion. Brown's warming.'

Like a steaming turd.

The department store was large and soulless as a disused

aircraft hangar, yet Rob felt oppressively hot and hemmed in. He tugged at his collar, but it couldn't be any looser. His temples were damp with sweat, his armpits slick. Usually spending Mum's money was fun. A few clicks and then movies and games turned up on the doorstep. There wasn't usually a discussion. Mum wasn't usually there, giving her opinion.

'No, love, you don't want that game. It's got zombies in it. Ugh, horrible! What about this one? You get a pony and if you groom and feed it right, it turns into a unicorn!'

She was talking to the sales assistant. An eighteen-year-old boy with high cheekbones and big eyes. He'd rolled up the sleeves on his suit jacket.

Dick.

Mum turned and pointed to Rob and then gestured to the rails of suits. Her cheeks flushed pink and she beamed as she chatted away to the boy. Rob caught the odd phrase.

'...New executive position... suitable for... potential managerial...'

Her misplaced pride was almost sickening, but the boy nodded politely. He selected several items, reeling off facts and features.

'...frog-mouth back pocket... dry weave breathable top layer... tear-resistant hand-sewn lining...'

Barely out of school and completely at home in a suit, spouting bullshit.

There was a politician joke in there somewhere, but Rob lacked the energy to make it. The sales boy tilted his head back, swept his long fringe out of his eyes and smiled down at Rob's mother through thick lashes.

'I'll leave you to browse now, madam. Give me a shout if you need anything.'

Rob watched the kid sidle over to two teenage girls pretending to look at ties, but obviously actually there to ogle the young lad. He pulled the hair-sweep move again and the girls melted into giggles. All trendy and sophisticated in his stupid rolled-up suit.

Rob imagined himself in an office, sitting at a desk with an in tray and an out tray. There was one of those clacky little executive toys between the trays and Rob wore a pale blue shirt and smart grey pinstripe trousers. He had bright red braces that he'd never actually wear, but in the scenario, they looked pretty awesome.

Maybe it can be like that. Maybe I can pull this off.

Imaginary Rob swung his feet onto the desk. He was wearing socks with cartoon penguins on them and sock suspenders.

Imaginary Rob, you're a fucking let-down. Who am I kidding? Putting me in a swish suit is like putting Sharon Silk in a lab coat. She's not going to cure cancer. She's just going to get her tits out and bend over the workbench like always.

'You all right love?' asked Mum. She'd taken one of the paisley shirts out of its packet and laid different-coloured ties on top, tilting her head to scrutinise the effect. It was the effect of vomiting onto some vomit.

'Yeah.'

'You sound glum. Cheer up! This is fun! Dressing you up all nice like when you were a little boy!'

Ah yes, trailing after his mother and her sister as they tried to find the perfect outfits for someone or other's wedding. They made out it was all about Rob, but his suit was an after-thought. They didn't make that many suits for seven-year-olds as it was and no one would really be looking at him anyway. At least, that's what he'd thought. Turned out groups of disapproving churchy elders found single mothers and their bastard offspring pretty interesting back then.

Then there were the late-teen shopping trips, usually serving as reprimand rather than treat. 'Well, if you can't keep your jeans nice, you'll have second-hand ones,' or, 'Auntie Joan shouldn't have to see that at her age. Wear pyjamas from now on.' That was how he ended up with those bloody flannel monstrosities.

Auntie Joan bathed me when I was a baby, why are my knackers such a big deal now?

Aren't you excited about the interview?' Mum was asking. 'I'm so proud. About time you had something go right for you. Lucky getting asked in so quick with the economy the way it is.'

'Yeah.'

Luck? That CV made me sound like I was slumming it even applying. The made-up credentials of an administrative god. Rob chewed a loose flap of skin at the side of his fingernail.

'Oooh – now this is really nice! Like it? Most people couldn't get away with teal, but I think it brings out your eyes.'

She was holding a suit the colour of a diseased mallard, looking embarrassingly pleased and proud. Rob glanced over at the sales boy. One of the girls leaned on a display table, scribbling something down on a scrap of paper. From the way the boy slid it smugly into his inside jacket pocket, Rob could tell it was a phone number.

If I'm going to get laughed out of the building, may as well be for my suit.

'Yeah, fine. Whatever.'

*

'So that's where you got that fucking awful suit.'

'I know you're finding this hard, but if you could try to take it a little more seriously?'

'I don't even know what "this" is.' Jules fidgets on the edge of the bath. I'm not sure what she means by 'this'. My attempt to explain why I'm terrified of my so-called son, or 'us'. Me and Jules. Jules and me. Is there an us? Am I ready for another us? It's been a long while since the last one but I'm still not sure I'm ready.

6

On the bus home, Rob swigged some vodka he'd ingeniously poured into a bottle of Coke at his mum's. If they really did have plain-clothes transport police on the bus, then they wouldn't know he was drinking. Although Rob suspected those signs were bollocks anyway.

He watched a kid at the front of the bus copying everything its mum did and said, driving her crazy. Rob sniggered to himself. The mum grabbed the child by the wrists and leaned forward to scold him quietly. Her cleavage was familiar. As she straightened back up, Rob realised with a start that the mum was Lisa MacFarlane.

His first proper girlfriend. His only proper girlfriend. Unless fingering the new checkout girl at Newridge's counted. *Probably not.*

And there she was, Lisa MacFarlane, looking like a proper grown-up with a kid and a pushchair and a shoulder bag full of juice cartons and wet wipes. Would their kid have looked like him? His and Lisa's? A mini Rob. Unlikely.

Lisa's kid looked just like her – big dark eyes and beetly brows.

She must have aggressive genes or whatever they call it. Rob read about it once in one of Bummer's science journals, but now he couldn't remember. Maybe it was for the best he and Lisa never had a kid. *Her genes would've stamped all over mine anyway.*

Rob sighed and took another swig of Coke. He tipped it up too fast and some escaped the neck of the bottle, splashing his chin and making him cough. As he wiped his face on his sleeve, Lisa stood on tiptoe and peered down the bus. Her eyes narrowed slightly, like she wasn't quite sure what she was looking at. Rob screwed the lid tightly back onto his Coke. His fist clamped the neck of the bottle. His breathing quickened. Lisa's face broke into a wide friendly grin. She gave a little wave. Rob swallowed. She wouldn't be waving at him, would she? They didn't part on very good terms, what with her brother's black eye and the broken garden furniture and all that.

But there's only me at the back. And she's looking right down the bus.

Lisa waved again, the motion bigger this time. She added a little 'Wooo!' Rob dropped his Coke into his carrier bag and raised his hand.

Maybe she's a single parent. Maybe she's gotten over the thing with her brother. Maybe she wants to—

The old lady in front of Rob wobbled to her feet and shouted down the bus: 'Lisa? Lisa, is that you?'

Lisa laughed in delight. 'Mrs Leaming! Yes it is! How are you?'

Rob tried to turn his wave into a fly-swat. The kid had seen him do it and tugged Lisa's skirt.

'Mummy, Mummy!'

'Sssshhh baby – Mummy's talking to Mrs Leaming. You remember Mrs Leaming, don't you?'

'She buys me sweeties!'

'Yes, she does.'

Rob considered opening the fire door and throwing himself out. It wasn't as if the road was busy. Instead he hunched down in the seat and stared out of the window, praying Lisa got off before him.

*

'Ah, okay, I see.' Jules adjusts her position, slips with a screech against the shiny bath edge and manages to right herself without spilling her wine. We both freeze for a moment, expecting a small voice to shout up, to ask what we're doing in the bathroom, what that noise was. I like that about Jules, how she'll play along with things without knowing what they are. Although this may be pushing it. I'm holding my breath, but the kid either didn't hear or didn't care.

'You were saying,' I prompt her.

Jules bites her lip for a moment, tracing back her line of thinking until she catches hold of the end. 'Ah, yes! Lisa. You wanted Brodie because of Lisa. You saw her with her son and you were envious of the life you didn't have. So you… adopted him?'

Still with the adoption thing. I suppose if my theory's correct it's technically true, but if only it was that simple.

'No!' I say, exasperated, then quickly drop my voice again. 'Aren't you listening at all? This wasn't planned! How the hell could I have known it would turn out like this?! It was totally spur-of-the-moment. The guy at the interview backed me into a corner. It's not like I could ever go back to the Empornium.'

She purses her lips, still not getting it.

'Remind me why you're telling me all about your ex and her cleavage?' Jules's voice is bitter.

'I'm sorry,' I say, rubbing my aching head. 'I'm not telling it well. But I feel like you need to know all of it. *Someone* needs to know all of it to have any chance of making sense of Brodie.'

*

A large glossy table dominated the interview room. Gregory, the Credit Co rep, ushered Rob into a seat. Gregory had spiky hair, a feeble act of rebellion against an otherwise entirely unremarkable appearance. Rob rested his fingertips on the table's shiny surface, unsure what to do with his hands. He left sweaty prints like a jungle tree-frog and tried to surreptitiously wipe them with his forearms without Gregory noticing.

Gregory didn't notice. He bustled around pointing out notable aspects of the meeting room. 'It has a window,' he said, gesturing to a view of a derelict train station with pride.

'Um,' said Rob. Gregory handed him a copy of the company manual to leaf through until the interviewers deigned to arrive. Rob took it gratefully, and studied it cover to cover. Their mascot, Captain Credit, featured heavily. His cartoony lantern jaw and flowing cape jarred against the slick, distanced professionalism demonstrated elsewhere throughout the brochure. Every page was peppered with buzzwords in a large flowing font, rearing incongruously out of segments on HR and debt collection policies.

SYNERGY.
DYNAMISM.
HOLISTICISM.

Every image represented their diverse multicultural workforce; a beautiful wheelchair user enthusiastically high-fiving a handsome Sikh over the water cooler, a stunning white security guard swiping a debonair black executive's ID pass. Most of the people Rob had walked past on the way in were middle-aged white men.

A gentle tinkling sound from the jug of water in the centre of the table drew Rob's attention. Cubes of ice and slices of lemon bobbed on the surface, moved by the flow of the air conditioning. Five glasses were arranged neatly alongside. Rob's throat was biscuit-dry. He looked up to see what Gregory was doing. Gregory was by the window, gazing down at the view wistfully. Time stood still as Rob poured from the jug and cubes of ice plopped into his glass, splashing the table with water. He'd developed an irrational fear that the interviewers would walk in and tell him the water wasn't for him, or that Gregory would say he shouldn't have poured it until everyone was present. Eventually he sipped it, fighting the urge to roll the glass on his face, or, weirder still, pour its contents into his crotch.

The interviewers filed into the room. No one commented on the water. There were three of them. A hard-faced woman with distracting neon-blue eyeliner, a small, misshapen man with a meaty slab of a head and one eye bigger than the other, and a carbon copy of Gregory, although apparently they weren't related and this one was called Gustave. Shiny faces and spiky hair just seemed to be the trend at Credit Co. Rob wished there was another him to take the interview.

Each interviewer had an identical leather-bound clipboard with a thick sheaf of interview questions on the front and Credit Co's logo embossed in gold on the back. A fist holding a sheaf of cash. Gregory introduced the interviewers and Rob shook hands, aware his own hand felt like a day-old market stall fish.

'I like your tie, Robert,' the little troll man said. 'My son has the same one.' Rob was caught off guard. The man sounded kind, reasonable.

Perhaps this won't be so bad.

It was bad. They asked what he knew about Credit Co, but he could barely remember anything apart from the fact they prided themselves on giving credit to anyone, no APR too large, no repayment plan too long. He parroted this back at them like he was Captain Credit in their TV advert, only he didn't feel like a superhero, just some guy with his pants on the outside.

They asked weird questions like 'Why is a ring doughnut better than the holeless kind?' He spoke at length about wearing one on each finger and ended up talking about the shape of the universe with no recollection of how he'd got to that point. He contemplated just thanking them for their time and walking out, but there was never a good time and he didn't want them to see the sweat patch he was cultivating on his chair.

'So, you seem to have taken a seven-year break since finishing university. What happened?'

The woman asked that. He could barely take in the question, so mesmerised was he by that bright blue eyeliner. It made the whites of her eyes glow with a purplish light.

He had intended to explain that these missing years, the Sex Shop years, had been spent travelling. That he had broadened his mind trekking across Mongolia, building primary schools in India, monitoring a population of orang-utans in Borneo. He'd watched enough charity telethons to know what those places were like, and he'd even come up with the kicker closing sentence: 'And where better to apply such international knowledge than the international home of credit – Credit Co?'

Only, for some reason, he didn't say any of the rehearsed stuff. Maybe it was the guy mentioning his son, maybe penguin-socks Rob was in the driving seat, maybe it was some weird manifestation of jealousy for Lisa's lifestyle, or just the distraction of that blue eyeliner; Rob still couldn't be sure why he said it, but the words came out just the same: 'I was raising my son.'

*

'Ah-ha!' Jules interrupted triumphantly.

'Sssh!' Rob hissed before returning to his story.

*

'You didn't mention you were married on your application form,' the woman said, inclining her head and pursing her lips, reading back through her notes as if she may have missed something pertinent.

'No, I, err,' the words tumbled on, like he was Sharon Silk, just going through the motions, getting the job done. 'My wife… died. I'm a widower. A single widower.'

'Oh.' She nodded as if he had given the only possible correct answer.

'That's wonderful!' the little troll man cried out as Gustave beamed. 'I mean, sad news about your wife, but... I would have loved to be a stay-at-home papa! Alas, it was not to be. Still, Gerta did a wonderful job.'

'Gerta's your wife?' said Rob, taking another quick sip of water, trying desperately to replenish the sweat he'd lost into the leatherette seat.

'Our au pair,' he said, and his eyes dropped quickly to his clipboard before finding Rob's face again. 'And your son? What's his name?'

'His name?' Rob thought about Lisa MacFarlane, about her boring, plain little son, who was probably called Oliver or Jack or Charlie. 'Bodie.' *Dog's name! You can't give him a dog's name!* 'Ahem, sorry, Brodie. His name's Brodie.'

'These modern names, eh?' said Gregory.

After that it was like the Gregorys and Blue Eyeliner weren't even there. It was just troll man and Rob, comparing fatherhood stories, boyish likes and dislikes, minor scrapes and trips to A&E, unfortunate pets and beloved friends. By the end, when Rob said: 'Yeah, Brodie's a great kid. Great kid,' he meant it wholeheartedly. As the interview finally wound to a close, troll man pumped Rob's hand and offered the parting shot: 'Maybe Brodie could come to the rugby club with Austin Jr some time?'

No fuckin' way mate. Kid sounds like a freak.

'Count on it,' said Rob, making finger guns for some reason.

Finally it was just Rob and Gregory in the room. Gregory clapped Rob on the shoulder enthusiastically.

'I've never seen Austin take to anyone like that before. I'd say you're a shoo-in, mate.' He said this carefully, like someone practising a foreign tongue, unused to words like 'shoo-in' and 'mate'.

'Really?' said Rob. 'I guess it was down to Brodie.'

*

'He's right out there, Rob.'

'Mmm?'

I look up. I was so caught up in the retelling, I'd almost forgotten she was there.

'Brodie. He's right outside playing PlayStation. So this idea that you... made him up to score points with Austin? That's just fucking crazy town!' She makes a loony gesture alongside her head, more vigorously than she would have if she was sober. But she's more amenable than if she was sober, too. Sober Jules would have probably stopped me at the beginning, around the part with the hippy policewoman, and walked out.

'Keep your voice down! He'll hear!' If he is a he. Maybe he's more of an it.

'He's yours, Rob. Anyone could see the resemblance. And there's Bummer. Bummer loves kids and there's no way he'd let you just take someone else's.'

'I already told you. Bummer remembers it wrong. It's not how he says.'

'Even by your own logic, your so-called made-up child doesn't seem that spur-of-the-moment,' says Jules gently. She stands and arches her back, pushing one fist against her spine until it pops. 'You could have phoned Credit Co at any moment and backed out. Or just kept quiet about the kid in general, hoped they didn't mention it.'

I feel like I'm losing her in more ways than one.

'If I'd told them I lied about the kid, that was me out of a job, and I thought me and Bummer were done. What was I gonna do? Go crawling back to Mum and Gordon and see Lisa on the bus every day? No way. And not mentioning Brodie at work...' I'm not sure what to say to that. Truth is, it never even occurred to me. As soon as Brodie had a name, that was it, he was real. Even though obviously, he wasn't. Not at that point, anyway.

7

'So, as a final question, I'd like you to tell me why you think ring doughnuts are superior to the holeless kind?'

Rob reached for a cashew nut from the glass bowl on the table. The interviewee's eyes flicked over to them. At the beginning of the interview, Rob had told the guy refreshments were for the interviewer only. Just to fuck with him. Now he could see it was all the poor idiot could think about, that can of Tizer and the bowl of cashews. The room was hot and airless and the cool can of Tizer, sides beaded with condensation from the fridge, must have looked like heaven.

The guy wasn't as bad as Rob expected from his CV. He used to be a tour manager for some death metal singer, so Rob had hoped for tattoos and nose rings and evidence of a drug habit. But he was just sweaty and harried-looking, with dark rings under his eyes and scruffy hair. His suit was almost as bad as Rob's – shiny grey polyester with purple suede elbow patches. He was clearly still thinking about the doughnut question, sucking on his teeth and staring up into space. At least he hadn't burst into tears like the homeless guy.

'Because you can fuck it?' he offered in a slow American drawl.

Rob doodled a cock on his notepad, then underlined it to make sure it looked like he was writing. He rose to shake the man's hand.

'What the hell are you doing here?' Bummer appeared in the doorway with a ring-binder tucked under his arm. Behind him the real interviewee waited politely, looking far too smart and together to work in a sex shop.

If Rob had spent more time carefully crafting Brodie and less time sneaking into the Empornium to interview completely inappropriate replacements to amuse himself, things might have turned out differently.

'Get out,' said Bummer, and his eyes, they were like nothing Rob had ever seen before. Beyond management eyes, beyond angry disappointment eyes. They were eyes of hate and disgust. Enemy eyes.

*

'I'm Rob.' This prompted a daggered look from Shiny Face Greg. Nicknames were a major no-no at Credit Co. 'Err, Robert and... And...' *Hi, I'm Robert Buckland and I've sold vulcanised rubber cocks to the county's leading educators for the last seven years.*

A vivid smell-memory of the used bin's piscine tang stung Rob's nostrils.

Never again. I'm Robert Buckland, completely new and exciting guy.

'I'm Robert and my dad's a retired astronaut.'

There, stick that in your pipe and smoke it, Mr Shiny.

Gregory, to his credit, looked impressed. It was Rob's first day in the new job, but it felt more like the first day of school. He had the uncomfortable clothes, the fear that no one would like him, that he'd get lost in the maze of rooms and corridors, that he wouldn't understand what he was supposed to do. The only thing he didn't have was Bummer, ruffling his hair and telling him it wasn't so bad once you got used to it.

Gregory was playing teacher, making Rob present himself to the class. The others took their turns. Most were boring as wallpaper. Even the curvy redhead. But there was one hottie. Little brunette with twinkling eyes. She stepped forward and said: 'I'm Jules. I like windmills,' with a quirk of her eyebrow. Some of the others sniggered. Rob couldn't decide if he liked the idea of a woman being office joker or not.

'Thank you, *Julia*,' sneered Gregory. Clearly he was in the 'not' camp.

Gregory took Rob on a brief tour of the M&A department, as he was fond of calling it. He seemed to like acronyms in general. M&A, HR, CUL, CCCS. Rob thought this the hallmark of a CUNT. The tour basically involved pointing out the toilets, photocopier and vending machines.

'Credit Co cut a deal with a massive drinks corporation,' said Gregory, beaming with pride. 'As a result, all our soft drinks are trade price!' Rob felt slightly sorry for him. It didn't seem like there was much going on in Gregory's life beyond work.

'I'm afraid the only space is next to Julia,' Gregory informed Rob solemnly, leading him across to the empty desk. 'She doesn't work well with others, but you seem to be a real people person, so we're hoping you can turn that round!' He patted Rob on the back. 'I'm sure she'll brief you on the latest project.' Gregory headed for his own desk. Rob noted it was larger than anyone else's, as was the monitor. So much for the lack of hierarchy mentioned in the brochure. Rob sat down as quietly as he could. For some reason it felt as if making noise would highlight his lack of credit knowledge. Jules carried on typing.

He opened his bag and took out the photos. Spent time carefully aligning them, rolling the Blu-tack steadily between thumb and finger, almost fashioning a penis but remembering not to.

He'd put even more work into these photos than into his inflated CV. Well, Tenike had, following his directions. She'd emailed them to him with the words: 'Dad will be mad if he finds out I did this. Bye for ever.' What a drama queen. Delete.

Rob was pleased with the results. She'd altered an old school photo just enough that the kid resembled him without too obviously being him. Darkened the hair from carroty orange to a deep russet red. Changed the eyes from grey to brown. Added a dusting of freckles and a gap between the two front teeth. The result was a devastatingly cute kid, a kid who'd break hearts when he was older.

'Who's that?' asked Jules, swivelling in her seat.

Rob realised he'd been gazing fondly at the photo and smiling. He was actually thinking about the Blu-tack cock, but she didn't know that. *Can come off as the doting dad from the get-go.*

'My son,' he said, puffing himself up with paternal pride. He set the photo down by his mouse mat.

'Oh,' said Jules, turning back to her work.

Not good. Probably thinks I'm married now. I mean, not that I'm interested in her specifically, but it's a start and I wouldn't want her telling all her little friends I'm unavailable.

'My wife she, err...' *Did I say the cause of death before? Is that the kind of thing they ask in interviews?* 'She... died. Giving birth.'

'Oh, God!' Jules turned back to face him, eyes wide with concern. 'I'm so sorry!'

He took a few more photos from his bag in silence, trying to look hurt but not offended. He pinned them up on his noticeboard. The kid at the beach, the kid playing in the snow, the kid holding a hamster. All the necessary childhood memories covered. None with the dog; that would have made things too confusing. Bodie, Brodie. He could've made up a name for Bodie, too, of course, but that seemed wrong, since he was real and dead. And it was more stuff to remember.

'Don't you have any pictures of her?' Julia asked, her voice hushed.

'Who?'

'Your wife.'

'Oh. No. It's... too painful.'

Jules smiled, reflecting his own fake sadness back at him. He sat down to review his handiwork, stealing a glance at her out of the corner of his eye. *She's really going for this shit. Maybe I can do this. Maybe I can pull the whole thing off.* The cork noticeboard looked almost as good as Bummer's wall of photos. A real family man. *That reminds me. Need to make crib notes on the dead wife.*

'What's his name?'

'Brodie.'

She paused. A slight wrinkle appeared between her eyes. She was clearly stifling laughter. Not the reaction he was going for.

What's wrong with Brodie? Good, solid name that is. Name of a rock star, or a Premier League striker. Doesn't know what she's on about.

'Didn't Greg say your last name was Buckland?'

He nodded, mute.

'Brodie Buckland?' she asked, then turned away, muttering under her breath: 'Gonna be a porn star when he grows up?'

He could not believe she was mocking his pretend son.

'Actually, my wife chose the name,' he said. 'She named him after her grandfather. It was her final wish.' He leaned down to turn on his computer, knowing she was watching in open-mouthed horror.

In your face. Not so funny now is it? Laughing at my wife's dying breath. How do you like that?

Jules said sorry very softly and then talked him through their current project.

*

'You're saying you PhotoMorphed Brodie into existence?' She's flipped back to incredulousness, verging on anger. 'It's a good program, but it's not that fucking good.'

She gets up and with one stride she's at the door, fumbling with the lock. I leap up, put my hands over hers, desperate to stop her opening the door.

'Don't! You can't!'

'Because if you see him you'll be forced to confront how insane this is?'

*

Rob was studying the gigantic cafeteria's extensive wall-mounted menu when two M&A guys came to join him. Both wore pastel coloured shirts, ties in complementary colours and glasses with thick, stylishly geeky frames.

'Robert, hi!' said Pink Shirt. 'Good to have you on the team!'

'Shame they've stuck you with *Cruel-ia*, though, eh?' said Green Shirt, clinking trays with Rob. Both Shirts burst into guffaws of laughter. Rob hated the way Green Shirt laughed, tucking his chin in and shaking, like he was trying to channel the laugh down into his shirt. *What a tit*.

'Did I miss a good joke?' asked Jules, appearing behind them. They were holding up the queue and people behind were becoming impatient, so Rob was glad when the two pastel shirts slid their trays along to pick up identical tofu curries. They continued sniggering and didn't acknowledge Jules.

'Fuckheads,' Julia muttered under her breath. Rob hid his smirk by rereading the menu once more. If she really had ridiculed his dead wife's legacy, he wouldn't forgive her that easily.

'Look, Rob.' She touched his arm. 'We got off on the wrong foot there, and I don't need another person in the office that hates my guts, so...' She took one of the double chocolate muffins off her tray and perched it on his. '... Peace offering.' She saw his eyes flick to her own muffin and added: 'Okay, so I got me a peace offering, too, but...'

He would've liked to see her squirm a little longer, but

decided enough was enough. Karen (that was dead wife's name, now) would want him to forgive her. She'd want him to have a new woman in his life.

Giving lady, that Karen.

'Thank you,' he said, then inclined his head towards the menu. 'What do you recommend?'

She chose a stew with dumplings for both of them. Rob was relieved. The tofu curry looked like the contents of a newborn's nappy. Jules sat down at a nearby table and asked: 'So, how did you end up here?'

For some reason, he felt uncomfortable giving her the interview spiel. Lying to Jules was different from lying to four pricks in blazers, somehow. He stalled, trying to think of ways of telling the truth without revealing the lie.

'What do you mean?'

'Well, you don't seem like a money-grabbing arse-wipe like most of these twats.' She indicated the cafeteria with a sweep of her fork. 'So what's your damage? What makes a normal guy want to work in this capitalist hellhole?'

Oh, she thinks I'm normal. 'What about you? You seem to hate the place. How did you end up here?'

'Never been stuck in a job you hate?'

If you only knew. Instead he nodded. 'I was a supermarket shelf-stacker when I was sixteen.'

She laughed. 'Cute, but not comparable to this place. Especially when you're a former library-dweller.'

'You were a librarian?' He couldn't keep the surprise out of his voice.

'What were you expecting? Mohair cardigan and horn-rimmed glasses? Douche!'

He'd never felt so wrong-footed. He was used to chatting to Heather, the conversational equivalent of a child's toy with a pull-string in its back. Thankfully Jules continued. 'I just wanted to earn a decent wage in a nine-to-five. If I can't do what I want, then I better get paid. This or stripping. Although stripping's looking more appetising daily.'

*

She digs her fingernails into my hand and I let go with a manly squeal. She flings the bathroom door open with such force, Brodie drops his PlayStation controller in surprise.

'Sorry Brodie,' she says, one hand still on the door handle, the other still clawing my flesh. 'Just wanted to check you're okay.'

He nods, mute. Picks up the controller and returns to his game. My mini-me, only with big dark eyes and better hand–eye coordination than I ever had. Sure he's playing now, while Jules is around. Soon as we're back in that bathroom he'll be analysing and studying again. Last week he drew a circuit diagram of the toaster from memory. At least, I *think* it was a circuit diagram and I *think* it was the toaster. Who knows what he's really doing when my back's turned?

'When's tea?' Brodie asks.

'In a bit.' I pull Jules back into the bathroom and slam the door.

'What the hell was that?' Jules's angry eyes make Bummer's look positively welcoming.

'I don't care what you say.' Another lie. 'He isn't normal. I'm not even sure he's—'

I stop myself just in time. If I tell her what I suspect she'll have me sectioned. I suddenly wish I had told her this in that little café in town she likes. Bought her a big hot chocolate with marshmallows and sprinkles, slice of cheesecake on the side, kept her sweet.

'Not even sure he's what?' And she's looking at me like she did about the Amber episode, like she did at the fun run. Took the return of a made-up boy to straighten those situations out. Sprinkles won't cut it.

'Proof,' I say, knowing that for all her open-mindedness she's a sceptic, thriving on facts and figures. 'I'll prove to you he isn't what he seems.'

She huffs out through her nose, rolling her eyes.

'Fine.'

8

It got to three o'clock and Rob didn't dare say anything, just continued copying and pasting. He was relieved to find that a Junior Market Analysis Assistant was essentially a 'copy and paster'. He'd spent most of the morning copying names and numbers out of sales spreadsheets and pasting them into the company database. It seemed to Rob that a large part of Credit Co's work consisted of taking simple processes and making them appear difficult and intricate to increase their monetary value. He was considering going to the library after work and getting a book on industry buzzwords so he could throw them into conversation now and then. Everything was going great, apart from the whole finishing-early thing.

Can't just get up and walk out. What if they don't remember? I'll look like a right arse. He looked at the clock in the corner of the screen again. 15:01.

'Hey hard worker!' Gregory appeared behind him and leaned on the back of his chair. 'Don't you need to be somewhere?'

Thank God for Gregory, the interfering shiny-faced git.

'Yeah.' Rob grinned sheepishly and went to the coat stand for his jacket.

'Wouldn't want to leave little Buckland Junior standing at the school gates, would we?' Gregory laughed heartily.

'Brodie,' said Rob, quietly, checking his phone and wallet were still in his pockets. 'His name's Brodie.'

*

Rob got right up to the gates of his former primary school before realising what he'd done. He'd headed to the school as if he really did have a child to collect. He looked up at the big oak tree in the corner of the playground, its bark even rougher and hornier than when he used to try to climb it all those years ago. He was seven in the Brodie photo. He'd thought primary school was a drag, but God, if he'd only known. At least at primary school he'd grown up with everyone there, so his ginger hair wasn't a novelty. At secondary school, he may as well have had leprosy.

It wasn't so bad when Bummer was around. Not that Bummer was a hardnut – Rob had never seen him raise a fist to anyone – just that he gave the impression of being one. That beneath the dopey grin and pot belly there was a metal skeleton with laser eyes.

Unfortunately Bummer left school the year after Rob started, so then it was wedgies and toilet dippings day in day out while Bummer started on the road to his porn empire working as a glamour photographer's assistant. The models loved him because of his shabby, gentle ways and purposeful, professional disinterest in boobs and minges.

Everything's different now. Striking out on my own. The plan is working.

'Miss, miss, there's a man!' A kid with bunches and a checked dress ran over to the teacher on playground duty. Rob had heard that his old headmaster, Mr Ibsen, was still there. Amiable old sort, but even he was unlikely to welcome a former pupil staring into the playground with their hands in their pockets. Rob waved to the teacher as nonchalantly as possible and walked on.

*

I slide the lock back in the tiniest increments, holding my breath, and look at Jules pointedly with a finger to my lips. Move the door open millimetre by tiny millimetre.

Outside, Brodie is still playing the game. I let my breath out carefully, disappointed that the effort was unnecessary, but still not wanting to blow my cover. Jules rolls her eyes and opens her mouth, no doubt to point out how dumb this all is, but I wave my hand at her urgently and she shuts up once more. She seems intrigued if nothing else.

I tiptoe closer to Brodie.

I fucking knew it.

Brodie has a notebook open on the floor in front of him. Rather than playing the game as intended, he's watching how the enemies move, marking down their patterns in his large childish handwriting so he can avoid them rather than kill them. I point this out to Jules triumphantly. She looks at me like I'm the one behaving oddly.

'You never played a fucking video game? I've got books

full of hand-drawn maps and codes at home and I'm a thirty-year-old woman!'

'Sssssh!' And that insane fear's back, the fear of the banshee wail, of the pod person tendrils, of becoming a puppet at the mercy of some alien child.

Brodie doesn't look round, just says quietly: 'I'm really hungry now, Dad.'

That word. I am a puppet at his mercy and it's mostly because of that word.

Defeated, I turn towards the kitchen.

'Fine, I'll get cooking. Jules, a little help?'

Maybe on another page of the notebook there'll be the evidence I need. Next time he's sleeping, I'm going to find it. Those diagrams – surely if Jules saw those she'd agree something was up.

*

That first afternoon was magical. Rob got some beers from Mr Singh on the way home and drank them in the bath listening to the radio. Although when he told Bummer about it later, he said he'd had an illicit wank watching Sofia Marriott's leaked sex tape, because it sounded edgier than Irish folk music and a marshmallow madness bath bomb. He'd never seen Sofia Marriott's sex tape, because the way her eyes looked in the infrared freaked him out.

After his bath he air-dried, playing PlayStation in the nude until his eyes felt crunchy. Then he dug his bag of weed out of the sock drawer and smoked a skinny spliff in bed and drifted into a dreamless herbal sleep.

Lather, rinse, repeat. By Wednesday, it was already getting boring. He wanted to phone Bummer to try to make amends, but there was a New Guy working at the Empornium now and Rob didn't want to ring up and get him. Instead he wandered down to Baby World, almost hoping Poo Witch was there. He imagined a showdown where he put her in her place and she dropped her petition and her protests and Bummer was so grateful they became best friends again, just like before. Poo Witch wasn't there, though. Just Heather, leaning on the counter, drawing something on a big sheet of card. Her face was close to her work, the tip of her tongue poking out of the corner of her mouth. She leaned back to inspect her handiwork and spotted Rob.

'Rob!' Her delight was obvious and at first he thought she'd hug him, but she just clasped her hands together against one shoulder and shifted her weight coyly like an elephantine approximation of a Southern belle.

'You're closing down?' Rob asked, nodding towards her big blocky capitals.

She shook her head, frowning. 'No, it's a clever play on words, actually it says— Oh no! I *did* put Closing Down! It was meant to be Clothing Down. There's an offer on newborn clothes.'

She stamped her foot and looked like she might cry. Rob felt oddly paternal. *Must be what it's like having a kid. Suddenly, you want to care for everyone.*

'Katherine will be so mad,' Heather continued mournfully. 'She says the card's too expensive to not get it right first time.'

'Tell you what,' Rob said, gently taking the marker pen from her. 'If you draw a capital T round the S like this... And then fill all the other letters with a loopy pattern, too, like this… Katherine need never know.' He did a couple of letters and then handed the pen back to her. She snatched it eagerly and tried to copy his examples, pressing the pen down so hard it squeaked. 'Who's Katherine anyway?' he asked, gritting his teeth against the sound.

'My boss,' she said. 'And she's also— PAUL!'

He'd only ever heard her use that tone with him. It was odd that it rankled him to hear it used for someone else.

'Hello sunshine!' The man was tall and handsome in a generic sort of way, if you were into curly dark hair and long straight noses. Rob took in the oversized knitted pullover and boot-cut cords and felt an instant and inexplicable twinge of hatred. If doughnut-fucker had got the job, they could have been mates, but not this guy. 'Can I get some pound coins off you please, lovely?' the man asked, furtively glancing around. 'We're all out again and Victor hasn't had chance to talk me through the banking.'

Rob wasn't sure what annoyed him more – the fact that this suave, sophisticated streak of piss was his replacement, or the fact that he hadn't acknowledged Rob in any way in all the time he'd been here. He contemplated clearing his throat and offering his hand: 'Good afternoon. You got my sloppy seconds.' But he didn't. The way the guy kept nervously checking behind him made Rob edgy, too.

Probably one of those buttoned-up psychos, all sensible shoes and polite chit-chat until the day he flips and goes slicing and dicing pensioners with a rusty machete. Where was he when the petitioners were out in force?

'So anyway, Heather,' Rob said loudly, because Heather had disappeared out back getting change for his replacement. 'I'll be off.'

Usually, Heather would come running out to say bye, much to Poo Witch's chagrin. This time all he got was a muffled 'Mmm.' He was relieved when his mobile rang.

Somebody loves me!

He hurried out of the shop before answering. Traffic passed, drowning out the background hubbub of protesters, although there were far fewer than when Rob worked there. New Guy really landed on his feet.

Rob's shoulders sagged at the voice on the other end of the line and he realised he had been hoping for Bummer. It was just Mum.

'Big news!' she cried without even waiting for him to say hello. 'We're moving to Malta!'

'WHAT?'

Nobody loves me.

'Come round Saturday, we'll fill you in on everything. There's still so much to get sorted, got to go. Kisses!'

She sounded breathless and happy. Way happier than when he'd told her about the new job. He'd thought that that was the pinnacle of her existence.

*

I'm holding the Kenny Ketchup bottle and staring into its moulded plastic face, so I can't see her expression. This Kenny Ketchup is an astronaut. There are versions where he's a cowboy, or a policeman, even a bear, but I usually buy the astronaut. At least now I can pretend it's for Brodie. I sniff and twitch my nose. I won't wipe my eyes. No need. That would be stupid.

Jules reaches for the Kenny Ketchup. She gives his neck a quick twist to make sure the lid's on properly but it looks like she's putting him out of his misery. She takes him out of my hands and puts him back in the cupboard, in the sticky brown ring left by Billy Barbecue's leaked contents. For a moment her fingertips rest lightly on the backs of my hands. I take a breath, about to tell her something else, something nothing to do with all this. Well, sort of to do with this, because I wouldn't have met her without it—

'It can't have been all bad?'

'Sorry?' I register that she's saying words, quietly, but I can't absorb them.

She steps back, brushing the hair out of her eyes and then lowering the oven temperature at arm's length.

'Your mum, Bummer, Brodie.' She says it even quieter and nods towards the seated child. 'All difficult stuff to cope with, but it can't have been all bad, surely?'

My mouth twitches, knowing something's expected of it. It seems like she wants me to say *her*, that she's the good thing to come out of all this, but I may be misjudging the situation. I've misjudged a lot of things recently. I don't really want to tell her the next part, but like everything lately, I feel I don't have much choice. My path is set, and it's a collision course with the sun. I glance at Brodie again. The music I put on earlier is still playing. The PlayStation game's theme tune is still competing with it. Brodie can't possibly hear what we're saying. Unless he can, of course. He could be sitting there looking all innocent with his superhuman ears tuned to the frequency of my voice, taking in every word.

*

No one at Credit Co ever called him soulless, or degenerate. Well, Jules did sometimes, but only for a laugh. He didn't have to clean up any mysterious residues, or listen to graphically detailed accounts of fetishes and fantasies. He just had to copy and paste, and add up and forward emails to the relevant people. And when he'd done that a few hundred times, he got to go home and put his feet up.

Which is where the plan stalled a little. What next? If he'd sucked up to the boss, he could probably have scored a promotion, but Austin had recently talked about organising a playdate, which was impossible.

A lady in his life might have been nice, but it turned out luring office hotties back to the flat wasn't as easy as he'd thought. Bummer had no problem with that sort of thing, but for Rob, nothing worked.

When Jules appeared by his desk, he almost made that dreadful sphincter-clenching mistake of calling her Mum, but managed to rein it back to: 'M'Jules.'

'What's happening M'Rob?' she asked. 'You look sad.'

He considered lying, saying he wasn't, or that his dog had died. He considered being truthful, but enigmatic, saying he was contemplating the futility of existence, or the relative emptiness of the universe. His mouth had other ideas.

'Mum's moving to Malta,' it said, quite against his own wishes.

'Sucks,' said Jules, pulling up her chair. 'My parents are dead.'

'What?' Rob turned to look at her, troubles forgotten. 'How?'

'Murdered.'

'Christ.'

'Yeah.'

Suddenly Malta didn't seem so terrible. At least he could visit Malta.

'What happened?' he asked, wondering if it was okay to ask. She'd offered the information in the first place, so it seemed acceptable.

'Shot in an alleyway.'

'They ever get the guy?'

She shook her head. Poor, brave Jules. She seemed remarkably together. Rob would have been a puddle on the floor if his mum had been gunned down in an alleyway. Although at least if they'd got Gordon, too, that would've taken the sting out of it a little.

'Was it a long time ago?' he asked, hoping it wasn't last week because he'd feel absolutely terrible for putting that thumbtack on her chair a few hours back.

'Yeah,' she said. 'I was ten, they were millionaire philanthropists...'

'You're joking about your dead parents.'

'My parents aren't dead. They live on a caravan park by the coast. But don't you feel better about your mum going to Malta?'

He had to admit that he did.

9

Rather than heading straight to Bummer's after work, Rob crossed over and called in at Happy and Tasty Food. He asked for three different chow meins without looking at the menu. One each for him and Bummer and one for the kid he'd doubtless find hoovering the flat, or picking through Bummer's CD collection. Mrs Chen grinned broadly as she prepared Rob's order and, along with two bags of prawn crackers, she added a bottle of white wine to his bag for free.

'For the lady,' she said, winking at Rob.

Rob knew the wine would only be useful if the lady wanted to clean any old silver she had lying around, but it was the thought that counted.

'Thanks, Mrs Chen,' he said with a smile, not bothering to correct her. Bummer was the closest thing he'd had to a girlfriend in years. The sex shop repelled normal women. Getting out of there was the best thing he ever did, it was just the circumstances that were wrong, and he was going to sort that out right now.

As he neared the shop, he saw that someone had daubed a message on the metal shutter in dripping red paint. 'Filth Mongers', it said, in shaky, uneven writing. Rob smirked.

If ever Bummer wanted a new name for the place...

Nestled between Baby World and the Empornium was the other entrance to the flats. Rob prepared himself for the smell of damp and decay and pressed the buzzer. After a moment, the door clicked and Rob pushed his way inside and climbed the stairs. He knew the door to Bummer's flat would be open. Bummer only locked it when he was in bed, which was rare. But things were different now. Rob couldn't just walk straight in. His invitation had been revoked, like an unwanted vampire.

'It's me,' he called from the landing. 'I brought chow mein.'

'Bagsy chicken!' Tenike's light, tinkling voice called out.

'No,' said Bummer. 'We don't want any.'

'Why don't you have the pork?' Rob entered the living room and held the bag out to his friend. 'You like all the pig products.'

The TV was the room's only light source. The curtains were perpetually drawn in Bummer's flat. Rob had never asked why. Tenike lay on the floor with homework books spread out around her. She'd removed her cornrows, and her hair spiralled down her back in luxurious tangles. Occasionally she glanced up from her work to watch TV. A group of pseudo-celebrities were camped out in the catacombs of an old church. The infrared cameras picked up their large, scared eyes and every now and again, one of them screamed and set the others off.

Bummer snatched the bag from Rob's outstretched hand, flopped back down on the sofa. It was a start. Rob hovered uncertainly by the armchair, watching as Bummer opened the chow mein and picked out a big lump of beef with plastic chopsticks. He'd chosen beef on purpose, knowing it was Rob's favourite, trying to get a rise out of him.

'How was work?' asked Bummer. Rob wondered if there was a hint of a challenge in the question. The hint was confirmed when Bummer leaned across and wiped his chopsticks clean on Rob's trousers.

'Pretty cool,' said Rob, trying to ignore the splodge of black bean sauce soaking into his leg. 'Had lunch with Jules again. There's a coffee house inside the office. Did I tell you that already?'

'Yes!' Bummer sprayed half-chewed bamboo shoots onto the floor. 'You told me telepathically while not speaking to me for the last week.' He got up and stalked off to the bathroom, still sucking noodles noisily. Only Bummer could convey his fury through eating.

Rob sat in stunned silence. Bummer had thrown him out, told him he wasn't welcome, and now it seemed like he was the one waiting for an apology. It just didn't make any sense. The celebrities continued shrieking on the television and it gradually became clear Bummer was prepared to eat his meal on the toilet. Rob looked to Tenike for help.

'How do I make it up to your dad?' he asked.

'God, you're thick.' Tenike stabbed a chunk of chicken with her chopstick and ate it like a lollipop. Rob stared at her blankly, wondering if he'd missed the class on reconciliation the rest of humanity got. He opened his mouth to question her further, but she scowled, so he shut his mouth again and went to find Bummer.

Bummer was eating his noodles on the bog. He'd propped the little polystyrene cup of black bean sauce on the sink next to the toothbrushes so he could still dip his food with ease. He was scowling, too, just like Tenike.

'What can I do?' asked Rob.

'Oh, I dunno,' said Bummer, putting his noodles down on the edge of the bath. 'Maybe not walk out on me. Maybe not make out I forced you into working for me and made your life a living hell. Maybe take responsibility for your own stupid decisions for once in your worthless life.'

'Maybe,' Rob agreed thoughtfully. 'Are there alternatives?'

He'd hoped Bummer would laugh at that, but he just turned away to pull up his jeans and flush.

'And now you've got a new high-flying job and new high-flying friends...' He spoke sullenly to the emptying toilet bowl.

'Aww, Bummer.' Rob clapped his friend's shoulder awkwardly. 'No one could replace you, mate.'

There was an uncomfortable pause, broken only by Tenike making spewing noises from the living room. Bummer turned and hugged him and easy as that, they were brothers again.

'I don't get it,' said Rob a little later, reading the TV Guide description again. 'Is Alfred an alien, or does he control the aliens, or are they like his pets or what?'

'Doesn't matter,' Tenike replied, rolling her eyes. 'Point is, every eight-year-old boy thinks *Blight Brigade* is cool. So Brodie should, too.'

'Can't he stand out from the crowd and like something old-school like *Galaxy Squad*?'

'If he wants to get his head kicked in for being a loser.'

'Parents talk about weird stuff at the school gates,' Bummer piped up. 'You need to have his viewing habits down, just in case.'

Rob sighed. 'Fine. *Blight Brigade* it is then.'

Bummer and Tenike took it in turns quizzing Rob to make sure he knew his stuff. And it was weird, but he remembered every little detail about Brodie, even things they hadn't discussed, like how he loved dinosaurs, and said he wanted to be a palaeontologist, even though he was such a good footballer. Rob would have preferred him to go for Man U trials instead, but maybe he could do both.

Rob pictured Brodie as a young man, looking kind of like Rob, but better looking and with cooler hair and clothes. He was standing at a podium in the atrium of a museum. A huge crowd had gathered to watch him speak. Rob was at the front, and before Brodie started speaking, he gave his dad a little wave. Behind him there was the complete skeleton of a massive dinosaur. It was similar to one of those duck-billed ones, but with huge wings. Brodie explained how it was the missing link between dinosaurs and dragons everyone had been looking for for centuries.

'And I named my discovery... Robasaurus. After my dad.'

Stop that. You're getting too far into this shit. He's not really real. Just you remember that.

'...but don't mention what school he goes to.'

'Huh?'

Tenike and Bummer were both looking at him expectantly, expressions eerily similar despite their obvious differences in age, weight and skin colour.

'You can't mention his school,' Bummer reiterated. 'It's too easy for people to check up on, or for someone to say, "Oh, my Julian goes there, he'll have to keep an eye out for little Brodie," and before you know it, the gig is up.'

'What if someone asks?'

'You'll think of something.'

The spooked-celebrities thing had finished and in its place was some glossy American cop show, where all the police looked like ex-models and the cases always strangely mirrored issues they were having in their own lives.

'This is rubbish,' Tenike complained.

'Maybe he could be home-schooled.' Rob reached for the remote.

'Are you kidding?' Bummer nearly spat out his beansprouts. 'Home-school kids are freaks. You don't want a home-school kid.'

'The home-school girl at my ballet class said I shouldn't eat wine gums because the sweet factories murder horses to get hooves for the gelatine. Don't flick off that one! I like it, it's really good!'

It was a glossy American hospital programme where all the doctors looked like ex-models and the cases always strangely mirrored issues they were having in their own lives. Rob sighed and threw down the remote.

'How about you've got a sister who had to give up a promising teaching career due to a wasting disease and now she educates Brodie?'

'Was there just someone in this show with a wasting disease?'

'Maybe.'

'I've just spent two hours working on a made-up kid. I'm not doing a sister, too.'

Bummer paused in licking the foil container. He had black bean sauce on his nose and forehead.

'Said the bishop to the rabbi,' he said with grin.

'Can't you just lend me one of yours?' asked Rob. 'You don't need both the twins all the time. We can dye one ginger and call him Brodie.'

*

'Fucking hell!' says Jules, twisting the oven glove like it's her blankie. 'You actually did it? You actually took one of Bummer's kids?'

'No. How many times do I have to tell you, I made him up!'

'Does his mum know? Is she in on it? Did she secretly not want him?'

'What I'm trying to tell you,' – I lean close, speaking into her ear as if that might keep Brodie's crazy sonar or whatever the fuck he has from working – 'is I'm not sure Brodie is a boy.'

'Oh.' Jules looks relieved, like finally she understands. 'There's nothing wrong with him being intersex, Rob.'

Why are all her assumptions based on me being a total git? That I don't want to acknowledge my child. That I'd steal a child from a friend. That I'm an intolerant arse. Do I seem that terrible?

*

Gregory's nose was red and chapped. He looked like he'd gladly crawl home and lie under a duvet feeling sorry for himself. But it was Team Meeting day, and Gregory was Team Leader, so being away was not an option. At least, for Gregory it wasn't. In his brief time at Credit Co, Rob had learned that Gregory took his job very seriously. He was like a Credit Co policeman, only he didn't get paid any extra for being that way.

'Okay,' said Gregory, with stuffy-nosed faux brightness, 'as this is Robert's first team meeting, let's show him what team meetings are all about!'

After an hour, Rob had a really good idea what team meetings were all about. They were all about talking about things they'd spent the whole rest of the week discussing, only in a claustrophobically formal setting, with Gillian taking minutes in the corner as if her life depended on it. Some redhead using corporate buzzwords she clearly didn't understand, and Gregory beaming at her each time like she'd delivered the secret truth of the universe. Simon, a compulsive blusher, being forced to stand up and give a presentation about his role in the latest project, which Rob missed entirely because he was captivated by the rivulets of sweat racing down Simon's scarlet cheek from his hairline to the collar of his shirt. And what team meetings were about most, the worst, but most important aspect of team meetings was Fun. Organised, structured, strictly adhering to Credit Co's ethics and etiquette policies, F.U.N. Due to Gregory's failing voice and steadily rising temperature, this week's Fun was a hurried game of charades.

'Count yourself lucky,' said Jules as they headed back to their desks, 'last month, we had to have a three-legged race round the car park and Gillian slipped over and laddered her tights and got sent home for breaching dress code.'

Rob just stared at her, unsure whether she was pulling his leg. She'd caught Simon out with the dead parents thing, too, and her story had been even more outlandish that time. Rob liked that about Jules.

Always joking around. Like a bloke.

He took a seat and moved his mouse to get rid of the screensaver. Typed in his password – Brodie22 – and resumed work on his spreadsheet. But out of the corner of his eye, he could see Jules working on *her* spreadsheet and she was frowning slightly and he was forced to admit that although her sense of humour might be pretty blokey, she was most certainly female. While he was largely occupied with the soft downy hairs on her nose, his mouth went rogue again, blurting: 'Do you want to go somewhere after work?'

She laughed aloud and shushed him and then laughed again at his dismayed expression.

'Ethics, young Robert, ethics! No fraternising!'

He shrugged, feeling the colour tug at his cheeks in a pale imitation of Simon's earlier display. A moment later, Jules smiled and leaned across to him: 'I'd love to, but aren't you forgetting something?'

Shit. Brodie.

'I didn't say pub,' he covered smoothly. 'Can't stay out late. Just wondered if you wanted to come shopping.'

Late-night shopping. Genius.

'Okay... but don't you need to pick him up from school or anything?'

'No, a friend's collecting him. It's his... birthday.'

You dirty liar. Brodie's birthday's the twenty-second of September like his grandma's.

'Oh, wow, how old?'

'Eight.'

More lies, he's seven.

'So are we present-shopping?'

'Hmm? Oh. Yeah, yeah. Well, we've got to get him something, haven't we?'

*

I contemplate not going any further with the telling. Just leave it at that. Yes, you're right, Jules, I just had a temporary breakdown. I'm fine now. Brodie *is* my son so let's all just live happily ever after and not worry that one day he might show us his true face and lay his eggs in our hollowed-out carcasses.

I stop abruptly and she smiles, hopefully remembering how great that shopping trip was, how it really seemed to be the start of something and—

She moves away from me to sit with Brodie. She keeps looking at the spare controller, clearly wants to be asked to join in. Brodie's too absorbed in his non-game, slipping past waves of enemies to the end of the map, even though the level won't end until everything's dead. I cough and he turns to Jules.

'Would you like to play, Julia?' he asks. His hands are still moving on the controller, the burly marine on the screen continuing to deftly dodge enemy after enemy despite the fact Brodie's not even looking at the screen any more.

A shiver runs down my spine. I think about yelling to Jules, 'Look, look at that, it's NOT NORMAL!' But then the oven timer buzzes and instead I call them both over to the table for dinner while I retrieve the pizza from the oven. Maybe I will just leave it at that. Maybe after dinner we'll get to be a normal family, the three of us. No need for any more lies, or any more truths.

10

Crossing the road to the shopping centre, Rob felt conflicted. He looked at Jules out of the corner of his eye. Her hair was loose round her shoulders and she was wearing knee-length shorts with knee boots that didn't quite meet them and red tights underneath. In the past he'd always thought that looked really stupid, but he liked it on her. Her cheeks were flushed and she was talking animatedly about something, but he couldn't concentrate on that, because he was too busy thinking about what to buy Brodie. This gift was very important. It could determine their whole future relationship... His and Jules's, of course. Not his and Brodie's.

'Okay,' she said as they entered through the sliding doors, 'where do we start?' She linked her arm through his and he wanted to do a little victory dance, but instead he looked left and right and nodded towards the catalogue shop: 'How about in there?'

She frowned. 'Really? Don't you want to go to a proper toyshop?'

Good job I asked her along or I'd have gone home with some right shit.

'Uh, yeah, yeah, of course.'

'Upstairs then, c'mon!' She tugged him towards the escalator, as excited as if they were picking something out for her.

At the back of the upper arcade, there was a huge toyshop called The Big Top. A tall wooden ringmaster welcomed shoppers through the red and white striped frontage. Rob swallowed at the sheer size of the place. Jules instantly disappeared into the maze of aisles. He hurried after her into 'MiniWorld', a section laid out with miniature houses, toy cars, plastic farmsteads and animals. He felt better among these and pushed a shiny blue sports car up the in-ramp of the multi-storey car park with his fingertip.

'Ehhhhhehheehehehehehehehe!' Jules leapt out from behind a three-foot-high Victorian mansion and made what Rob could only assume was her interpretation of a machine gun. She fired at him repeatedly with a pump-action water gun. Fortunately, it wasn't loaded. Her eyes were alight with a mischievous fire and she would probably have continued shooting until he was a sodden heap on the floor if she'd had access to a bucket of water.

He gave her a devilish grin of his own and barged past her to get to the weaponry section. Snatching up a plastic broadsword and shield, he knocked the gun from her hands with his blade, put his foot on it to stop her picking it up and laughed triumphantly.

'That was a crap gun noise,' he told her, swivelling his sword round so it formed a makeshift bazooka. 'You should do it like this—'

'Sir, could you take your foot off the product please?'

Rob looked round to see a woman dressed as a circus ringmaster. She was around Rob's age, dressed in a black top hat, red tailcoat and cream breeches. Rob came very close to laughing in her face, but there was something familiar about her that pushed him towards politeness.

'Sorry ma'am.' Rob stooped and picked up the gun. 'I'm going to buy this and...' He snatched up a cuddly German Shepherd. 'This little fella for my friend here, and...' He cast around and spotted just the thing. '... this, too.'

'Uniform makes her look like a right gimp,' Jules muttered behind her hand. Rob flinched at the choice of insult. The sales assistant didn't hear. She was too busy examining Rob's selected purchase with undisguised delight.

'An Optibot 7000? You have a very lucky little boy waiting at home!' And that's when it clicked. This woman had a little boy back home. Rob had seen him in his pushchair outside the shop, holding a placard and wearing a poorly knitted woollen hat.

'Wow,' said Jules, 'he sure is! I don't know what it does, but it looks cool.'

Rob tried to focus on Optibot 7000, hoping the protester didn't blow his cover somehow. The toy robot was beautiful. Beautiful and mean, like a futuristic diva. His body was smooth metallic-purple chrome, his large feet, fists and domed head matte silver. His moulded face was set in a permanent scowl, with deep-set blue lights for eyes. His box claimed he could say over fifty phrases, was programmed with thirty sets of movements and could be taught over two hundred more.

As the assistant rang the toys through the till, Rob thought there must be some mistake. He wanted to say: 'Hang on, I'm buying a toy robot, a cuddly dog and a gun, not a holiday villa with a pool and maid service.' But the assistant and Jules were both looking at him with such adoring admiration, he couldn't ask to put the robot back. Optibot had transformed him from a grubby little man selling dildos and anal beads into the best dad in the world.

Move over Bummer.

Rob reached into his inside jacket pocket for the credit card his mum had given him for emergencies.

*

'Could you pass the ketchup, please, Julia?' Brodie asks. She hands Kenny over.

I'm not massively experienced with kids, but I'm pretty sure Brodie's table manners aren't the usual. Not just the politeness, which is fairly weird if I'm meant to be his dad, but the cleanliness. He's been with me a week now, and he's never spilled anything. He's never got food round his mouth, or played around with it, or showed me what he was chewing. I remember Gordon telling me off for all those things as a kid, and even when I was much older than Brodie.

Jules doesn't seem to notice anything's amiss, though, so maybe it's just me. Maybe I always had Brodie and he did get kidnapped and returned to me. Maybe everything else is in my head. Like the conversations I've heard him having that stop the moment I open the door. Not just a kid talking to his toys, but both sides of the conversation, one voice crackly like it's over an intercom. Or the strange symbols that are sometimes left in the steam on the bathroom mirror, too high for Brodie to have been able to reach. I caught the kid flicking a towel at them once, trying to clean them away before he went to bed. Trying to destroy the evidence?

*

'Your mum's gonna go spare!' Bummer held Optibot upside down, pressing the controls on the soles of its feet. All the kids were with their various mothers, so Rob was round keeping him company.

Serves her right for making out she's going to Malta. Gordon won't even go on the Eurostar. As if they'd go to Malta.

'She won't.' Rob chewed his fingernail.

'She will, and she'll want to know what you were doing spending that much at The Big Top. It'll come up on the statement you know.'

'I know.' He did know, but he hadn't thought about it. He'd been too busy enjoying being respected and respectable for a change. 'I'll tell her it's for deprived kids in Africa. For some charity drive at work.'

'Aww, shit!' Bummer probably didn't hear him. He'd been trying to get Optibot to break-dance for two and a half hours. Optibot preferred to moonwalk and say: 'Crush them!' The instructions said it was easy to give Optibot commands. Rob had given up after fifteen minutes, but Bummer had now proved categorically that it wasn't easy.

Saying goodbye to Jules wasn't easy either. She clearly wanted to go back to Rob's flat. She was more than willing to call in at the babysitter's and pick Brodie up along the way. So naturally,

Rob had to make his excuses about Brodie missing his mum more on his birthday, what with it being the time she died and all, and so another woman turning up might upset the apple cart, and he came off sounding incredibly heroic and selfless, but no closer to easing his aching balls. It wasn't like he wanted a relationship or anything. If he'd wanted that, he could have stayed with Lisa. No. Time to reap the benefits of all that hearts and flowers crap.

'Bloody piece of foreign shite!' Bummer threw Optibot onto the sofa.

'High-five, buddy,' said Optibot, raising his silvery fist.

'So, how's New Guy getting on?'

'Not bad,' said Bummer, suddenly looking perkier. 'Used to work in corporate law. He thinks we may have grounds for a harassment case against Poo Witch.'

'Oh, right.'

Rob tried to find something on television that wasn't about people in love, or having sex, or having successful, fulfilling lives.

Bummer picked Optibot up again and cradled him in his lap, twiddling his radio antenna back and forth absent-mindedly. 'It's all going to be fine. She's not going to bankrupt me, or anything. Everything will be totally fine.'

'Good, good.'

Everything comes up roses for Bummer again.

*

'You see, at the time, I wasn't looking for a relationship, just pure sex.' That was meant to make my eagerness to bone sound better, but I realise it probably makes it sound worse.

It's not how I meant it at all. I want to show her how much I've grown, how much I've changed, because of her.

'So that's why you ended up shagging Amber?'

She's finished her wine now and is rolling the glass back and forth in her palms like a movie villain. She doesn't seem particularly jealous, which makes me feel even more hopeless. She found another bottle of wine in the back of the cupboard, so that's perked her up a bit. Must be another one of Mrs Chen's 'gifts'.

Brodie's doing the dishes while we talk on the sofa. Didn't even have to be asked. Can't she see there's something seriously up with that?

'I didn't shag her.'

'Oh? How come she was so pissed at you if not for your disappointing penis?'

The light hurts my eyes. I have this weird tension headache that's growing steadily worse. I could skip over this part, but I'd like to see Jules jealous. She probably won't be, but I have to try. At least she seems to have temporarily given up trying to prove that Brodie is real. Maybe she thinks she's already won that argument, what with him being there doing the dishes and all.

*

Rob swiped his card at reception and sauntered through the building. He stopped off at the coffee shop and bought two cappuccinos and two chocolate chip muffins. On his way up the stairs with his carefully balanced tray, the two pastel-shirted M&A guys caught up with him. He couldn't really claim not to be going their way, so he was forced into polite corridor chit-chat.

'So,' said the taller of the two, Rob thought he was called Toby, not that it mattered. 'We couldn't help but notice you've been seeing a lot of Julia.'

Rob shrugged. It wasn't a question. This all felt very playground.

'Yeah,' the other one – *Stanley?* – took up the interrogation, 'you do know it's against ethics?'

'Oh, well, wouldn't want to breach ethics now, would I?' said Rob, wanting to flick cappuccino foam onto their expensive glasses and leg it.

'No,' said Toby, in a tone that could have been considered threatening if he wasn't wearing a lemon and cerise tie. 'You really wouldn't.' There was an uncomfortable silence and then the pair moved off to talk to a man in a wig and braces. Rob amused himself creating puns about company bigwigs. Hopefully one of them would be good enough to share with Jules.

When he got to his desk, the first thing he noticed was the relaxed atmosphere. Gillian was sitting on the edge of her desk, talking to a couple of M&A girls about last night's soaps. Simon, usually hunched over his computer typing feverishly to reach a deadline, was reading his emails, chuckling now and again. The second thing he noticed was Gregory's absence.

'Greg's off sick,' said Jules, licking her lips. She was munching a tub of coleslaw at her desk. It stank like a runner's armpit, but Rob just smiled to himself. She'd smell better once she'd got the muffin down her neck.

'I got you a muffin,' he said, handing it over. 'And a cappuccino.'

'Oh, you're sweet,' she said with a sigh, 'but I can't. I'm on a diet. I'm getting pudgy.'

'Oh. Right.'

This forced Rob to do a reappraisal. The Jules he had fixed in his mind had a devil-may-care attitude. She didn't worry about her looks, or her hair, or her make-up. She just told jokes and talked about zombie movies and ate junk. This woman, he suddenly noticed, had her hair tied back, and earrings in and a magazine article about Bikini Bodies open on her desk. This wasn't Jules. It might've been Julia, but it wasn't Jules.

He didn't comment on her new look, because he knew he wouldn't be able to sound positive about it, and she'd just get all huffy. So he gave the muffin to Duncan, the office dustbin, and the extra cappuccino to Simon, who was far too calm for Rob's liking.

In most ways, the day went really well. Because Gregory wasn't there, and Sales couldn't spare a manager because they were far too important, there was no team meeting. Everyone used the time to get the day's work done so they could spend the rest of the time flirting and chatting on Instant Messenger. It was a Friday, so everyone was fairly upbeat anyway, and it was payday. The only downer was Julia's weird behaviour. She worked nearly all day and hardly told any jokes and every time she came back from the toilets, she'd reapplied her lipstick and adjusted her hair.

Not that Rob would usually notice that kind of thing.

As she was returning from one of those breaks, Rob decided to make his move. 'Hey,' he said, as if he'd just thought of it. 'It's payday and it's a Friday and—'

The bing-bong of his Instant Messenger interrupted.

> U out tonite?

The sender was ARSimmons. Rob frowned.

'Who's A. R. Simmons?'

'Amber. What were you saying?' Julia turned fully away from her computer screen for the first time that day.

'Which one's Amber?'

'Sits at the back near M&A... You were going to ask me something?'

> Cmon. Every1s out.

Rob stood up at his desk and peered over the rows of cubicles. The pastel brothers saw him looking and glared, shaking their heads. A vision in a pencil skirt sat between them. Long red hair and breasts that deserved a round of applause. Well done that woman. Rob sat back down to reply.

'Hmm?' he asked, as his fingers flew over the keys. 'Oh, I was just going to say – everyone's out, are you coming?'

'Uh, yeah, sure,' Julia said very softly on the edge of his hearing. 'Sure, I guess.'

*

Rob was sitting in the bar with Amber on his knee, determined not to feel guilty.

Why should I feel guilty? Just because Jules is sitting there with a face like a smacked arse and no one's talking to her, that's not my fault is it? She wanted to come didn't she?

'Us ginges have to stick together, don't we Rob?' said Amber, ruffling Rob's hair. He turned his attention back to her.

She really does have a cracking set. I mean, it's not like that's all I look for in a woman, but they are exceptionally good.

'We sure do,' said Rob, trying hard to maintain nipple cont— eye contact. Trying hard to maintain eye contact.

Jules continued stirring her drink with a straw, making little whirlpools and staring at them. She'd been doing that for ages. She nearly knocked her drink over as the two pastel shirts barged past with trays of cocktails. Rob had never been anywhere where they let you have trays. In most of his usual haunts, a tray would be too much like a potential weapon. He'd never been anywhere so full of pine either. Pine floorboards, tables, chairs.

More like a furniture showroom than a pub. *Sorry, bar.* The others all laughed at him every time he called it a pub and said he was 'old-skool'. They definitely pronounced it with a k, somehow.

Toby set his tray down in front of Rob, blocking Rob's view of Jules.

'Where's my pint?' asked Rob, taking in the array of brightly coloured but distinctly non-beery drinks before him.

'We got you a Mephisto Fisting instead,' said the other pastel, who Rob now knew was Spencer. He laughed at Rob's bewildered expression and said: 'It's a cocktail, dummy!'

Who says 'dummy', dickwad? Rob thought, but didn't say, because for some reason Amber and Spencer seemed to be bumchums or something. He didn't want to ruin his chances just yet.

'And where's my change?' Rob added as Spencer and Toby took their seats opposite.

Everyone laughed.

'Oh, Rob, you're so quaint,' said Toby, sniggering into his drink. It looked like lager, but it couldn't be, because it was in a fluted glass with a piece of lime in it.

A chair scraped back and Rob watched Julia hitch her handbag farther up her shoulder as she got to her feet. She hovered by the table, like she was weighing something up in her head. Eventually, she said: 'So, I'm heading off then?' the hint of a question in her tone. Conversations carried on around her. No one else looked her way. She sighed and turned towards the door.

'Bye then,' called Rob over the hubbub, trying to be friendly. She rounded on him like he'd just called her a crotch pheasant or something and narrowed her eyes.

'Shouldn't you be going, too, Rob?' she asked.

Spencer and Toby paused in their attempts at charming a girl and a guy from accounts and turned to watch this unfolding scene. Identical smirks touched the corners of their mouths. They elbowed one another and muttered their amusement.

Rob's balls dropped into his shoes. Any sense of arousal developed from having Amber sliding around in his lap shrivelled like a worm in the sun.

'What, er, what do you mean?' he asked, throat suddenly dry. *Why do I feel so guilty? Don't remember signing any contract. I'm not tied to her. I'm too young, for Christ's sake.*

'Don't you have a son back home? Or have you forgotten about him?' She turned and flounced out of the p— bar.

Rob realised he was turning red – not a good colour with his hair. Amber shuffled away onto the bench at the side of him, waiting for an explanation.

'He's at my sister's,' said Rob, draining his drink. *Hell, I've invented a son, why not a sister? Better than saying: 'I made him up so girls like you would shag me.'* 'She doesn't have a wasting disease, though.'

Amber smiled weakly. 'That's nice.' She fiddled with the gold chain on her wrist. 'You've got a son, how... nice.'

This is all wrong. A man with a kid is meant to be like a chocolate-covered handbag to a woman. She's supposed to go all gooey-eyed and think I'm all responsible and mature and stuff without actually having to care about politics or stop playing computer games. But this one's acting like, like... like it's a bad thing! Maybe... maybe, some women don't... Nah, it was Jules. Emitted an off-putting-girlfriend vibe or something. Need to stop thinking about Jules and get to know Amber, find what she's attracted to.

And there's an easy way to learn more.

'Shots anyone?'

*

'Why are you telling me this?' There are tears in Jules's eyes now and she keeps wiping her nose. 'I know you picked her at the start, but now... I thought...'

She looks down at her knees, then across at her freshly poured glass of wine.

Maybe she's going to chuck it in my face. It's what I deserve, after all.

When I started telling this part, it felt like the key to everything. Amber came back with me and Brodie wasn't there. Where was he if not home with me? The sister was clearly made up, even Bummer wouldn't say he was babysitting, so where was Brodie? And better than that, telling this part will show Jules how Amber was nothing, just a pair of tits and a bad attitude, a horrible mistake I'd never repeat.

11

Amber stumbled backward onto the sofa, dragging Rob by his tie.

'Your flat's nice,' she told him between kisses.

'Is it?' asked Rob, enjoying the gropey, scrabbley kissing and not really paying attention to anything else.

After shots, shedding the two pastels was easy. They weren't big drinkers, and when it became clear Rob and Amber were on for a killer sesh, they mumbled something about going for kebabs and meeting up later. Rob made damn sure that wasn't a possibility, moving from bar to bar a drink at a time.

He avoided anywhere he might see Bummer's mates, because they were sure to come rushing over and make him look uncool. They all had names like Pop-it-in Pete, and Sticky and Gooser. Amber didn't need to be introduced to people like that.

He spent the night nodding appropriately at her small talk, even though he didn't know who Loz and Shannon were, or if she was actually prettier than the two of them put together, or even if they genuinely were a pair of fat, untalented bitches.

On a scale of Jules to Heather, it was towards the Heather end of the spectrum, but at the time it seemed worth it.

He didn't even have to try to trick her into going back to his flat by saying his contact lens had slipped, or anything. She suggested it. She seemed to have forgotten all about Brodie, and if that was what it took to get laid, then so be it.

'It's really nice,' said Amber, slipping a hand inside his shirt and caressing the flesh, sparking a chain reaction of goosebumps up his chest and across his shoulders. 'What's the bedroom like?'

Rob was suddenly glad he hadn't got round to making the flat look too much like there was a kid there. There were a few of Bummer's finger-paintings on the fridge and a couple of cool toys, but that was it. Otherwise the quintessential bachelor pad.

Smiling, he took Amber's hands and pulled her to her feet and into his arms. After some red-hot kissing action, he led her through to the boudoir. His hand hovered by the light switch, but he decided to leave it off. He didn't want Amber being put off by the poster of Mimi Winters.

No sense in making her feel inadequate right before the act.

He reached for the lamp instead and lowered her onto the bed. Her hair fanned out across his duvet, shining and silken to the point of feeling like a wig, not like Jules's hair at all. He pretended to smell it, surreptitiously sniffing the bedlinen over her shoulder.

'Aww, were you smelling my hair? That's so sweet!'

'Yeah, well, it just smells so great, I couldn't—'

'Intruder! Intruder! You are in breach of the Intergalactic Code! You have five seconds to exit the area!'

'What the hell is that?' asked Amber, pulling her bra strap back onto her shoulder.

Oh.

Fuck.

'That?' said Rob, trying to sound casual as he shuffled round the room, trousers round his ankles. 'Oh, that's just—'

'FIVE!'

'Optibot...'

Fucking Bummer. The total, total arsehole. Rob kicked his feet free of his trousers and scrabbled under the bed. *Where has he hidden the damn thing?*

'FOUR!'

'...it's Brodie's favourite toy.'

'Then what's it doing in your room?'

'THREE!'

Rob drew the curtains and felt all along the windowsill. Had to be somewhere near, or the motion sensor wouldn't have triggered when they sat on the bed.

Bloody Bummer. Couldn't make the thing break-dance, but managed to set Guardian mode.

'Just a little game we like to play. Hiding it in each other's rooms, that kind of thing.'

'TWO!'

Rob couldn't remember exactly what Optibot did when he reached the end of his countdown, but he was pretty sure it wasn't a good thing to happen at two in the morning in a flat with chipboard walls.

Amber was not amused. She sat in the middle of the bed, arms folded, jaw set. Jules would have been annoyed, too, but not like that. Her glare would have said he was an annoying dick rather than the worst human alive.

'ONE!' Optibot emitted a terrible sonic sound, one that

was felt as much as heard. Rob's eyes streamed and he felt that if he didn't cover his ears, his brain would dribble out of them. Amber screeched and leapt off the bed to flick on the light.

'Can't you help me look?' bellowed Rob, his face wet with tears and snot forced out of his head by the aural onslaught.

'What's it look like?' Amber screamed back, her eyes screwed tight shut.

'Like a robot!' Rob roared. 'And it might help if you opened your fucking eyes!'

He knew immediately that was a mistake. Amber wasn't a girl you could swear in front of, never mind at. She opened her eyes but only to glower at Rob and then survey his room disdainfully.

'What about those?' She pointed at his shelves.

'What? Not those! Those are collector's items – didn't you see the movie?' She tilted her head and gave him a look she usually reserved for Jules or girls with VPLs. 'Fine, whatever, I'll find it.'

Ten minutes later, Rob found Optibot at the bottom of his laundry basket. How the hell the infrared tripwire feature worked from there was beyond him.

Got to hand it to those Japanese, they make quality action figures.

As Rob looked down at Optibot's sculpted metallic face, his anger ebbed away. The desire to rip Bummer's throat out through his arsehole slowly dispersed.

It was a pretty funny prank. If Rob had been the one to think of it, he would've laughed until he bawled.

That Bummer.

'I found him—' Rob strolled into the lounge and waved

the toy sheepishly at Amber. His hand dropped to his side, still gripping Optibot tightly. Amber had pushed the sofa up against the front door and was sitting on it, crying.

'What are you doing?' he asked.

'Someone's trying to get in!' she almost screamed.

It was only then that the ringing in his ears subsided enough to allow him to hear the clamour outside. Someone *was* trying to get in. The door handle was turning and someone was hammering on the door violently, powerfully enough to bow the centre inward.

Rob pushed the sofa aside a little and opened the door the tiniest crack. A huge, dark, malformed shadow loomed forward, causing Rob to leap back. As he did so, the hallway light flared brilliant white before exploding, raining glass onto the hallway carpet.

'What the hell was that?!' yelled Amber, sobbing harder.

'There was someone...' Rob nudged the sofa further with his hip and opened the door fully. The hallway was empty. He looked up at the light bulb. It was intact. No glass on the floor. He scratched his head. Maybe he was more drunk than he thought.

'Your stupid mates and their stupid pranks!'

'Yeah,' Rob agreed uncertainly, even though he knew Bummer wouldn't be out in the middle of the night, and he didn't have any other mates. Maybe it was neighbourhood kids messing around? Yeah, that made sense. And the smashing light? Some kind of sensory hallucination caused by the Optibot? Yeah, like when that cartoon gave kids weird seizures or something.

Having suitably convinced himself nothing was seriously

amiss, Rob respectfully waited for a lull in Amber's drunken crying. When she'd reduced the noise to a fevered sniffling, he said hopefully: 'Shall we return avec le boudoir, then?'

*

'You prick! You're lucky she didn't punch your lights out!'

I suppose that's fair. Unexpectedly, the Amber story seems to have softened Jules towards me. She's pushed all her sadness down inside and the gold in her eyes twinkles like a supernova.

'Oh, wait,' she continues. 'Is that why you were off work afterwards? She smashed you in the balls like you deserved?'

I shake my head, smiling in spite of myself at the eagerness in her voice. We're silent for a moment. I watch a woodlouse navigating the lumpy pile of the rug, aware that I'm getting closer, closer to the really bad stuff. The stuff that obviously she knows about, but has probably never thought about too deeply. And now she will. But I have to tell her, to tell someone. And we've already established that Bummer can't grasp the reality of the situation.

'That make-up and hair stuff wasn't about you, you know,' she says slowly, getting to her feet again. She stands on her tiptoes, then rocks back on her heels to stretch her calves. 'I was just trying something out.'

'I didn't think it was about me.'

Until now. She can see it in my face, I know it, because she suddenly looks annoyed again.

'All right, I need to pee, back in a minute.'

'What?'

For some reason, the thought of being left alone with Brodie terrifies me. He's paused his video game and is sketching in his notebook, drawing the alien. If Jules leaves, I can at least close my eyes, just for a second. The throb in my head is already diminishing at the prospect of shutting my eyes for a moment, escaping that harsh light.

'I need to pee. I need the toilet to pee in. Ergo, I'm going to the toilet and will be back in a minute.'

'Fine, fine.'

As the bathroom door closes behind her, the sounds of the flat rush in around me. I nearly buckle under them: the urgent music of Brodie's video game, the gentler guitar jangles of my competing track, the hum of the extractor fan from the neighbouring flat's kitchen, the pots adjusting their position on the drying rack, threatening to crash into the sink. Brodie puts down his pen and turns to fix his big dark eyes on me and just like that, I feel better. Way better, like someone injected me with a wonder serum.

It's a trick. Must be.

'You've been talking for ages,' says Brodie.

'Got a lot to talk about.'

'Are you going to kiss her?'

'What? No! What makes you think I'll do that?'

Brodie just smirks that little knowing smirk of his and it's as maddening and beautiful as Jule's.

*

'Aww, no way man, didn't mean to cockblock you!'

'Don't worry about it.'

'Totally forgot I'd put him in there! I'd've warned you if I'd known you were taking a fitty back with you.'

'I know, I know.'

'You just don't usually pull.'

'I— Thanks a lot, Bummer.'

Rob threw down the PlayStation controller and slumped on Bummer's sofa. He was irritated because if it wasn't true before he invented Brodie, then it was definitely true now. Most of the girls at work avoided him like the plague these days. Rob supposed word had gotten round that he had a kid at home.

*

'Or maybe they heard what a massive arse you were to Amber?' Jules interrupts.

'Maybe,' I concede, returning to my story.

*

Approaching any of them, even just about work stuff, got him cold, hard stares or turned backs. Jules was still speaking to him, but even she seemed a bit funny about something. At least she'd quit all the weird hair and make-up stuff.

Rob contemplated going home, taking down all Brodie's drawings and paintings and pasta pictures and burning them on the stove, but for some reason even the thought gave him a strange feeling in his stomach. Bummer's oldest son, Neil, was in the kitchen frying bacon so Rob assumed the smell was making him hungry. He wanted to leave, but his flat seemed all wrong somehow. He didn't want to go back to it.

There was a pair of kid-sized trainers in the hallway that freaked him out. He'd ordered them from a catalogue without really knowing why and when they arrived and he put them on the shoe rack, he felt oddly sad. Those shoes haunted him. They were too clean and unused. He came close to putting his hands in them and walking them about, kicking at the cupboard doors to scuff them up a bit. Fortunately he realised that to do that would have been proper mental. He was already flirting with madness; doing the shoe thing would be giving it a big ol' snog on its cold-sore-encrusted mouth.

'It's like he's taking over my life,' Rob said suddenly, causing Bummer to start and misfire. He shook the controller frantically, trying to waggle himself free of the zombie's clutches.

'Who?' asked Bummer.

'Brodie. Your kids are real and they don't cramp your style like he does.'

'I love my kids, no matter what,' said Bummer with a shrug. 'You gotta take the rough with the smooth.'

'There isn't as much smooth as I thought there'd be.'

'Well, what are you going to do? If you hadn't said the kid's mum was dead, you could've palmed him off onto her.'

Rob let his head fall into his hands.

'It's all too complicated. Wish I'd never started it.'

'Well, you have started it. Real or not, Brodie's yours now and you're stuck with him.'

Neil came in carrying his sandwiches, licking ketchup from his fingers.

'Why don't you just say he's been kidnapped?' he asked. 'Kids get kidnapped all the time.'

*

'I just want to be absolutely clear on this,' she says, now nursing a bottle of pop and a bag of tortillas filched from the kitchen. 'You're saying at this point, Bummer remembered that you made up Brodie. A fact he's now magically forgotten?' I nod, trying to ignore the harsh edge to her voice. 'And the Brodie you're talking about here, the one you were planning on having kidnapped—'

'Not *having* kidnapped! He didn't exist!' I stop, forcing my voice lower, not wanting to wake Brodie, who is now in bed asleep, allegedly. 'He wasn't real.'

Jules rolls her eyes again, stabs a tortilla chip so savagely into the dip it breaks and disappears, submerged.

'I'm trying to help you work through this, Rob, I really am. I just want to know that it wasn't the Brodie in there,' she jerks her head towards the bedroom, 'that you were talking about having kidnapped.'

'Yes. No! I mean, I wouldn't have a real child kidnapped, would I? I'm not a monster.'

She wrinkles her nose and I remember I told her about how I'd considered claiming someone else's dead kid just to make it all end. My non-monster credentials probably aren't looking too good. I'm surprised she didn't come back from the kitchen with a can of mace.

Maybe she did. Maybe fetching the pop and tortillas was a front. Her bag's on the kitchen counter, after all.

She picks the broken tortilla out of the dip, tosses it into her mouth and sucks her fingers clean. Her eyes are searching, scouring my face, no doubt looking for the lie.

I wish it was there. I wish this was the lie and the lies were
the truth. Her brow crinkles and eventually she says: 'You
ever consider another reason the women in the office might
have avoided you?'

*

'Everything all right?'

'Mmmm?'

'You've been staring at Brodie's picture for ages. Gregory'll
start dropping hints before long.'

Gregory's hints were damn annoying. Little tee-hee asides like
'Ho-hum – these spreadsheets aren't going to fill themselves in!'
Ho-hum. Berk.

Rob traced the outline of Brodie's face with his fingertip
and pictured it on a missing poster. Tears welled in his eyes.

Holy shit. What the hell is wrong with me?

Jules hadn't been exactly full of sympathy over the whole
Amber debacle, would probably be even less so if she knew the
full story, but she looked genuinely concerned about this.

'Has something happened to Brodie?'

*The perfect in. But I can't do it. Can't let some imaginary
kidnapper have him.*

'No, I'm sure everything's fine.'

*May as well lay the groundwork, just in case. I mean, it's
not as if I'm actually going to say he's been kidnapped, is it?
That'd be crazy.*

Jules reached over and laid her hand on top of his. Her
palm was small and hot, her fingertips soft as they gently
stroked his index finger. He glanced at her from the corner

of his eye. It was clear she'd forgotten all about Amber and the almost-sex. She leaned forward and it made her shirt gape. Her skin was creamy white, almost translucent, so you could see the faint blue-green outline of her veins. He'd take that over Amber's fake-tan cleavage any day of the week.

*

'You like my... skin?' Jules's hand has gone to her chest and she's stroking it self-consciously.

I'm doing my best impression of Simon the office blusher again, my cheeks warm and glowing as the bare bulb overhead. I really need to buy a lampshade. Her eyes are wide and she seems a little afraid of me, which is weird, because I'm the one who's afraid. Afraid of Brodie, afraid of the police, afraid of Jules and the fact I'm handing my bare and beating heart to her and she's hardly noticed. Bare and beating heart? What the fuck have they done to me? I don't think like this.

The pain returns, lancing through my hindbrain in regular throbs timed to match my pulse. I sit with my eyes closed, listening to the sound of my own blood, and eventually she speaks.

'At this point, you could still have just... shut up. Shut up about Brodie, let people forget. You hadn't been to the police, you hadn't notified anyone official.'

I wait, feeling the colour ebb from my face until I'm as translucent as her chest. She could see everything, all of it, if she'd only look.

'So, why didn't you? If all this is as you say it is, which I don't for one fucking second think it is, then why didn't you just let everyone forget all your bullshit and move on?' And I realise this is why she's the one I had to tell. Because she will ask the difficult questions. She'll demand the answers I don't want to give.

12

Mum and Gordon still seemed insistent about Malta. Every time Rob went round, they were poring over travel guides and tourist maps. Showing him pictures of big craggy rocks in turquoise sea, old men playing bowls in the sun, coastal villas with mosaic floors. Almost like their childhood holidays, apart from the turquoise sea, the sunshine and the villas. That morning, his mum rang to say she'd booked the flights, and did Rob want to have a final look through all their stuff before they car-booted it. He decided he would, just to make sure they didn't get rid of anything they needed, because it was pretty obvious they wouldn't go through with this.

As he brushed his teeth, Rob oscillated between joy at getting Mum's house ahead of schedule and a profound sense of loss that there'd no longer be anyone to cook him Sunday roasts and buy him little presents when he needed them.

If they actually go, of course. He spat and watched the frothy toothpaste swirl down the plug hole.

The bus journey made him nervous, but there were no

sightings of Lisa MacFarlane, which was good. He imagined living in his mum's house and having to see Lisa on the bus to work every day. He got older and greyer, and she stayed permanently youthful and beautiful, even while her family continued to grow and she got on the bus with three kids, five, six. She got on with her husband and he was the guy who replaced Rob at the Empornium, with his handsome chin and attractive hair. Imaginary elderly Rob got imaginary elderly Jules to ride the bus with him, and she looked Lisa up and down and said: 'Wow, you're right, you really aren't good enough for her.'

Rob breathed out heavily through his nose as if he could expel his imaginings and inhale something better.

Should probably just sell it. Get myself somewhere proper.

When he got to the house, he expected it to look different, somehow. It didn't. The privet hedge still formed a spindly arch over the gate, the hanging baskets still twirled slowly on their hooks on either side of the door when the breeze caught them.

Getting rid of those will be my first job. He looked up at the red-brick building. It was an ex-council house, built back when they made council houses a reasonable size.

Rob stepped over the threshold and, rather than being met by a cavalcade of cats, he came face to face with Gordon, standing right there, who embraced him awkwardly. Rob's arms locked to his sides in panic. He couldn't have hugged Gordon back even if he wanted to.

Gordon took a step back, but kept a hold of Rob's arms, as if he might run given half a chance. 'He's here!' he shouted into the house. 'The boy's here!'

'I'm twenty-nine, Gordon.'

'Yes,' Gordon said sheepishly, stepping away. 'Yes, of course. Sue! Come on!'

'I'm just getting the— Smile!'

The flash left Rob reeling. Coloured lights spangled the air around him like he was imprisoned in a kaleidoscope. His mum beamed.

'I want to record every bit of today!

'Why?'

'Because today—' She pressed her lips together firmly and breathed in sharply through her nose. 'Today's probably the last full day we'll have together. We fly out on Friday.'

'What?'

'I told you, hon, the flights are booked. And you'll be working, won't you, so we might not see you again.' Tears flowed down her cheeks and she embraced him tightly, stroking his hair like when he was little. Rob wondered when it would be appropriate to raise the issue of getting the house signed over.

Maybe after dinner.

Dinner was weird. Mum had done enough food for ten people, and refilled his plate as soon as it was empty, like he'd be living off water and Pot Noodle when she wasn't there to cook for him.

'There's dessert after,' she said, pushing the same piece of meat around her plate with her fork. 'Cheesecake, meringue or chocolate cake. Or you can have a bit of each if you like.'

'I think I'll have a bit of each,' said Gordon, getting to his feet.

'It's not for you, Gordon!' She said it so savagely, Rob flinched, too.

'Hey, it's fine.' Rob suppressed a belch and waved his

stepfather towards the kitchen. 'I'll just have whatever's left. You get stuck in, Gordon.' Gordon didn't need telling twice. He hurried to the kitchen clutching his plate, blinking rapidly like a kid who'd got an unexpected telling-off.

Knew this was coming. She's going to break down and say she can't leave after all.

Mum suddenly looked very old and small. The grey in her hair was more prominent than the chestnut, the lines under her eyes more noticeable than the sparkle in them. Her knuckles seemed bonier, her clothes baggier. She was disappearing before his eyes. She took a deep breath and he was relieved when she breathed it out again.

'I'm glad you've found this new job,' she said, reaching for his hand across the table. He let her take it. 'Although it was good that Victor could look out for you at your old place.'

Rob nodded. Her hand was very hot and dry, like a leaf in a sunny windowsill.

'We... we would have liked to have left you more money, but there are the flights, and the shipping...'

He squeezed her fingers gently.

'Don't worry about the money, Mum.' *I'm a great son. So selfless.* 'The house will fetch a few bob.'

Her eyes widened and then filled with tears.

Awww – overwhelmed by my generous nature.

'Oh, Robert!'

She's going to hug me now and tell me she can never leave me.

She pulled her hand away from his and covered her face.

'Oh, Robert, you didn't think you were getting the house?'

'I— what?'

'Robert, where did you think we'd get the money to start a new life in Malta? Gordon sells reclaimed fireplaces. I used to clean hotel rooms. We don't have money, Robert. This house is all the money we have.'

'Oh.'

'You have a flat and a well-paid job. That's more than a lot of boys your age.'

Most Premiership footballers are younger than me. Most A-list actors, too.

'You're going to be all right, aren't you Robert?' Finally the hug came. He was too big to be properly held by her fragile bird body, so the majority of the hugging had to come from him. Tears wet his hair as she leaned her cheek on the top of his head and stroked his face.

'It's better that I leave, Robert, it really is. I feel like you'll never stand on your own two feet with me around.'

Why bring a child into this world only to abandon him?

*

'So, this is it then,' said Bummer, his voice slightly echoey in the empty house. Mum and Gordon were in a taxi outside, waiting for Rob to finish up so they could wave goodbye and head to the airport. He would have gone with them and waved them off, but he couldn't drive and it would've been weird to take a taxi with them and then have to make his own way back. Or worse still, return with the same taxi driver, all their small talk already exhausted, listening to talk radio and praying for an early death. He wondered what Mum and Gordon would do if he just stayed here. Just sat on the stairs as their taxi fare climbed and climbed, red digits clicking up on the counter. Probably nothing. Probably just go to the airport and ring when they get to Malta. Rob felt like he was drifting. Like his body was filled with helium, and if a gust of wind blew through the open door, he'd be off into the street and up into the air and away. Higher and higher, until—

'Come on, mate.' Bummer threw an arm round him and gave him a squeeze, anchoring him back to the world again. 'Let's turn the leccy off and get the hell out of Dodge.'

'Why don't we leave it on? Give the new residents a nice surprise?'

Bummer looked at him, the shadow of a smile crossing his lips. 'Kidder, if this wasn't your mum's house, I'd have done a shit in the attic and wiped my cock on all the door handles. But it's nicer to keep all the good memories, isn't it?' He ruffled Rob's hair and held the cupboard under the stairs open.

Rob leaned in to flick the switches on the fuse box. His hand hovered. To the left of the fuse box were two fiercely scratched pencil lines, one saying 'Rob', the other 'Vic'. Bummer was as tall as the fuse box. Rob was tiny. He must have only been up to Bummer's armpit back then. Maybe that's why Bummer was still bigger in Rob's mind even though he was the taller one now.

'Shall we go to the pub after this?' Rob asked. 'There's something I've been thinking of doing.'

If she can abandon a child, so can I. At least Brodie's imaginary.

'Sure.'

'Thanks.'

He flicked the switch.

*

I wipe my nose. Jules is looking at me like I'm broken. I'm not sure if that's better or worse than looking at me like I'm a kidnapper.

*

Rob had never been to a police station before. He had vague flashbacks of collecting Bummer from the station one Christmas because he'd been running down the main street in town with a traffic cone on his head telling everyone he was the King of Farts, screeching and laughing like a madman. The police were more bemused than angry and only took Bummer away at all because the local residents complained and, once they'd got him in the car, there wasn't anywhere else to take him. Bummer couldn't remember where he lived and none of the pubs were willing to phone a taxi. Rob's recollections of that day were hazy. He'd been fairly hammered himself and the hangover was already pounding when he went to fetch Bummer. He'd been too inebriated to feel the roiling terror that plagued him today. Austin's stubby fingers tightened round his forearm, banishing any thoughts of escape. Why did it have to be Austin again? What was it about that pompous little man that made Rob blurt things he'd soon regret?

That morning, Rob had gone into his monthly appraisal as normal, ready to drop in the usual buzzwords and make the odd spreadsheet joke. But rather than getting straight to business, Austin had instead enquired after Brodie and when he might be taking up the playdate with Austin Jr. Before Rob knew what was happening, he had blurted: 'He can't!' and then the only thing he could follow that with in the face of Austin's open-mouthed shock was: 'He's missing!' The words tumbled out, about how Rob went to pick up Brodie from school, and he wasn't there, and some of his friends and some of his teachers had thought he'd gone to music group because he had his guitar with him, but he hadn't, and actually, as they traced it back, no one had seen him since lunch, when he was talking to a man with a dog by the school gate, and now four days had gone by and he still hadn't turned up and it was looking more and more like he'd been kidnapped. Hadn't Neil said that was common? Kids get kidnapped all the time, he'd said.

Austin had listened attentively, and then told Rob he could take as long as he needed on full pay. It was then that some naughty little voice in the back of Rob's head raised its fist and yelled: 'Score!' and that made Rob realise that he wasn't actually a grieving father at all. He was actually a bit of a shit, doing something really awful, deceiving everyone around him, most of them good, kind people who had never done him any harm. He had to stop this, had to find some way out of the lie. But from then onwards, things happened very quickly. Austin phoned his secretary and told her to cancel all his meetings. He put on his coat and then helped Rob into his, one arm at a time like a child, snatched one of the Brodie photos from Rob's desk as they hurried past, and then marched him down to the underground car park. Speaking authoritatively the whole time about the importance of timeliness in child abduction cases, he got straight into his huge shiny BMW and whisked them to the police station.

He was still fully in control of the situation now, in a way Rob found almost comforting. He explained confidently how he could organise things like helicopter flyovers and reconstructions with actors and television campaigns. When they reached the desk, Austin slapped a hand down on it, startling the receptionist. Beside him, Rob twisted Brodie's picture in his sweaty hands, hoping he didn't resemble any wanted child molesters.

'Uh, I, uh,' he stuttered to the lady behind the desk.

'My friend's son is missing,' Austin barked. 'What are you going to do about it?' The woman behind the desk merely nodded and reached for a form from a filing tray.

'How long has he been missing?'

Oh Christ. Rob's mind was blank. He couldn't remember what he'd already said to Austin and his ad-libbing skills had deserted him, like when he was in the school play as the Innkeeper and he only had one line but when he came to it, all he could think of was the Arrowfat's Marrowfat Peas advert, so he sang the words to that instead.

Peas that please, peas that please
They're Arrowfat, Marrowfat
Peas that please.

'Sir?' she said, looking concerned. 'Your lips are moving, but I can't hear what you're saying. Could you repeat that please?'

'Have some compassion, woman!' Austin was going red in the face with fury. 'His son is missing!'

Rob had been mouthing the pea advert lyrics, so he didn't repeat himself. Instead he said: 'He didn't come home from school.'

The woman laid down her pen and smiled. 'Sir, it's only four o'clock. Couldn't he have gone round to a friend's house?'

'He doesn't have any friends,' Rob barked and then, in an effort to sound less angry and crazed, he added: 'Friday. He didn't come home from school on Friday.'

The woman shuffled in her seat. She was wearing a white starched blouse, already completely devoid of creases, but she tucked it in more firmly at the waist and smoothed it down further anyway. Picked her pen back up.

'So,' she pursed her lips and made a mark at the top of her form. 'Mr...'

'Buckland,' he said hesitantly, realising as she wrote it down that Bummer was right; pretending Brodie was kidnapped would be a plain terrible idea.

On record now. No going back.

'Mr Buckland, your son went missing on Friday and you are reporting it now on Monday?'

'Yes.'

'He is dedicated to his job!' said Austin, a man who clearly wouldn't have noticed if his own son had gone missing unless the au pair let him know about it.

'And how old is your son?'

'S-eight. Erm, this is him.'

He pushed the photo across the counter to her. Her eyes shifted from the picture to his face and back again.

'The two of you look very alike.' She smiled grimly. 'Take your time and fill out this form and I'll send someone to talk to you.'

Good work.

Only it wasn't his greatest work, as it turned out. Because first Rob had to spend forty minutes filling out the paperwork, chewing at his cuticles, which helped with the image of the overwrought father figure but was actually due to the strain of creative thought. Austin quietly retreated, embarrassed to be witness to such a raw emotional moment. And then a detective turned up, a big, bluff, hearty man with kindly eyes.

'Hello Mr Buckland.' His voice was gentle but booming, the sort of voice an enchanted tree would have. He shook Rob's hand, a curt, firm twist of his thick wrist conveying strength and professionalism. 'My name is Detective Bellamy. I'm from Missing Persons. I specialise in abductions, so you're in safe hands with me.'

Rob knew instantly that this man was telling the truth. If Brodie wasn't made up, this man would definitely find him.

'...I know it's difficult,' Bellamy was saying in his rumbling tree voice, 'but I need you to answer all these questions as fully as possible. To help Brodie.'

'Help Brodie,' Rob echoed, delving into the fantasy once more.

For an hour he answered questions about Brodie's likes and dislikes and friends and enemies and past, present and hopes for the future, until he started to feel like he really had lost a son, and the tears that came were real, and he wanted to shout: 'I made it all up, he's okay, he's still living his imaginary life at home with me!' But he was too far in by now.

And then, last of all, because he'd sobbed and wailed so loud and for so long, they brought in a counsellor to talk him through the next steps. She sat and put her hand over his and talked in soothing rhythms with a voice like the ocean, while Bellamy slipped out into the corridor to make some phone calls and at the end of all that, Rob was so emotionally exhausted, all he wanted to do was go to the pub and drink it all away.

13

'Oh, Rob. It's clear you believe all this, I can see that, but—'
Her eyes are pitying and I can't take that just now, not her pity.
Knowing what I've done, knowing I don't deserve her pity at all.

'Please, just let me finish. I'm almost finished.'

Almost finished. Now there's an understatement.

*

Slumped over a pint of bitter, Rob thumbed in a text to Bummer.
He hoped Bummer would join him. He didn't want to be alone
right now. Without Brodie, without Mum, maybe even without
Gordon, all the significant parts of him had gone and he was
just meaningless atoms. Strange and empty like his life.

He'd come further afield than usual to avoid running into
anyone from work, or Bummer's gross mates or Lisa. Caught
a bus out to what passed for countryside around these parts
and got off when he saw a pub. It had a low ceiling with heavy
beams that trailed dusty tendrils of spider silk, and several old

men were defiantly smoking pipes. There was a guy at the bar in a tweed jacket who could have been the frotter, but Rob couldn't 100 per cent remember what he looked like.

Rob sighed and pressed send. At least when he was texting it looked like he had the vague vestiges of a social life. Now he was just a lone drinker cradling his mobile and staring at the screen like some poor sad fuck.

Stop staring at the screen, you poor sad fuck.

He pocketed the phone and scanned the bar again, nearly falling off his seat when he spotted Amber on a barstool further round. She was playing with her hair and talking to the barmaid, who looked similar but with shorter, blonder hair and a dumpier figure. Rob looked away quickly, hoping she hadn't seen him and wasn't in the process of telling the barmaid what a massive dickhead he was. This was the last thing he needed. They hadn't exactly parted on the best of terms, and she avoided having anything to do with him in the office. In fact, the closest he'd come to a conversation was when he overheard her say his name, and looked round just in time for her to announce to Spencer and Cody or whatever the fuck his name was: 'Colossal wanker!', which of course they brayed at, like the asses they are. Letting out a slow breath of suppressed rage, Rob realised he'd crushed a handful of aged bar peanuts to dust in his palm.

'Oh, God, that's *him*!' Amber squawked in horror.

Fine. Whatever. Give her both sodding barrels.

'Hi Amber,' he said sweetly, flashing his best sarcastic smile. Bummer once said that Rob was always an arsehole after drinking bitter. Hopefully the pints he'd soaked up so far were doing their work, because he missed Brodie too much to take any prisoners.

'What are you doing here?' she said with a sniff, draining her short like she was considering glassing him.

'What are *you* doing here?' Rob snapped back, aware he might be slurring, but committed to seeing this through anyway. 'This is an old man's pub. You're not an old man. Or are you?'

Hah. Try that one on for size.

He knocked back the rest of his pint with a flourish and indicated to the barmaid for another. It was then that he noticed the barmaid looking at him like he'd just wiped his arse on her favourite dress. Pretty much the exact same look Amber was giving him, in fact.

'This is my sister,' said Amber with a smug incline of her head. 'She's the landlady. She could have you thrown out.'

'Oh, get over yourself, Amber.' Rob was bored of the whole scenario now. He wished he'd gone straight home and taken Brodie's finger-paintings down off the fridge. 'So you got a nasty fright from a robot alarm and didn't get to have sex. Boo-hoo.'

Amber and her sister exchanged incredulous looks and then rounded on him together.

'Actually, you shit-stain, it was the complete lack of decorum you showed when I was drunk and upset. You carried on like nothing had happened and tried to feel me up!'

'Get out of my pub!' said the sister, advancing on him. Menacing if she wasn't five foot nothing.

'Decorum?' asked Rob, on a roll now, bitter and bitterness mixing together inside him, egging each other on. 'If you want decorum, go out with someone from the seventeenth century instead of getting pissed up on tequila slammers, you dozy tart!'

'Right, that's it,' said the sister. 'I'm throwing you out!'

'Oh, yeah?' said Rob. 'You and whose army?'

*

'Brodie's finger-paintings?'

'Hmm?'

Jules's voice is insistent, hurting my brain in the same way the light did earlier. 'You said Brodie's finger-paintings this time. When you spoke about it before, you claimed Bummer did it.'

I keep my eyes closed and forge on, pushing her voice, the agony, down small and compact inside, burying it under the memory of a different, more bearable pain.

*

Bummer's scuffed trainers sloped into view. They stopped by the drain, kicking at the gravel.

'Aww, Kidder.' Bummer's voice seemed a million miles away, lost in the stratosphere. 'You look like shit.'

Bummer's strong hairy arm reached down and helped Rob into a sitting position. Rob hadn't realised the kerb's coldness was actually numbing the pain a little, or he would have stayed lying down. He took the corner of his shirt away from his lip. It had done a good job of blotting the blood and was now reddish brown and soggy with slaver.

'Got in a fight,' said Rob. Although he knew as he said it that it wasn't true. A fight was generally a two-sided thing.

When one combatant lay on the floor and took repeated stomps to the ribs and face, it was less a fight and more a kicking. 'You should see the other guy.' He tried to smile and split his newly mended lip open again.

Yeah, Bummer really should have seen the other guy, because he'd realise what a miracle it was Rob was still alive. The other guy was 'roid rage personified, a broad-shouldered, thick-legged, walking headbutt of a man with knuckles as hard as his steel toecaps. In fact, the more Rob thought about it, the more he wondered how he *did* make it through. He had a vague recollection of a crackly, distant voice saying help was coming, but whoever it was obviously didn't stick around.

'How did you know where to find me?' he asked Bummer.

'Don't you remember? That guy must've really twatted you. You sent a pin to my phone. Thought I should check it out, the way you've been behaving lately.'

Rob checked his phone and saw that apparently he had, although he didn't remember doing it.

Bummer took Rob home, back to the Empornium, where a few picketers were still stoically waving their words of moral outrage. They soon got out of the way when Bummer indicated Rob's broken face and said, 'Haven't your lot done enough?' They went into a hushed huddle to discuss who among them had overstepped the mark.

Bummer cleared the sofa of crisp packets and sweet wrappers so Rob could lie down and, once he'd settled, fetched a hot-water bottle for his ribs, a pack of frozen chicken nuggets for his face and a magazine to lift his spirits. Rob turned the pages.

Amber was right. I have no decorum.

*

Rob spent the next few days hiding out at Bummer's, terrified that his phone was going to ring and it would be the police saying they had found out everything. The kid didn't exist, he'd wasted police time and he was going to prison. An unknown number rang several times, Austin rang several times, and Rob's voicemail slowly filled up with messages from Bellamy sounding increasingly urgent. Finally Rob supposed he would have to take the risk that he was being surveilled and head back home. There would be a plain-clothes officer waiting for him and he could tell them it was all a hoax and get some time off his sentence. Make the best of a bad situation. There were fewer stairs if he went via the Empornium, but he hobbled down the main stairwell anyway. His face compared even less favourably with the New Guy's in its current state.

There were no protesters, so he took his time at the crossing, waiting for the lights to change instead of chancing it. He watched the cars flash by, the tang of someone's catalytic converter assaulting his nostrils. He hadn't heard from his mum yet. She'd sent a postcard with a tacky primary-coloured map showing all the places he'd never visit and their new address. As if he was going to write to her like it was olden times. No phone call, no care package of whatever sweets and snacks were popular in Malta and no baseball cap from Gordon. Gordon always bought him horrible baseball caps with regional logos on even though he'd never worn one in his life. Cornwall, Scarborough, Grimsby. They were all in a drawer somewhere.

At the entry door he swiped his key fob over the panel. The lock clicked open. The lift was out of order again. His right knee was swollen from where Mr Steroid had stamped on it, but there was nothing else for it. He hiked up the pissy-smelling stairwell, pulling heavily on the banister rail for support.

The front door was open. He was fairly sure he hadn't left it that way. He pushed it as quietly as possible. He didn't think a plain-clothes detective would break in, but he wasn't sure of the procedure. What if they thought he'd topped himself from grief? They'd break in then for sure.

Every drawer and cupboard in the house was open, its contents emptied onto the floor. What if they were looking for evidence of his lies? What might they find? Maybe he should be pretending he hadn't come back from Bummer's, in case he needed some kind of alibi. For what, he wasn't sure. He peered into the kitchen, flicking on the light with his elbow, because he'd noticed CSIs on telly never touched light switches with their hands. There must be some reason for that. He padded into the bedroom, accidentally kicked the chest of drawers and ground his teeth together painfully so he didn't cry out.

The wardrobe was open and all his clothes were on the floor, still on their hangers. New possibilities cycling through his mind, he checked them over to see if they'd been slashed.

Wouldn't put anything past Amber now.

All were still intact, although every pocket was inside out, even the tiny ones on the backs of his jeans. Optibot had been taken off the shelf and placed on the bed, in the centre of the pillow.

Satisfied that there was no burly constable waiting to slap handcuffs on him, Rob went to get a beer.

At least they haven't emptied the fridge-freezer onto the floor as well.

As Rob selected a bottle from the bottom shelf, he noticed that every item in the fridge was turned so that its label faced outwards. Every pizza, every can of Coke, every microwave macaroni cheese carton, all accusingly pointing their labels at him.

Fucked-up OCD detectives.

The beer had been organised in the same manner, labels perfectly aligned.

He found the bottle-opener on the floor among packets of spaghetti and tubs of dried herbs. Opened one bottle. The lid clicked off properly with a little shushing sound and he drank in long, grateful draughts. At least he could rely on beer. *Beer didn't buzz the Feds in to ransack the flat. That was one of the other cretins in this building.*

Rob sat down on the sofa and turned on the TV. It slowly dawned on him that if they were gathering evidence, they would probably have taken some stuff with them. His laptop out of the bedroom for instance, or even the piles of old receipts in his desk drawers. It didn't look like anything had been taken. Nothing at all.

A knock at the door sent Rob's heart pounding. He hadn't *really* thought the police were surveilling him, not really, and yet now it seemed they were. He leapt to his feet and glued his eye to the front door's peephole. There was Bellamy, filling the whole hallway, it seemed to Rob.

'Mr Buckland?' he called as he thudded on the door with a powerful fist. 'Mr Buckland, are you all right?' He moved aside, and behind him Rob could see two uniformed officers hefting a battering ram between them.

This was it.

'Just a minute!' he yelled, downing the beer just to get rid of it, and then instantly regretting it. He cast around frantically, thought about trying to tidy up and then realised how futile it would be. It was over. Time to face the music.

14

Rob fumbled with the lock, fully intending to confess everything as soon as the door opened, but when it swung inward and he was faced with the looming hulk of the detective, he found himself temporarily stunned into silence. Bellamy looked around at the piles of debris and then at Rob, face better but still bruised, and after a long moment, said: 'Well, I suppose now we know why you weren't answering your phone.' And Rob started trying to construct his answer, trying to calculate what they'd found and how incriminating it was, wondering if it was better to come clean completely or deny all knowledge or plead temporary insanity, but before he could say anything, Bellamy said, his voice filled with concern, 'You're having a rough time, aren't you Mr Buckland? Were you in the house when the burglars came? Do you think it was connected to the kidnapping?'

Rob's mouth dropped open as Bellamy waved the uniformed policemen inside and one started taking photos while another radioed in for a forensics team.

'I know it's no great consolation with everything that's

happened,' said Bellamy, folding his arms across his barrel chest. 'But the headteacher of Brodie's school is still attempting to locate Brodie's missing file, and it seems his teacher has confessed to failing to report him missing and has been suspended pending an investigation.'

'She has?' Rob's stomach knotted. He couldn't remember who he'd said Brodie's teacher *was*.

'Mr Buckland, what used to be here?' Bellamy had moved on, unaware of the terror he was eliciting in Rob. He was standing by the fridge, pointing.

Rob joined him. There were four blobs of Blu-tack on the fridge door. A cold shiver passed through his stomach.

'It must have... fallen...' He crouched and searched the floor. Bummer's finger-painting wasn't there. He peered under the fridge. Just fluff and silverfish. He straightened, dusting his knees and frowning. 'It was a painting,' he said, as Bellamy nodded and scribbled in a notebook. 'Brodie did it on his first day of nursery so I saved it.'

Rob had thought about this little scene so many times now, he actually saw it in his mind's eye as he said that. Himself, racked with worry, waiting outside the nursery school gates. All the other kids piling out, running to their parents, carried on a wave of noise and motion. His stomach twisting with angst that Brodie had spent the day crying and missing his daddy. And then, finally, the nursery teacher holding the door open again and Brodie running out, a big smile on his face and a crumpled painting for Rob clutched in his pudgy fist.

'...bed?' Bellamy was saying.

'Mmm?'

'I'm sorry, I know this is difficult. Brodie's bed, his things, where are they?'

Oh, crap.

Panic leaked onto his face.

'I thought so.' Bellamy made another note. Rob felt like he was going to puke.

'I think there's a strong likelihood this is connected to Brodie's disappearance. Now, could you tell us about what happened to your face?'

Fortunately, the forensics woman arrived right then, giving him time to process. They didn't know. For whatever reason, they really thought Brodie was a real missing boy. How could he say anything now? How could he admit it wasn't real when they were all working so hard? The forensics woman had a suitcase full of intriguing pots and brushes with her. As she got to work dusting for fingerprints on the greasy kitchen countertops, Rob was gripped by a new fear.

Hope they don't notice there are no children's fingerprints. Can you be arrested for an absence of fingerprints?

*

'Can I take a look at something?' Jules asks suddenly, getting up off the sofa. I stay sitting, waiting for her to clarify. 'Brodie's room?'

Ah. So she picked up on that.

'Sure. But we'll have to be quiet.'

I lead her to the bedroom. My bedroom. Brodie's bedroom. The only bedroom. My collectible action figures are still on the shelves, in various poses thanks to Brodie's investigations.

Brodie is in the bed. My bed, with its dark grey quilt cover and mismatched pillows. Two blue, one pale grey, one cream. Brodie's head is resting on the cream one. In this light his hair has the dark red glow of an electric hob. He moves in his sleep and I try to pull Jules back from the open crack of the door, but she won't move.

She's looking at the ancient sagging camp bed that used to be Bummer's but is now mine. The sleeping bag that's become my permanent bedding. She slips inside and opens a drawer. I'm not sure what she's looking for, but all she finds are my old band shirts. She crosses back over to me, closes the door softly.

'Where are his clothes?' she asks. 'His toys?'

'I told you,' I say, 'I made him up. He's not real. He doesn't have anything.'

'He has you,' she says and it's like a rebuke and a reward at the same time.

'I'm not good at this.'

*

Rob didn't go to the office for a couple of days. He couldn't face Amber, or Jules, or the picture of Brodie on his desk. He didn't want to know about whatever awareness campaign Austin had set in motion for the return of a fake boy. And anyway, his knee still hurt. He limped down to the Empornium stockroom and priced French ticklers to keep himself busy. Bummer tried to talk to him and regularly brought him cups of weak, sugary tea, but he couldn't explain how he felt to his friend. He couldn't even explain it to himself. He felt guilty and lonely because he'd reported an imaginary boy missing.

It didn't make any sense. Fortunately, Bummer seemed to think it was to do with Mum and Amber and the burglary and getting a pasting. He kept saying things like: 'What a shitter, eh Kidder? What a shitter,' and 'Plenty more fish in the sea, Kidder.'

But then Bummer had to go and sort something out in town, leaving the New Guy in charge.

The New Guy came in and eyed Rob suspiciously every so often. He seemed to think Rob was there to take his job. He disappeared off to mop the toilets. When he came back, Rob had become a little distracted and priced the same French tickler three times with different prices, one on top of the other. Newbie looked at it for a long time. Rob carried on pricing the rest of the shelf. Newbie picked up the multi-priced tickler and carefully peeled off the prices, sticking the correct one on very neatly, perfectly aligning the bottom corner of the sticker with the bottom corner of the packet.

Is he the one who ransacked my fucking flat?

New Guy noticed Rob watching him, and shrugged. 'They look better straight.'

Rob nodded, adjusting the pricing gun until it read £750.00. 'I'm surprised you're not with Bummer,' Newbie continued, moving on to organise the condoms by colour and flavour.

'We don't do everything together.' Rob carefully mixed the £750 ticklers in among the rest.

'I know you don't, I just thought what with the— Did you put this in here?'

He was holding up something called a 'Nomdom'.

'I don't even know what that is.'

'It's an edible condom. It's a novelty item, not a contraceptive.'

Rob wondered whether anyone could sue if they were too dumb to realise something made out of stretchy sugared jelly couldn't prevent pregnancy.

At lunchtime, Rob nipped in to see Heather. He didn't know why. To see a friendly face probably. To see a woman who wouldn't call him a wanker and then set a bouncer on him, or save all his files as Work_by_Dickhead.

She looked overjoyed to see him. It was nice and heart-rending at the same time.

'I can make some extra sandwiches,' she told him joyfully. 'I've got all the stuff in the staffroom.' She toyed with the gold chain round her neck. 'You could maybe come and eat them with me in there.'

Rob looked around. 'Where's the Poo Witch?'

'Huh?'

He suddenly realised he'd never called her that in front of Heather before. It was his and Bummer's secret name for her.

'Your boss.'

'Oh. She's doing something in town at the minute. She said she'd be back in time for close. So you should be safe.' Heather batted her eyelashes and Rob realised that she was trying to flirt with him. Horrifying. It would be perverse to lead him on. 'Well?' she continued. 'Are you coming for sandwiches or what? They're roast beef.'

I am hungry.

*

'You are the absolute worst,' says Jules, but absently, like her mind's still on something else.

*

Heather took her gum out of her mouth and delicately stuck it to the inside of her bright pink Hiya Puppy lunchbox. The lunchbox matched her fingernails. The chipped polish had flecks of glitter in it.

'Auntie Katherine says gum's a disgustin' habit, but Paul says everyone's allowed one vice and that's mine.' She bit her lip and looked at him shyly.

Rob nodded, trying to shovel the sandwich down his throat as quickly as possible so he could leave.

This was a bad idea. A lump of gristle stuck in his throat and he gulped frantically to dislodge it. *It isn't even good beef.*

There was a long, awkward silence, filled only by Rob's chewing and the fluttering of Heather's eyelashes. She'd doused herself in a floral perfume, the cheap, cloying kind sixteen-year-old girls wear when they don't know any better. It was making Rob feel sick, but he tried to ignore it.

'What happened to your face?' she asked eventually, just as he swallowed and said at the same time: 'So does Po— the manager leave you in charge often?'

They both laughed nervously and started to answer at the same time, too. Rob stopped and let Heather go first. He'd rather be eating anyway.

'No, she's just busy with the court case at the moment. And your face?'

'I fell down a manhole— she's where?'

'Court. A manhole? That's terrible. You should sue the council for that, you should, it's illegal isn't it?'

Rob put his sandwich down. Between the sugary flower scent and the terrible feeling he had about Poo Witch's court case, his appetite was pretty much gone.

'Thanks for the sandwich, Heather,' he said, standing up and pushing his chair in. He shoved the remains of the sandwich across the table towards her. 'Finish it if you want.' She looked at it like he'd just presented her with a bar of Aztec gold. 'I've gotta go and check something.'

Rob had his mobile phone out of his pocket before he'd even left Baby World. As he waited for Bummer to answer, he noticed it. The picketers hadn't been around all day. Usually, even if they didn't come to do a full-blown protest, one or two would come by and try to discourage a few patrons. They didn't like to let their guard down completely in case there was a sudden rush of customers intent on buying vibrating anal plugs. But right now there was no one there. Not even the old guy with the walking stick who always used to tell Rob he didn't fight two wars so young men could peddle filth.

The New Guy, Paul, had been surprised Rob wasn't with Bummer. And what was it Heather had said? Poo Witch was at the court case? Why had Bummer said he was going into town? Did he say?

The line connected, but Bummer didn't say anything.

'Hello? Hello, Bummer?' Rob called out desperately.

Bummer finally answered, hushed and apologetic: 'Rob, I can't talk, the magistrate is looking at me all funny.' The line went dead.

Magistrate. Did he say magistrate? 'The magistrate is looking at me all funny.' That was what he said, wasn't it?

Oh, crapping Christ.

But Rob didn't have time to think further on it, because as he pushed into the Empornium and ducked under the display of whips and chains to return to the stockroom, his mobile rang. The number was an unfamiliar one.

'Hello?'

'Hello?'

The voice brimmed with forced joviality. Not one he recognised, but just the kind of voice a magistrate would have, the kind of magistrate who took Bummer's phone off him in court and then rang back to try to trick Rob into saying something incriminating.

'Who's this?'

'Robert Buckland?'

Not on your nelly, sunshine!

'Who's this?' Rob repeated, ignoring Newbie in the doorway holding up one of the £750 French ticklers in front of his face and tapping the price angrily.

'It's Gregory. From work...' Gregory trailed off into nervous laughter.

Oh, cocks. It would be, wouldn't it?

'Right. Okay.' Rob swiftly changed his tone from indignant to pitiful. 'Sorry I didn't ring.'

'That's okay. Austin told us not to bother you, that you were having personal issues and would contact us when you were ready, but then Amber said we shouldn't expect you back any time soon, which sounded a little ominous, so I thought I'd best ring.'

What has that cow been saying?

'Yeah, yeah, well actually,' – *I'll show her* – 'it's not about what Amber thinks it's about.'

'Oh?' Gregory sounded confused. 'She said you fell and hit your face on a kerb or something?'

'Well, I did, but the reason I've not been at work is actually,' – *come on tear ducts, come through for Daddy* – 'it's actually about my son.' And as he said that word, that golden, magical word, all the terrible feelings he'd been battling came racing back to the surface. All the guilt, all the hurt, all the loneliness welled up inside him and rushed out of his face in a loud sob that shocked even him.

'Robert?' Gregory sounded genuinely concerned, bless his shiny little face. 'Oh, Robert, what happened?'

It was an even richer and more vivid telling than either Austin or the police counsellor got, and now Rob was so caught up in the lie, he was starting to think there must be some truth in it. An externalisation of something that happened to him as a child, some memory he'd repressed, because otherwise he wouldn't be feeling all these genuine, terrible emotions, would he?

As he wiped the tears and snot from his face, he remembered the New Guy, who was still in the doorway, now staring at him open-mouthed.

'What's your problem?' snapped Rob. 'You some kind of grief tourist? Can't you leave an anguished father in peace?'

15

Back at his flat, Rob flicked through the channels until he found *Blight Brigade* and settled back on the sofa with a can of Special Brew to watch it. He started out watching it so he could have convincing conversations with other parents about the nonsense their children watched, but then got really into it, and he wanted to see whether Alfred's snooty sister would ever find out that the monster under her bed was actually Alfred in one of his alien forms.

As the bright colours from the screen washed over his face in a soothing balm, Rob leaned back and dozed. He drifted into a hazy dream where Brodie was both a real boy and himself as a child and they followed Rob's mum around like cuckoo chicks, telling her they were 'the real one'. A voice like static whispered in his ear that everything would be all right, which was the point when he became aware he was dreaming, because how could any of this ever be all right?

A knock at the door jerked Rob awake. On TV *Blight Brigade* was over and there was an even weirder cartoon about a care home for abused imaginary friends. The knock came again. Rob sighed, wondering which twat let this one into the building.

Rob unzipped his sleeping bag down to his waist and shuffled to the door. No point in getting spruced up for Jehovah's Witnesses. Flipping back the latch with one hand, he turned the handle with the other, poised to slam it in the God-botherer's face. But it wasn't a God-botherer. It was something much, much worse.

'Surprise!'

This is bad. This is so, so bad. This is ultima bad.

The whole office was on his doorstep with flowers and cards and boxes of chocolates. Simon at the back, glowing scarlet like the helium balloon he was holding, cord gripped tight in his sweaty palm. Gregory and Gillian in the middle, holding a giant basket of fruit and nuts between them. Toby and Spencer with carrier bags of gifts and their hands in their pockets, sheepish carbon copies of one another. And right at the front, Jules, holding the new game he'd blabbed on about to her ages ago.

'For when he comes back,' she said gently, and with such genuine conviction Rob wanted to take her in his arms and kiss her on the mouth right there.

But instead he scratched his head awkwardly and shuffled backward so they could squeeze past him and said: 'I suppose you'd better all come in.'

He held the door wide for them and noticed there was no sign of Amber. *Couldn't come down off her high horse even for a kidnapped child, the cow.*

The one good thing about the whole situation was they didn't expect him to say much. He saw their eyes darting to the pictures on the noticeboard and the framed photos on the side table.

The lack of a child hung over them all like a spectre and none of them dared mention it, so they made polite small talk among themselves instead. This meant Rob could sit and stare at his feet and try to think of a way out without losing face. The only thing he came up with was burning the flat down with them all inside so the story never got out, but that seemed a bit extreme, even for him.

But you can only talk about the weather and what Helen from accounts has done to her hair for so long. Eventually, Gregory stood up and said: 'Robert, I have an announcement to make. Everyone, listen up...'

He's starting a team meeting, right here in my lounge.

'You may have noticed Austin's not here, and it's not because he doesn't want to be. It's actually because he's pulled some strings with the Powers That Be at Credit Co.' Gregory said this with an ironic little chuckle, as if he'd just made a funny, funny joke. 'And they have agreed to fund the media campaign to get Brady back.'

'Brodie,' Jules hissed.

'Sorry, of course, Brodie. Austin is personally overseeing everything. So, err, if you just provide us with a few photos, the posters will go up ASAP and the TV campaign is pencilled in for a fortnight's time. We all wish it could be quicker, but you know...'

Having never run a TV campaign for the return of a kidnapped imaginary child, Rob didn't really know, but he nodded instead and thanked them all for this wonderful opportunity to have his son restored to him.

*

'So why did you let it go that far?' Jules sounds exasperated and her cheeks are pink. I can't blame her. I'd be annoyed at me for pulling something like this. I am annoyed at me. I almost shrug, but if she's anything like my mum, that would just send her flying into a rage, so instead I say: 'It was real now—' I stop, try to squeeze a few more drops from the wine bottle into my glass.

'Go on.'

Now I shrug. I can't say it. I'll make up something else instead. I'm good at that.

'Prison. I could've gone to prison. Wasting police time and that.'

'That's not what you were going to say.' Her hazel eyes narrow and it's like she's peeling back my skin with a scalpel. A few more layers and she'll realise there's nothing inside.

'I kinda wanted them to bring him back,' I admit finally, as I'm forced to accept the bottle has nothing more to offer. 'I know it's crazy.' I grimace as I wrench at the bottle, holding it in my lap now, still twisting the neck, hoping it will break in my hands. A theme when it comes to me holding glassware. 'But it felt like I had to do something about him being missing.' My palm is raw and still the bottle is intact, defying my wishes, like everything. 'Even though I knew—' I try again. 'No matter how weird...' It's no good. 'I don't expect you to understand.'

She lifts my hand away from the bottle and gently strokes my reddened palm. It tickles, but I don't stop her doing it.

'I won't ever understand you, but I think I'm starting to.'

*

'No, really Bummer, what have I become?' Rob tightened his fist round his pint glass, wishing it would break and lacerate his hand because that's what he deserved.

'Maybe you have a mental condition,' offered Chloe. Chloe was Bummer's oldest. Twenty-one, which really freaked Rob out, because it meant Bummer was having sex long before Rob was. 'Some kind of compulsion, or a neurosis.' Chloe had just finished her law degree and was training as a forensic psychologist. If she hadn't been lumbered with a share of Bummer's DNA, she'd already be running the universe.

'You've always seemed wrong in the head to me.' Tenike smirked into her orange juice.

'Shut it,' said Rob. 'How come you lot are all here anyway?'

Rob had never seen this many of Bummer's children in one go. Tenike was a pretty permanent fixture, but now there was Neil and Chloe, and Chloe had brought her boyfriend along as well, an unbearable toff with a plum in his mouth and a double-barrelled surname.

'Scheduling conflict.' Bummer shrugged and smiled. 'I like having them all around, anyway.'

Rob didn't. It meant they had to sit in the pub's family room, where toddlers stumbled around bumping into chairs and parents gave him nasty looks when he referred to Credit Co as the Twat Factory. He wanted Bummer to himself so they could get pissed and come up with an incredible plan that probably wouldn't work, but would make him feel better, like when they finalised Brodie's details. Rob had had more one-to-one conversations with Bellamy over the last few weeks than he had with Bummer.

Bummer wasn't himself. He was being all quiet and boring, like he was trying to show the kids he was a responsible adult so they'd respect him and shit.

'It seems to me,' said Neil, furtively sipping Bummer's Guinness and then making a face, 'you need to cut your losses and get a new job.'

'Fuck off, Neil!' said Rob, ignoring the nearby mother pointedly covering her offspring's ears. 'This was your stupid idea in the first place, so I'm not taking your advice again in a hurry! And anyway, I can't switch jobs again already. How would that look on my CV?'

Neil shrugged. 'I'm sixteen, my CV's empty.'

'You could always lie about it. You know, like with the kid,' said Chloe.

Before Rob could come up with a witty retort, Chloe's boyfriend, Roderick, drew attention to himself by putting his wine glass down on the beer mat and taking a deep breath. The group eyed him expectantly. He hadn't said much since Rob said he spoke like that MP caught trying to auto-erotically asphyxiate himself with a pair of fishnets in the House of Commons.

'It seems to me,' he said, running a finger thoughtfully around the rim of the wine glass until it sang. 'Seems to me the only option you have is to go along with it.'

'What?' asked Rob. 'So I just go on TV and weep and wail and beg for my kid back?'

'Well, yes.' Roderick nodded, slowly meeting Rob's eyes. 'It'll blow over eventually.'

'Blow over eventually?' Bummer was incredulous. 'And the waste of police time? The real kidnapped kiddies missing out on

TV campaigns 'cos of yours? Lying to everyone, everywhere? What if your mum finds out? What then?'

'She's in Malta,' said Rob softly. *Although this might bring her back.* 'Horrible as it is, they can't go on looking for him for ever. And, well...' *Bummer's right, everything he just said is absolutely right.* '... it's not as if they're going to find him, is it?'

*

Rob didn't really know what he was expecting a kidnap appeal to look like, but it certainly wasn't this. The terrible thing about Credit Co was that it applied its brand values to everything. Literally everything, from the drinks machines in the lobby to the way it held a kidnap press conference. If it wasn't big and public and attention-grabbing, then, in the eyes of Credit Co, it wasn't worth doing. How could you stop something that big and powerful? Rob wanted to now, he really did, but it would be like throwing himself in front of a combine harvester to save a field mouse. There were too many moving parts, and even if he managed to salvage something, the cost would be too great.

They were using the cafeteria, the biggest space in the building. All the chairs and tables were pushed back against the food counters, the kitchen staff in front of them, arms linked, each solemnly holding a candle. Staff from every department lined the mezzanine above, secretaries and underwriters standing shoulder to shoulder with consultants and office managers. They'd unfurled a huge hand-painted banner from the balcony railing. It said 'Bring Back Brodie' in huge black letters, with the Brodie Kidnap Hotline number neatly printed at the end. Around the edges of the room were all the concessional staff; the cleaners, the security guys, the girls from the snack shop, all earnestly gripping large glossy copies of the Brodie picture, some of them crying.

Rob wanted to run into the middle of them all and scream. He wanted to stand on the press conference table and face the camera and tell them he made it all up. He wanted to shake the sniffling snack-shop girl and ask her why she was crying over a kid she didn't even know. But his throat seemed to have devolved into a second urethra, capable only of pissing out useless sentiments.

'Thanks, Dan,' and, 'Cheers for the support, Michael,' and, 'This means a lot, Hazel.' Even though he didn't know who the fuck Dan and Michael and Hazel were. He'd accused New Guy of being a grief tourist to piss him off, but this lot were the real deal. Competing to be the most affected by this terrible tragedy. This terrible, fake tragedy.

Detective Bellamy sat at the middle of the press conference table, broad shoulders square and determined. Either side of Bellamy were chairs for Rob and Gregory. Somehow, Gregory had become the spokesperson and coordinator of the whole event. At some unknown signal from Bellamy, Gregory took Rob gently by the arm and led him through the crowd. A reverent hush fell and they parted respectfully to allow the pair through.

As Rob dropped quietly into his seat, he was briefly amazed to find he had any back teeth left, his jaw had been so tightly clamped and grinding, grinding, grinding for the last few days. As he looked into the black eye of the camera, he spotted that Jules had somehow shouldered her way to the press line.

He nodded to her feebly and she gave him a thumbs-up. If he wanted to tell anyone the truth about this, it was Jules. His stomach lurched, and right then, he knew he couldn't go through with it.

I can't do this. I just can't. I'm worse than those people who hold press conferences knowing they've killed their own child.

Gregory gently coaxed Rob into a seat.

Well... not worse.

The camera panned down the line as Gregory thanked everyone for coming.

I mean, I haven't killed anyone or anything.

Gregory led a round of applause for the event sponsors and the camera swivelled up to take in the banners and the crowds of mourners. Gregory finished talking and the silence sucked at Rob's ears, demanding his attention.

I'm going to a special hell.

Bellamy leaned forward and spoke intently into the camera. He outlined the whole thing: how Brodie disappeared from school, his likes and dislikes and the many avenues the police were considering. He didn't mention the burglary, like he didn't want to show all his cards to this kidnapping super-villain. And all the time, Rob was thinking:

They're going to end up making some terrible TV movie about this unless I come clean right now. There'll be some ex-soap actor playing me in He Made Up A Child, *unless I do something. Just speak up, you gutless git, come on!*

And then he realised all eyes were on him. The only sounds were the low hum of the air-conditioning units and the stifled sniffling of the exhibitionist criers. Rob took a slow breath, aware that what he was about to say would change his whole life for ever. But it had to be said, it must be said. He cleared his tight piss-tube of a throat and said:

'I just...'

Say it, SAY IT, what's wrong with you?

'I just want my son back!'

And his head slumped onto his arms on the desk, and those sobs came again, those crazy, over-the-top repressed sobs came flooding out of him.

16

Talking's becoming more and more of an effort. The kitchen tap's dripping and I desperately want to go over and try to turn it off. I'm pretty sure the constant drip, drip, drip is what's causing my headache. Maybe I should get my bag of wrenches from under the sink...

'Weren't you worried they'd come after you?'

As if I have a bag of wrenches. I doubt I have a wrench singular, never mind a bag of them.

'They who?'

'The police.'

My headache intensifies. I vaguely recall a weird old cartoon where the main character's forehead vein would grow huge and pulsate and threaten to kill him. That's exactly how this feels right now.

'Even if they did,' I say, gritting my teeth against the pain, 'it would have been way after all that, wouldn't it?'

Like, maybe more around the time they found out I'd claimed a child that wasn't, that couldn't be, mine.

*

Rob tried to avoid talking to Bellamy after the press conference by ducking into the toilets and spending an age in a stall, pretend-crying just in case anyone was listening. When he came out, rubbing his eyes vigorously to make sure they were suitably red, Bellamy was still there, broad and constant as the Major Oak. There was no escaping it.

'All right?' said Rob, unsure what protocol was for this sort of situation.

'You were very brave,' said Bellamy, clapping Rob on the shoulder so hard, his knees almost buckled. It was like being clubbed with a caber.

'Thanks.' Rob looked down at his shoes.

'Now, I don't want you to worry yourself looking for Brodie's birth certificate.'

'Oh?' *Oh. Oh shit.*

'We've got a team on it. All we need is Karen's maiden name.'

'Karen?'

'Your wife.'

Shit. Of course. 'Smith.' *Stroke of genius.*

Bellamy looked at him for a long time. His eyes were large and blue and unblinking. Rob held his gaze for as long as possible, but eventually he had to look away, had to break the connection, and he almost blurted: 'I made it all up, it's not true, none of it!' but before that could happen, Bellamy blinked and gave a curt nod.

'Very well then,' he said. 'Might take them a while, but, well, y'know...'

And he winked and walked away, leaving Rob propped against the toilet door, weak-kneed, unsure what just happened.

*

I look at her out of the corner of my eye. She's biting her bottom lip, brows drawn together. Did she pick up on it, that little breadcrumb I left for her? Bellamy's wink.

That wink's kept me up at night. A wink. Why would he wink unless he was in on it? But then, I don't know him. He might be a winker. You know, one of those guys who just winks whenever he's said anything vaguely pleasant, like you won't realise the pleasantness is directed at you unless it's accompanied by an ocular cue. I've never winked, because I worry people would think I was coming on to them. A winking pervert, that's what I'd look like. Not Bellamy. His wink was kind, inclusive. But indicative of what, I'm still not sure.

'You think Bellamy's wink meant something, don't you?' Her tone suggests that if I do think that, I'm stupid and mad and paranoid. 'You think he's involved in all this somehow.'

'I don't know.' I really don't know.

She shakes her head and I want to eat my breadcrumbs.

*

Rob went straight back to work after the press conference. Not through any sense of guilt but because he feared the police would soon start delving deeper. The lie was never intended to be so in-depth. Rob needed paperwork and evidence, not just a plausible backstory. Imported Japanese robots and finger-paintings on the fridge weren't going to swing it this time.

Bloody Roderick. This is bloody Roderick's fault for talking me into going through with the press conference. Well, he'd better be damn good at forging stuff. And brainwashing teachers into believing they taught an imaginary child for a year or two.

Rob sat heavily on his office chair. It sighed even louder than him.

Oh Christ. I should just sell the movie rights now. That ginger bloke from the war series, he could play me. He'd be all right.

He turned on his computer, grateful for the reassuring monotony of his spreadsheets. But all around he could hear his colleagues whispering quietly to one another, words like 'stalwart' and 'bearing up' and 'putting on a brave face'.

I should probably just slip to the toilets and slit my wrists. They'd just think it was the grief, or something.

He clicked and copied and pasted, trying to let the background susurrus of pity wash over him. He copied three columns into his new spreadsheet, deleted them from the original and closed it. The first column needed highlighting green, the next orange, the third red, like traffic lights. The final column stayed white, and he put in a formula so it showed the total when red and orange were deducted from green. He tried working the first few out manually to make sure the formula was correct, but all he got was the Arrowfat's peas song and maddening murmurs of sympathy.

Fuck, how can I get out of all this?

Jules turned to him and said: 'Why don't we blow this popsicle stand?' And somehow he let her lead him by the hand, out of the office and into the centre of town. No one tried to stop them or even asked where they were going. The privilege of the suffering father.

Next thing he knew, he was sitting in the arboretum with an ice cream dribbling out of the cornet onto his hand even though the wind was bloody freezing. Jules sat down on the bench beside him, sucked the last of her cornet into her mouth with a satisfying smack and asked: 'Better?'

Rob looked at the sticky mess oozing its way down his wrist and shook his head. Jules took a tissue out of her pocket, wrapped the whole lot up in it and dropped it into a nearby bin. She used another tissue to dab his hand clean.

'I've got a can of Coke if you'd rather?' she asked, reaching into her pocket.

He nodded. She put the can in his hand and tugged the ring-pull. He took a sip and leaned back, watching a family of moorhens skim across the surface of the lake.

'I've fucked it all up,' he said, to no one in particular.

One of the baby moorhens was more adventurous than the others. It raced off ahead, paddling into the middle of the lake, neck outstretched for speed.

'Oh, Rob, don't say that.'

'It's true. This whole mess is all my fault!'

The baby moorhen stopped dead in front of its mother, spun round and tried to peck her in the eye. She responded by holding the ungrateful little bastard underwater in an effort to drown it.

'You can't blame yourself.' Jules reached for his hand. 'As terrible as it is, these things happen.'

'No, they don't,' said Rob, desperately. He could stand pity from anyone else, but not her. Not Jules, she's a mate. 'Jules, I've got to tell you—'

With the impeccable timing of a soap opera ad break, Rob's phone rang. He broke free from Jules's grasp to answer it.

'Hi Rob. I know you're quite busy and all. It's just that—'

'Come on Bummer, spit it out!' snapped Rob.

'Looks like I might end up losing the shop, Kidder.'

*

'Yes,' says Jules firmly. 'Yes Rob, we're mates. I want you to remember that.'

I'll never forget it.

*

When Rob arrived at the Empornium, it was eerily quiet. No protesters outside, shutters pulled down; even the busy main road out front was void of traffic.

He slipped in through the side door, and found a similarly subdued scene. Bummer and New Guy sitting by the till, drinking beer and reading legal papers.

'What's gone off?' asked Rob, pulling up a stool and helping himself to a can from the cooler bag.

'What do you think?' asked Bummer glumly. He slung a thick sheaf of paper towards Rob. Poo Witch's petition. It had over two thousand signatures. Rob skimmed through the long lists of names and addresses.

'But half these people don't even live round here! Why do they care?'

'There are two schools and a nursery up the road,' New Guy pointed out. 'Their kids probably go to them.'

'Not that I was talking to you. My point remains – what's it got to do with them?'

'They think the Empornium attracts paedophiles.'

'Perverts,' Rob corrected New Guy. 'The Empornium attracts perverts.'

'No difference to these people.' Bummer sighed.

Rob had never seen him so forlorn. There were only two things Bummer truly loved, apart from being on the bog. His shop and his kids. And without one, he could quite easily lose the other.

'They can't really prove that anyway,' said New Guy, wearily. 'But what they can prove is the corrupting influence of the shop on children. Directly.'

'Bummer, will you explain this to me properly, please.'

'They've got a photo of Tenike.'

'Doing what?'

'Wearing a gimp mask.'

'Oh, shit, that?!' Rob burst out laughing and then realised that probably wasn't the appropriate reaction. 'She just put that on to make me jump. Why don't you get her to say that? That she just did it as a prank, not for... I dunno, sexual thrills or whatever.'

'That's what I said to my solicitor. But he thinks drawing attention to my home life would be a bad idea... Thinks I'd come across as a bad father.'

'Then he's a bellend. You're a great father.'

Bummer was a great father. Despite only getting to see most of his kids when their mothers needed a break, he remembered everything about them. Their best friends, foods they liked and disliked, favourite toys and clothes, even nitty-gritty stuff like blood types, allergies and medical histories, all locked away in Bummer's underused brain. It always amazed Rob that a man who couldn't remember to do up his flies after taking a piss could recite his daughter's school timetable without having to think twice. It could also be the key to Rob's dilemma, if not Bummer's.

'Bummer, your youngest two, the boys...'

'Joel and Jacob,' Bummer supplied automatically.

'Yeah, them, they go to primary school right?'

'Of course they do. Councillor Dupois Infant and Junior School.'

'Right, right, Councillor Dupois...' Rob laid a finger against his lips thoughtfully. 'And if I was to tell the police Brodie went there, would they be able to find out otherwise?'

'Who's Brodie?' asked New Guy, frowning.

'Fuck off Newbie, no one likes you.'

'Yes, Rob,' said Bummer, cracking a smile, 'they would find out otherwise. Teachers tend to know the names and faces of their kids. Well, apart from Mrs Ferry. Poor cow.'

'Mrs Ferry?'

'You know – the one who went nuts.'

'Oh yeah, her...' *Nervous breakdown. That could work.* 'And she's back at school now, is she?'

'Yeah. Some of the parents aren't too happy about it, even had the police in, I hear, but she's harmless enough. Just calls all the kids – boys and girls – Mark MacDowell after that one troublemaker kid. I'll be glad when Joel's out of that class.' He affixed a paperclip to the sheaf of legal papers. 'I hate the name Mark.'

So, at least now Rob had a teacher and a school for Brodie.

Maybe this can work.

'When are you next going to see Joel and Jacob?'

Bummer slipped the legal papers back into their cardboard folder and pushed it across the table to Newbie. Newbie dragged his hands down his face and sighed.

'I'm your manager, remember, mate,' said Bummer, patting him on the shoulder.

*

'Wow.'

I open my eyes. Hers are flat, deadened with disgust. Not a good wow, then.

'You actually almost thought of someone other than yourself for thirty seconds,' she continues. 'Almost.'

'What?' I expect her to be mad at me for being a liar, a faker, a creep, but selfish? I took Brodie into my life. I stood aside when Mum and Gordon announced their insane immigration plan. I was still going to shag Amber after she failed to recognise my collectible action figures. I may be many things, but I am not selfish.

'Bummer,' she says. 'He was your best friend. He supported you through everything, all your craziness, all your stupidity, and the moment he needs you, you use him instead of being there for him.'

'I...' I'd never thought of it that way. He's Bummer. It's not selfish if it's Bummer, is it? He's my best friend. That's what he's there for.

17

Meeting with Mr Ibsen was nerve-wracking. Rob hadn't wanted to go, but Bummer and his kids insisted that if they were going to do this, the only way it would work would be for Rob to go in person. Rob felt sick, standing there in Mr Ibsen's office, certain this would be the moment the lies unravelled.

Rob had only vague recollections of Mr Ibsen all those years ago, standing at the front of assembly, telling stories that evidently had some kind of moral. He couldn't remember a single one of those stories, but he remembered things that happened next to him. Richard Brant doing a wee, an ever-expanding puddle that everyone had to shuffle away from. Katie Morley puking a porridgey mess onto the shiny hardwood floor, triggering a Mexican wave of heaving and gagging around the hall. Chileshi Derbyshire standing up and pointing because there was a dog in the playground and everyone behaving as if they'd never seen a dog before.

Rob hoped something like that would happen during this meeting. A dog running through the corridor or the secretary walking in and emptying her bladder in front of Ibsen's cluttered desk would be the perfect distraction against what was going on in the bushes outside.

'Yes, yes, I remember young Brodie well, credit to the school, credit to the school.' This was the first time a stranger had built on the lie without any prompting from Rob. He could see in the man's face, in the pursing of his lips, the twitching of his moustache, that he was searching for something, anything about the kid. He wanted to remember Brodie, because he didn't want to be the heartless headmaster who couldn't remember the missing child. Amazing how it only mattered now. He didn't remember the boy standing right in front of him, even though he'd stood there years before, right in this spot, looking exactly like Brodie. He was even oblivious to two of his current pupils, crouching in the bushes outside with their father.

Fortunately Mr Ibsen had his back to the window, where Bummer squatted among the rhododendrons with Joel and Jacob, awaiting Rob's signal. Rob couldn't even remember what the signal was. He just stared hard into Mr Ibsen's eyes as the aged headmaster racked his brains for a memory of an imaginary boy. His clear, soothing voice lapped at Rob like a gentle tide and he let it, paying about as much attention as he had in assembly. Finally, a light went on in Mr Ibsen's eyes and he smiled and said: 'His performance in the Christmas play was enchanting.'

Rob knew that every kid in the school got to be in the Christmas play, regardless of if they were thick, or blind, or some other religion. Even if they just had to hold tinsel and pretend to be a Christmas tree, they were all in it. Rob had played the star. He hadn't really been listening and thought they meant the star of the play, as in Jesus, so he'd eagerly raised his hand. He'd ended up just standing on a stepladder for the duration of the performance with his face through what was essentially a gold toilet seat because his mum was terrible at art. The glitter was in his clothes and hair for weeks. He'd never raised his hand for anything after that.

He wanted to respond with: 'Actually, Brodie missed out, he had chicken pox,' or 'Yes, playing second sheep on the left was a big moment for him,' but Ibsen was really trying, and Bummer was waiting for a signal, so Rob gave them both a break.

'It was. I was so proud.' And he coughed.

The window behind Mr Ibsen slowly slid open and just as slowly Jacob was lifted inside, dropping soundlessly to the floor. He gave Rob a huge gap-toothed grin, clearly enjoying the adventure, blissfully unaware of the potential legal ramifications of their actions.

'And may I say how glad we are that you're being so understanding about Mrs Ferry's... situation. The last thing that poor woman needs is the local media pointing the finger of blame.' Mr Ibsen picked up a trilobite paperweight from his desk, tossing it lightly from hand to hand. 'And the lost file. We are making a concerted effort to find it, and I can assure you, this is the first time something like this has ever...'

Rob watched in terror as Jacob crawled behind the desk, over to the filing cabinet in the corner of the room. He narrowed his eyes, fearful that Ibsen would see the scene of subterfuge reflected in his pupils. Jacob tugged at the bottom drawer, failed to open it, turned the little key and tried again. The drawer slid out silently.

'Hey,' said Rob, setting his jaw in what he hoped was a dignified manner. 'The only one to blame is the scum that took my boy.'

I'm getting good at this. Maybe when this thing blows over I should take up acting.

Jacob had retrieved a manila folder filled with someone's school records. It didn't matter whose as long as they knew the format everything was kept in, so they could successfully forge one for Brodie. It probably wouldn't fool the police for long, but what else could he do? Just tell them Brodie wouldn't have any paperwork, because he wasn't real? Impossible.

As long as the school's accountability wasn't in question, Mr Ibsen seemed happy. He dropped the paperweight back on the desk and shook Rob's hand heartily.

Jacob was back by the window. Bummer had to lean half in to lift him back out. His cheeks were pink with effort. As Bummer raised Jacob over the windowsill, the stupid kid failed to lift his heels high enough, and he snagged a trailing spider plant perched on the windowsill. It rattled in its tray and for a moment Rob thought it was going to smash and ruin everything, so he did the only thing he could think of. He launched into a fit of racking sobs, gripped Ibsen's hand extra tight so he couldn't get away and buried his face in his former headmaster's lapel.

The plant rocked, but didn't fall, and now Rob was committed to weeping onto a man who remembered his imaginary son, but not him.

*

The low buzz of his phone. Bellamy again. Rob had been avoiding him, but he knew playing the stricken father would only get him so far. Failing to come up with a birth certificate, a note on the electoral register, anything, anything to prove Brodie's existence apart from some photos that just happened to be pretty much identical to all his own childhood photos, that was probably looking really suspicious. Forging the school documents would only go so far.

The phone stopped ringing. Against his better judgement, Rob called Bellamy back.

'Bellamy.'

'It's Rob— Mr Buckland.'

'Mr Buckland!' He sounded happy. Not like he was about to come round with an armed unit and attack dogs. 'I have some good news for you!'

'Really?'

'Whatever glitch in the matrix was keeping us from finding Brodie's files has been resolved.' Glitch in the matrix. That was what he called it. Strange.

'It has?'

'Yep, birth certificate, details from the nursery he went to as a nipper, the full works. We've even tracked down the guitar teacher he was due to meet the day he disappeared, which has set a few minds at ease. That one was a real stumper.'

'A stumper?'

'Had us all stumped, I mean.'

'Ah, I see.'

I don't see. I don't see any of it.

*

'You see!' Jules pats my shoulder. 'How would Brodie have any of that stuff if he wasn't yours?' She's back to comforting now, her annoyance at my shitty treatment of Bummer temporarily forgotten.

'I didn't say he wasn't mine, I said he wasn't real.'

Oh God, I've done it now. That's the distinction I've been trying to keep from her. The important distinction that makes me feel really crazy.

'How about we order a copy of his birth certificate?' Jules asks, and she's already online on her phone, searching for the right site. 'Maybe seeing it in black and white – that he's the baby you and Karen made, maybe that will help you come to terms with all this.'

'Karen's not real!' And I really yell that, way louder than I meant to, and from the bedroom, I hear Brodie's little voice, soft and frightened and alone:

'Daddy?'

Always playing the Daddy card. Sighing, I get up.

'We'll finish this in a minute.'

*

When Rob returned to Credit Co after a week's compassionate leave, things quickly got embarrassing. He'd got into a rhythm, a new normal, helping Bummer out at the shop and winding up Newbie, long lie-ins and sci-fi film marathons at home. It was almost like when he first invented Brodie, only a little lonelier, of course. But being at Credit Co, getting treated like a brave war hero all day every day, was starting to wear thin even for him. And those fucking t-shirts. Everyone, everywhere in every department had abandoned corporate dress code to wear a bright white 'Bring Back Brodie' t-shirt. Dark brown PhotoMorphed eyes staring out mournfully from every passing chest. The emergency helpline number emblazoned across every pair of shoulder blades.

Just when Rob thought he couldn't take being there any more, the other thing started happening. The first time, he was at the photocopier. Some girl from sales he barely knew came and stood behind him. She was a petite little thing, and her breasts brushed against the small of his back, her whispered words directed at his biceps.

'I think you're so brave,' she said huskily, a catch in her voice, 'carrying on as if nothing has happened.' Her fingertips grazed his elbow and he swallowed hard. 'You know, it's okay,' she dropped her voice even lower, until she was just breathing the words against his shirt, 'to show a little emotion.' And the most amazing thing happened then. She took his hand and led him into an empty conference room and shagged him senseless right there on the cold marble-topped meeting table. When he returned with ruffled hair and partially buttoned shirt, no one reacted like he was being an arsehole. Gregory patted him on the shoulder as he passed and even Amber had a wry smile and a distant look of sadness in her eyes, as if his previous behaviour all made perfect sense to her now.

'You know that's seriously fucked up?' Jules had asked as he manoeuvred his chafed nethers into his seat.

Okay, so maybe one person's treating me like I'm being an arsehole.

'Language!' He tutted, wincing and adjusting his position. 'Think of the ethics code!

'And nailing someone in the meeting room is within company policy, is it?'

'A woman,' Rob corrected, 'nailing a lovely woman, not "someone". I wouldn't just do it with a random someone like some kind of animal.'

'Oh really? Because it seems to me you'll knob any tragic bandwagon-jumper you come into contact with.'

Fortunately, Gregory chose that moment to materialise between them, a grave expression on his glistening face.

'Robert,' he said solemnly, 'the press are still asking for an interview. What should I say?'

Rob looked at Jules slyly, hoping to see her suitably impressed. She was reading her emails, eating a nougat bar.

'Tell them I'll think about it.'

18

When I get back from tending to Brodie, Jules is still browsing the web on her phone. She looks up guiltily as I sit down beside her. I glimpse the words 'Karen Buckland' in her search engine.

'Find anything?' I ask

Her mouth twitches. 'No.' She drops her phone back into her bag. 'But she might just not have much of an online profile. Fewer people were online seven years ago.'

I don't know how I feel about that. If Karen had a series of social networks, a blog, a collection of online photos of her and me and Brodie, would that mean I'm just crazy? Does the fact Jules didn't find any of those things mean I'm not?

'Was the interview to do with the race?' she says suddenly, maybe to change the subject.

'Probably. I didn't do it.'

I'm feeling weirder and weirder about telling her all this. I'm no longer sure what I've said and what I haven't. Which parts I elaborated or self-edited. Where in the midst of all the bullshit is the kernel of truth. I'm so tired. It's just a dull ache behind the eyes but it's always there. I want to roll into bed and sleep for a thousand years like a long-distance space traveller. Maybe I can just wake up after it's all over.

Right now, though, right now Jules is refilling her wine glass, the bottle glugging like an emptying drain. If I lie on the sofa with a cushion for a pillow and the rug for a blanket, she'll just wake me up. No hibernation for Rob. As long as I remember to leave out the bit with the girl and the dog, it'll all be fine.

*

Rob didn't do the interview, but that didn't stop the press sniffing around. He was finally glad about Mum and Gordon living in Malta in a self-contained bubble of darts and wine and cheese parties with their equally insular expat neighbours. Gordon would have denounced him as a cheat and a liar to the papers long ago if they still lived nearby.

Rob should have realised that Credit Co would never pass up free publicity. A chance to have their logo emblazoned all over a good cause was an opportunity too good to miss.

'What the hell is this?'

'I know that you meant heck,' said Gregory, moving between the desks, distributing the glossy packs, 'so I'll let that one slide. These are your Race for Brodie sponsorship packs. Aren't they wonderful? Marketing worked overnight designing them.'

Rob looked at the cover. Those eyes again, only this time even worse, because the picture was black and white. You could almost see the PhotoMorphing now. Brodie's grey face had a strange, ultra-smooth alien look to it where Rob had edited the freckles. Not that anyone would stop to notice that. Credit Co were far too busy enforcing their corporate branded Fun on everyone.

'...everyone to take part,' Gregory was saying. 'Inside your pack you will find a sponsorship sign-up sheet, a pen, a sponsorship fee money envelope, an application form for a Race for Brodie t-shirt and a Race for Brodie balloon.'

Oh good. So I can attempt to suffocate myself with an image of my fake, kidnapped son.

Rob pictured them finding his body in the flat, cold and stiff, the balloon stretched over his head, Brodie's distorted black and white face a grotesque rendition of his own.

'...up to it, Rob?'

Rob was wondering whether suffocating yourself gave you an erection, or whether the people who died auto-erotically asphyxiating themselves were already wanking. Now Gregory was staring at him with such grave concern, he wondered if he'd been mumbling aloud about it. He could get away with a lot of weird behaviour on the whole grieving father tag but that might be a bit much.

'Or would it be better if you just watched?'

Right, the running. He's talking about the running. Oh God. How to play this? Surely I have to do it. There's no way out of it without looking like a heartless cock. I hate running. No one should have to run unless they're being chased by a monster.

Jules was watching. Maybe he could win back some Brownie points with her by doing this.

A real dad would do it.

'I'll be there,' he said, and oddly, the catch in his voice wasn't put on, 'running as hard as I can for my Brodie!'

I mean, it's not like I've got to win the thing, is it?

*

'What are you doing?' Rob asked. It was a few days after the Race for Brodie roll-out. This had raised his profile with further reaches of the business, so he'd just got back from a quick fumble in the stationery cupboard with the one-eyed girl from accounting. She was surprisingly deft for someone with limited depth perception. Gillian and Jules were in the small clearing between everyone's desks. They both wore calf-length leggings and baggy t-shirts. Jules looked like her old self again, doing silly exaggerated stretches to make Gillian laugh. Rob wiped his mouth in case of lipstick stains.

'Training,' Jules said, and he could tell she didn't really want to invite him along, but was too good a person not to. 'You coming?'

He almost glanced down at his crotch.

You can take the boy out of the sex shop...

'I don't have any kit.'

'You could wear your Race for Brodie t-shirt. And I'm sure one of the guys would lend you some shorts,' Gillian suggested.

Fucking Gillian. So practical.

For a moment he imagined himself jogging down the street with Gillian and Jules either side of him. Mostly they jogged in companionable silence, but occasionally he cracked a joke and Gillian and Jules both laughed. Then imaginary him stepped in dog shit and Gillian and Jules both laughed harder and pointed at his dirty shoes and he realised they were the ones jogging together and he was just being tolerated.

'Nah,' he said, 'I'll give it a miss.'

He tried to ignore the relief on Jules's face. He'd thought they were mates, but apparently not.

Who trains for three miles anyway?

*

Jules rolls her eyes.

'Maybe I was a little overconfident,' I concede.

'You think?'

*

Rob was dying. His calves burned. His chest was tight. The edges of his vision were grey and fuzzy and he'd just been overtaken by a guy dressed as a hedgehog. Jules jogged alongside him, but clearly only out of sympathy.

She isn't even slightly out of breath. She could be up at the front with Gillian and Hedgehog Man if she wanted to.

'I... think I might... have to stop...' Rob panted, staggering to a halt and doubling over. Huge mistake. The world lurched violently and his stomach swirled in an effort to keep up. He gagged and swallowed. Sweat burned his eyes.

'All right Kiddo?' Bummer jogged over with Joel and Jacob.

Rob waved a hand at him and said, 'Pffak.' Sweat streamed from his forehead, tickling his nose, pooling at the back of his neck. With a massive effort, he straightened, squinting at Bummer.

Bummer had slightly rosy cheeks. The guy lived on a diet

of takeaway and pick 'n' mix and yet there he was, beer belly straining at his Race for Brodie t-shirt, not a bead of sweat anywhere on his pudgy frame. Joel and Jacob were running on the spot, knees flying, giggling and pushing each other. None of this made any sense to them – it was just all stupid adult stuff that they clearly weren't too worried about. Jules swigged from her water bottle, trying to make it look like she needed to stop, too, bless her.

'Who's this then?' asked Bummer, idly swinging his hands at his sides.

'Oh, sorry, do you actually know him?' said Jules, stepping forward to shake Bummer's hand. 'Thought you were just a concerned stranger. Jules.'

'Victor Harris.'

'Since... when?' gasped Rob. His head was a tiny bit less burny now and his legs felt like they might have bones in after all, but his eyes were still having a bit of difficulty with the whole seeing malarkey.

'Anyway, nice to meet you Jules. Later loser.' And Bummer was off again, jogging briskly, with Joel and Jacob easily matching his strides despite having much shorter legs.

'That was a little... insensitive,' said Jules thoughtfully.

'Him? Oh no, he's like my brother. That's how he shows affection.' Finally, Rob's breathing was more or less normal. He took a couple of steps and a stitch lanced through his side. 'Why don't you go on?' he said, sensing Jules's desire to be off and running again.

'Will you be okay?' she asked, already jogging slowly away from him, backward so she could keep talking.

'I'll just get some water and then I'll be fighting fit.'

Fighting off a heart attack more like. Does crossing the finish line in an ambulance count?

Jules spun round and disappeared into the crowd of runners. An overwhelming number of people were taking part. It was like everyone in Credit Co and all their friends, family and former lovers had descended on the park to complete the Race for Brodie. Rob might have felt guilty if he wasn't in agony from the lactic acid slowly devouring his muscles.

He limped over to the drinks station. One of the temps from his office was giving out plastic cups of water and bottles of isotonic sports drinks. She had long brown hair extensions and was wearing a ton of make-up, but beneath the fake eyelashes and the layer of bronzer, she was actually quite pretty. She was also about nineteen.

Girls mature quicker than guys anyway, so she's probably nearer to my age than Jules is.

Another bite of pain and weakness in his calves forced him to steady himself against the edge of her table.

Realistically speaking.

'Hi,' he said, smiling as best he could while his body imploded. 'Can I get some water?'

Her expression quickly changed from one of vacant pleasantness to one of vacant sympathy.

'You're him, aren't you?' she said in hushed tones, picking up a cup with fuchsia manicured nails. 'The one who this run's for? Well, his kid, anyway.'

Rob blinked, trying to draw the meaning out of the convoluted sentence. 'And you're Sarah, aren't you?'

'Sara,' she corrected.

Sarah for middle-class people.

'Of course.' He paused to take a sip of water. It was deliciously cool and the sip soon turned into a swig, which became a gulp. He lifted the empty cup to his forehead and rolled the cool plastic back and forth along his brow, living out his interview fantasy. What was reality anyway?

Sara watched, her thinly drawn brows pulled together in a frown, her full lips parted slightly in a confused pout.

'I think I need a sports massage,' said Rob, willing to be pathetic and needy if it got the job done. 'Would you be able to help with that?'

She smiled and under the circles of blusher her cheeks coloured for real.

*

Far away, Jules makes a small noise of distaste, but I'm on a roll now, like this voice is someone else's, like I'm listening to the story, too.

19

Rob pulled himself up into a sitting position. It wasn't a conventional sports massage, but it had made him forget about his aches for a bit. Sara was sitting alongside him, hitching herself back into her shorts. She had leaves in her hair. The tangled strands had a synthetic look and Rob became temporarily obsessed with looking for the glue joining each lock of hair to her own.

How long is her real hair? Shorter than mine? Wonder what it's made from?

There was a snuffling sound, and a springer spaniel broke through the undergrowth and jabbed at Rob with its damp nose. Rob got up and dusted soil and dry grass off his clothes. Sara was still fiddling with her shorts.

'Everything okay?'

'Yeah,' she said brightly. 'I've just got a touch of thrush, that's all.'

She must have noticed his face drop a couple of inches, because she laughed and patted his arm.

'Men can't get thrush, silly!'

'What?! Of course they—' Rob's leg grew warm and wet. He looked down to see the dog casually cocking its leg. He ached too much to get out of the way. At least the warmth eased the pain in his calf muscles a little and he didn't have to think about the fact that he now probably had thrush.

Jules burst through the low-hanging tree branches and said: 'There you are! The race is finished. Gregory wants you to make a speech. I think you can get out of it, but you should at least show your...' She trailed off as she noticed Sara, who was very obviously *sans* bra. She looked down at the dog, who was now scratching at the earth, flicking loose soil up at Rob. As her eyes travelled slowly up him, she couldn't fail to notice he hadn't entirely... gone soft yet, '...cock.'

Head held high, she turned on her heel and left.

*

'I hadn't even noticed you'd still got a semi. You were the cock in that situation. Did you really need to bring it up?'

'Sorry.'

I'd like to blame the Empornium for my boundary issues, but it would probably be unfair. Auntie Joan has already witnessed how little I care in that regard. Bollocks blowing in the breeze. I've always thought there was something majestic about male genitalia, the way it slowly rises to attention like a space shuttle being prepped for launch. I've yet to meet a woman who shares that sentiment.

'If it makes you feel any better,' I continue, wincing at the pain-memory of the hot itch in my groin, 'you weren't the only one who thought I was a cock. And I suffered.'

'My heart bleeds.'

*

'Why's she always got to put a – unh – dampener on everything I do?' asked Rob, rolling the bag of frozen sausage rolls across his inflamed crotch. 'Unless she's jealous.' He raised his voice so Bummer could hear him from the kitchen. 'Of all the attention I've been getting lately.'

Bummer was by the oven keeping an eye on the mini pizzas. Plates of cocktail sausages and some vegetable samosas covered the kitchen worktops, the other casualties of Rob's red hot penis.

'Yeah, she could be, yeah,' Bummer agreed quietly.

'I don't think these sausage rolls are gonna last much longer, mate.'

'Aww come on, Kidder!' Bummer groaned. 'I don't wanna have to cook everything out the freezer. We're gonna struggle to eat this lot as it is. Won't a cold towel do?'

'What about the cheesecake? You wouldn't have to eat the cheesecake right away.'

Bummer appeared at his side in a shot, still wearing his cow oven glove.

'I'm saving that cheesecake,' he said firmly. 'I'm looking forward to that cheesecake, and I'm not going to eat it after it's defrosted on your cock.'

Rob could see he was resolute on that one. Sighing, he unzipped his fly, working the sausage roll bag into the top of his trousers to get the cool plastic directly onto his skin.

'Oh, for Christ's sake, Kidder!' Bummer sounded genuinely horrified.

Incredible! From a guy quite happy to eat while shitting.

The cooker's timer buzzed and he hurried back to the kitchen, calling over his shoulder: 'Maybe she's just a real friend, and it bothers her that you're probably getting knob diseases and how does that look if you're called as a character witness and you can't go because you're in hospital with syphilis. How does syphilis sound when someone's trying to appeal against their ruling? Trying to prove they're an upstanding citizen? How does syphilis sound then?'

'Are we still talking about Jules?'

Bummer returned and rested a plate of cocktail sausages on the arm of the chair in silence.

Eventually the smell of the warm meaty snacks was too much for him and he snatched up a handful, still regarding Rob balefully. 'I don't get where all this comes from,' he said through his mouthful. 'You never used to be like this, Kidder.'

'Exactly!'

Bummer looked confused, wiping the grease from his fingers down the front of his shirt. 'Why would you want to be,' he indicated Rob's crotch with another sausage pinched between his thumb and forefinger, '... like that?'

'Oh, so it's good enough for you but not for me?' Rob's cheeks were warming to match his crotch as his anger rose.

'What? I've never had an STD. I always keep a lid on it, Kidder. Usually.'

'Not the lurgy, the sleeping around!' Rob was shouting, ashamed but unable to stop himself. 'You've always lorded it over me and now you've got five kids from four different women and you're not getting as much sex and you can't take it that I am.'

Rob realised he'd been pounding his fist against his chest as he bellowed.

Bummer's shoulders slumped. He looked old. Rob noticed the grey in his stubble, his sideburns, for the first time. The older Bummer looked, the younger Rob felt, until eventually he was eight years old again, giving Gordon a hard time over trivial nonsense. The sloped forehead, long thick forearms, pouched belly. To all intents and purposes Bummer looked like the old silverback turned out by the troop, barely able to accept his reign was over but lacking the strength to fight for supremacy. Rob waited for Bummer to bring his fist down on Rob's head, the elder putting a stop to the upstart pretender, but the blow never came.

'It was never just about the sex, never,' he said eventually, avoiding Rob's eyes. Then after another, shorter pause, his tone changed like he was trying to reaffirm their relationship. 'Come on then, get those out your pants so I can cook them. I'll make you a cold compress instead.' Rob handed over the soggy bag of mushy snacks and Bummer headed back to the kitchen. 'You're not having the cheesecake.'

*

'How long do we have to get this done?' asked Rob, sealing the Deluxe Debbies back into their box with packing tape.

'Two weeks,' said Bummer, climbing onto a footstool to unhook the bondage harnesses from the display rack.

'Then why are we doing it now?' Rob sank down onto the

box of Debbies and watched his friend becoming increasingly entangled in the mess of buckles and straps. He had better things to be doing with his time. Probably.

Bummer shrugged, causing the chains to shake and dance. One of the straps had snaked round his leg. As he reached down to unhook it, he overbalanced, falling onto the magazine table. His face turning red, he flapped around, succeeding only in tightening a studded breast strap round his neck.

'Fucking cocking wanking bastard bloody thing!' He went limp and burst into tears.

Probably not the best time to laugh. I mean, ordinarily, he'd be up for it, but he's a bit down at the moment, so laughing would be out of order. As Bummer struggled to regain his composure, the chains shimmied and tinkled against his heaving chest. *He does look bloody funny, though. Like those tubby little Shire horses on Nana's windowsill. Only on his back and all snotty.*

'Why aren't you helping him, you cretin?' snapped Newbie, appearing from the stock cupboard to untangle Bummer.

'I was about to actually,' said Rob as haughtily as he could manage. He stepped over to the table and fiddled with a buckle close to Bummer's wrist in an effort to make his statement true. Bummer pulled his arm out of reach.

'Let Paul do it.'

'Who?'

Bummer didn't even acknowledge that little dig. Newbie kept his head down, too intent on working all the twisted straps free to notice the tension in the air.

'Nearly got it,' he said soothingly. 'We'll have you up and about in a minute. How about a cup of tea?'

Rob shook his head in disgust.

So it's like that, is it? That's how it is now? Bummer and Paul, Paul and Bummer.

He was halfway down the street before he realised Bummer hadn't even tried to convince him to stay.

*

'You guys have made up now, though, right?'

It's clear Jules fears that if she walks out now the next time she'll see me will be as a blurred-out body on the local news. Tears of a clown, outwardly cheerful, a man with everything to live for, all those clichés spouted by newsroom types with no idea of what they're talking about.

'Right?' she presses, touching my arm again. I don't get the electric thrill this time, just warmth, tiny candle flames of hope against my skin. Reassurance that I can still feel, even if my thinking power's burning out.

'I guess. It's not the same.'

Paul's always there for a start, with his good looks and his easy charm and that weird edginess that Bummer seems to find endlessly entertaining for some reason. Waifs and strays, that's what Bummer's into. And now I'm not a waif, now I've got my own stuff going on, he's not interested in me any more.

She's rooting around in her bag now, stirring through the depths with little clinking noises, and I wonder if I've said something that's made her go for the mace. I tense, hoping there's an eyebath in the first-aid kit Gordon put in the cupboard. But she produces a little tin, a tin that used to hold lozenges, and she takes a lighter and some papers and tobacco out of it instead.

'I didn't know you smoked,' I say, forced to reappraise my view of her again.

'I don't.' She reaches into her back pocket and produces a tiny bag containing an embarrassingly small amount of weed. I could find more than that shaking out my bedding. But she's brandishing it like it's the answer to everything, so I just nod and let her get on with rolling. Maybe the police will bust in, declare me an unfit parent and take Brodie away. Maybe that would be a relief.

*

Rob had no idea why he used to hide his weed in a dominoes box in Gordon's shed, or why that suddenly came back to him, but his angry striding away from the Empornium took him to a bus stop and the bus he got on took him to his mum's house. If he wanted good weed, he could call up Charlie, his dealer, a fifteen-year-old with a BMX and an endless supply of illicit substances. But he didn't want good weed, he wanted that specific weed, however old and tasteless it might've ended up.

The house looked strange with no one in it. No moth-eaten cats in the front garden. They'd all gone into quarantine, apart from Queenie. She was too old, so Tenike had her, because Tenike's mum was one of those weird women who loved cats so much she put bibs and bonnets on them and took photos.

The lack of net curtains made the windows look empty and unloved.

Like me.

Mum made Rob drop the keys off at the estate agents the day she left, so even though the new owners hadn't moved in yet,

Rob couldn't go inside for one last look around. Not without breaking and entering anyway, and he'd been on the receiving end of that enough to know he didn't want to do it.

Instead he hauled himself over the fence and dropped into the back garden. It looked the same – lush patches of bluebells that Gordon couldn't get rid of no matter how many times he dug them up, a twisted old buddleia strung with bird feeders, a corrugated iron shed with a rusted door and a stand of tall conifers lining three sides of the garden, blocking out the outside world. Without Mum and Gordon and the cats, the lack of noise was stifling, the silence and stillness like being trapped in a vacuum.

He realised he'd been holding his breath and inhaled deeply. A breeze stirred the bluebells and goosebumps prickled his arms and neck. In a few strides he was beside the shed, glancing over his shoulder to make sure Sally from next door wasn't hanging out her washing. Her garden was equally still and silent.

The lock on the shed was old and rusted. Gordon hadn't even bothered doing it up. Rob pulled on the stiff old door and after a few tugs, it creaked open. The tool hooks along the wall were bare. Gordon's strimmer and lawnmower were gone. Rob thought about when he was eleven and mowing the lawn used to be his main chore. That mower seemed so big and heavy back then. He'd behaved like Gordon was a Dickensian workhouse master endangering a small boy with unsafe machinery. It had surprised him when he came to help out one weekend as an adult and saw how small and light the mower was. Ideal for a boy that age, really.

The only thing left in the shed apart from cobwebs and the lingering smell of cigar smoke (Gordon would come for a crafty one on Christmas morning every year) was the cabinet. Probably would have been a nice heirloom if it wasn't swollen from getting damp every winter. It usually housed Gordon's knick-knacks, things Mum would have liked him to throw away that he hoarded instead. Nails of varying sizes, some bent; elastic bands left behind by the postman; plastic moneybags harvested from the bank; old tins with half an inch of varnish or paint in the bottom. Rob rifled through all the drawers and cupboards. All were empty, save for a scattering of mouse droppings.

In the bottom cupboard, right at the back, was the domino box. He reached gingerly over the mouse shit and pulled the box to the front. Gave it a little shake. The contents rattled. He opened the lid. On top of the dominoes, there was a bag of weed, crumbly with age. On top of the weed, there was a note in Gordon's blocky handwriting.

I WON'T TELL YOUR MOTHER ABOUT THIS IF YOU DONT TELL HER ABOUT THE CIGGARS.

Bloody Gordon. If it wasn't for Mum he'd never have solved a crossword in his life.

Rob slumped to the floor and sat looking at the note for a long time. When he'd done he wiped his eyes on his sleeve and got up to go. After a final perusal of the empty cabinet and the empty shed, he vaulted back over the gate into the front garden.

He'd never been good at physical stuff and gate-jumping was no exception. He wrenched his ankle as he landed and pitched forward with a loud 'OOF!' Managing to regain his balance after a few staggered steps, he stood rubbing his ankle. The old pain in his knee flared up again, too, and he was forced to stay still, teeth gritted, until the pain subsided.

'You there! What are you doing?'

Shit.

Slowly he raised his head. On the street looking into the front garden was Lisa MacFarlane. Her tone changed from anger to incredulity.

'Rob? Is that you?'

No. It isn't. Bye. He pictured himself saying that and running straight past her, sprinting to the awaiting bus, poised to whisk him away. The reality was his ankle hurt like a bitch and he wasn't running anywhere.

'Hello Lisa.' He straightened his back. Her kid was with her, half-hiding behind her, peeping out from the safety of her coat.

'I thought your mum had moved out?'

'She has. I just... left something.' He waved the dominoes box at her briefly, then pocketed it again.

'Are you all right?'

'Me? I'm fine. Everything's fine.'

'You look kind of in pain.' She approached the front gate and leaned on it. Her nails were perfectly manicured. She had immaculate, womanly hands, not stubby and bitten down like Jules's, or chubby and girlish like Heather's. The kind of hands that would softly stroke your hair in the morning until you were ready to wake up and have sex.

'I'm good.'

'What are you doing with yourself these days? Not still at Vic's shop?' The distaste was evident in her voice. Heather didn't seem to mind the sex shop. Jules would probably be cool with it, too. Once she knew about it.

'Yeah,' he said boldly. 'I live upstairs with Bummer now actually.' He enjoyed her slight flinch at Bummer's name, her glance to her kid to see if he caught it, see if he was going to be saying 'What's a bummer, Mummy?' when they got home. 'We're raising his kids together.'

That was weird. Why did I say that? That was a really weird thing to say. I meant to come off like I'm all grown up and independent but that didn't sound right at all.

Her eyes softened as if a weight that had burdened her for years had suddenly been lifted.

No wait, I take it back, if I'm gay it's with the New Guy! He's good looking. Bummer's well below what I could achieve!

'Oh, I see,' she said quietly. 'Well, that's good. That's good Rob, I'm glad to hear you guys are doing okay. Give Vic my love.' And she strode away, no doubt bursting to tell her fucking boyfriend that her ex was now gay with his fat best mate.

'Lisa, I didn't mean—'

She stopped and turned, looking at him expectantly. He took in her soft dark hair and her crocheted beret. Her heavy wool coat and her soft suede boots. So put together, so carefully constructed. Her kid gazed up at her with undisguised adoration. Rob was probably giving her the same look.

I'll never be good enough for you.

He raised a hand.

'Bye then.'

*

'Oh, so she's too good for you, but I'll do?'

'I didn't mean it like that.'

20

Rob was dreaming that there were figures around the foot of his bed when the call came. He sat up in bed, panicked, half-expecting the shadowy shapes to loom out of the curtains, and was relieved to see Bellamy's number glowing out from his phone. The relief was short-lived. It was 2am. Why would Bellamy call at this time of night unless they'd found something? And the only thing they could have found was a horribly disfigured child's body that needed identifying.

'Mr Buckland?' It wasn't Bellamy, but some underling calling from his office.

Rob nodded for a few seconds before realising they couldn't see him, and instead squeaked, 'Yes?'

'Detective Bellamy has your son. At least, we think so. We need you to come and...'

All Rob heard for the rest of the call was a rushing noise in his ears. Perhaps it was the word son, echoing around inside his head, bouncing off his ear canals. Once again, he was desperate, screaming inside to tell this unknown caller all about his lies, that this poor mutilated thing they wanted him to look at couldn't be Brodie because Brodie wasn't real. But then he thought of all the consequences, all the police time wasted, all the company money spent, all of the colleagues misled. There was no coming back from that. He could go to prison. He would at the very least be fired, humiliated, shunned.

All you really have to do to make all this go away is say it's Brodie.

His stomach surged violently at the sound of that inner voice. It was dark and insidious, some part of his psyche he didn't want to hear, didn't even want to acknowledge.

'...car will be there in about fifteen minutes,' the voice was saying.

He was sweating and fighting down the urge to vomit, could only manage a strangled: 'Mmmhmmm.'

The police thought they had found Brodie, and Rob was just going to have to go along with it.

*

'They didn't tell you then and there he was alive?' asks Jules.

'I don't know, I wasn't listening,' I say, not really listening.

*

Am I really going to claim someone else's child? Because that's really wrong. Wronger than all the other stuff by far.

Rob gazed out of the police car window. In the pre-morning light, everything looked grey.

And what if it wasn't over there? What if they did DNA tests and found out the child wasn't his? Or what if they took his word for it, and he had to have a funeral for s—

*

'Wait, wait, you already did this part! So I guess that's it? Lisa's your unrequited love, Bellamy called, you got Brodie back, I'm all caught up with the story. Thank Christ, my arse has gone to sleep!'

You're my unrequited—

She gets up, punches herself in the arse a few times.

'There's still a few more bits.' I try to look pathetically needy, not difficult in my current mental state. 'I need to tell you properly about Bummer forgetting Brodie. And what Joel said after he first saw him. And you need to understand what I'm telling you.'

She rolls her eyes, then rolls her head, letting it loll on her neck to loosen it.

'Okay, fine.' She sits back down. 'Wrap this up, Bucko.'

At least she didn't call me Kiddo.

*

Bummer wasn't kidding when he said he'd come right over. All he had with him were Joel and Jacob, each clutching an identical *Blight Brigade* comic, and the jumbo bag of crisps he'd been eating on his way round the supermarket. Joel and Jacob dropped their comics on the floor and headed straight for the PlayStation.

'So, where is he?' asked Bummer excitedly, balling up the empty crisp packet.

'Bummer, you do remember...' said Rob slowly, already with a nagging suspicion he wasn't going to like the answer, 'you remember we made Brodie up?'

Bummer stared at him wide-eyed for a moment, then burst out laughing. He laughed long and hard.

Bummer, you old dog. You were having me on. One of your pranks isn't it? 'Ooh, what made-up son? Brodie's a real boy!' Classic Bummer!

'You nearly had me for a minute there, you sounded so serious.' Bummer clapped Rob on the shoulder as his laughter subsided. 'Stop holding out on me. I want to see my favourite godson.'

Rob watched, perplexed, as Bummer hurried through to the bedroom. Brodie was sitting upright, no doubt awoken by Joel and Jacob fighting over the PlayStation controller. Bummer walked straight up to him, arms outstretched, and lifted him out of bed. He raised him high above his head and twirled round and round, grinning like a lunatic. Brodie stared down at Bummer, brow slightly furrowed as if trying to remember who this guy was to him. Bummer let him drop and caught him under the armpits before he hit the floor, pulled him in tight and kissed the top of his head like he did with his own boys. Like he would if Brodie was Rob's boy.

'Bit quiet isn' he?' Bummer asked Rob, but Rob was unable to respond. Unable to think. 'We'll soon see about that!' And Bummer tickled Brodie's sides. Brodie jerked violently and the whites of his eyes grew bigger like a frightened horse and Rob thought *Now you've done it, Bummer, you cretin, now you've doomed the entire human race.*

But Brodie didn't unleash a thousand-decibel scream to attract his pod minions. He jerked and squirmed, and then started laughing. He laughed and shrieked and giggled until he was red in the face and could barely breathe any more and then Bummer set him back down on the bed. As the pair's hysteria subsided they gazed at each other with a look of such undeniable affection and familiarity that Rob was terrified. Bellamy thinking Brodie was his kid was one thing, but Bummer? Bummer knew he wasn't. So what was he doing?

'You okay?' Bummer asked later as Rob sipped a mug of tea. 'Your hands are shaking.'

'No,' Rob said, putting his mug down on the coffee table. 'No, I'm not okay. And I can't believe you're doing this to me. I'm sorry I left you tied up in the bondage stuff, okay, but this is taking it too far!'

Bummer was watching Joel and Jacob teach Brodie how to play *Hunter Vs XenoBot* but quickly switched his full attention to Rob.

'Taking what too far?'

'Oh, come off it Bummer. You know.'

'I don't know. All I know is you're acting all weird.'

They sat in silence, Rob's anger hanging in the air between them.

'Look,' said Bummer, 'if this is about Brodie—'

'How could it not be about Brodie?' hissed Rob, not wanting to draw the boys' attention away from their game. Joel glanced round anyway and looked at Rob, one eyebrow raised.

'Aww, gee man, I'm so sorry. I'm such an insensitive goon. Of course you're worried about him. Who knows what he's been through? But he'll be back to his old self in no time. You'll see.'

Rob was glad he'd put the mug down. It would be in pieces if he hadn't.

'Old self?!'

Rob was about to descend into a mad, spittle-flecked rant about how Brodie never *had* an old self. He felt it building within, the fury, an unfocused hatred he'd often directed at Gordon, but until now, never Bummer. Bummer looked so sincere, so concerned, like Gordon always used to, only this time Rob couldn't maintain the rage. It drained away like poison from a snake's fang and left him numb and empty.

This is madness. It's not happening. It can't be happening.

He sat and brooded in silence for hours, until Bummer said: 'C'mon boys, it's time to go home now.' They complained and wheedled, making out they wanted to stay and play with Brodie, when really they just wanted to keep shooting aliens in the face. But finally Bummer won the argument and they put their coats on and headed for the door. Rob followed them, expecting Brodie to do the same, but he was studying the game's box and frowning.

When Bummer and Jacob were out in the hall, Joel squeezed Rob in a tight hug, or his kneecaps at least. Rob didn't know these kids the way he knew Tenike. They didn't hang out at Bummer's a lot like Neil, or come to the pub like Chloe. This behaviour was new, but he was feeling so low, he wasn't about to question it. At that moment, he would've accepted a comforting hug from anyone. He crouched down and when Joel was close to his ear, the small boy whispered: 'Don't worry Uncle Rob, we know Brodie isn't real, even if Daddy doesn't.'

Rob dropped Joel like hot toast and stared after him open-mouthed as he trotted to catch up with his waiting brother and father. He didn't look round, didn't seem concerned by the bombshell he'd just dropped, just reached for Bummer's hand and disappeared down the corridor.

Rob let the door slam. Clenched and unclenched his fists. Rolled his neck. Paced a circle one way, a circle the other, and then marched into the front room, ready to confront the interloper.

'Right,' he said firmly, pointing a finger at Brodie. The kid looked up from the game box. His large dark eyes shone. 'What are you?' Rob said it with more force than he intended, but even so, he was shocked when the kid burst into tears. But as Brodie sat, sobbing and sniffing, all the anger drained out of him again and he realised that whether or not Brodie was real wasn't the issue at the moment. The issue at the moment was that there was a kid in front of him, scared and alone and upset.

'Look, I'm sorry, okay,' said Rob gruffly, and he sat down on the floor next to Brodie and wiped his cheeks and then held him until the crying stopped.

*

'That's not proof, Rob. Even if we were to ask Joel and he were to say the exact same thing, it isn't proof.' Jules is moving beyond exasperated again, back into angry. I wish she had more weed so she'd mellow out. That skinny little joint barely lasted an inhale each. Now we're sitting with all the windows open as if Brodie might somehow become a drug fiend if he gets the tiniest whiff.

Maybe he would. Who knows how weed might affect... whatever he is?

'This idea that kids never lie?' Jules is on a roll now, she's finished the wine. 'It's bullshit. Kids lie all the time. Everybody lies, Rob, everybody.'

'You don't.'

'What?'

'You're the most honest person I know. After Gordon.'

'Not long after we met, I told you my parents were dead. And Gordon lied to your mum about the cigars and the weed.'

He omitted the truth. That's not lying. Not proper lying.

*

Most of the time Brodie just read. Read and read. Read Rob's whole comic collection for hours while Rob watched fearfully, wondering if it was okay to leave the room while a kid was reading. Sometimes Brodie played, but in a weird way, like his heart wasn't in it, but he knew he should. He seemed more into examining things. When Rob first handed Optibot to him, he sat and studied the instruction manual for a long time and then regarded the robot carefully from all angles before placing him reverently on the sofa. At Brodie's age, Rob would have been racing round pressing Optibot's voice synthesiser button over and over until Gordon told him it was quiet time and took the batteries out.

He may look like me, but he's clearly not mine.

*

Rob spent the next few days phoning everyone he knew and casually dropping Brodie's name into conversation. The result was the same every time. First confusion, those few seconds where he thought they actually might ask him what the hell he was talking about, then the smile entered their voice and they asked how Brodie was finding school or if Rob was going to bring him round for a visit soon. He knew how his next call would go, and he wondered why he bothered saving it for last. Perhaps because until then, he could cling to the idea he was the sane one and the world was bonkers.

'Mum?'

'Robert? You don't ring for weeks and then you call up out of the blue just as I'm trying to cook a roast. There are a lot of elements on the go here, Robert. If the peas dry out or the potatoes go too crispy, Gordon won't like it. You know how particular Gordon is about his potatoes.'

'I know.' Rob looked over at Brodie. He was playing on the sofa with Optibot, glancing at the TV every now and then. 'You could have let the machine get it.'

'And would you have left a message if I did?'

'Probably not.'

It was bad enough talking to her across all those miles, worse when she wasn't even there.

'Well, then.'

Rob could hear her stirring frantically on the other end of the line, wooden spoon clanging briskly against saucepan.

'I was thinking about buying a laptop so Brodie and I can video call you. Using the emergency credit card. Is that okay?'

'That would be lovely!' There it was again – the smile in her voice. He could hear it, had become attuned to it over the course of his phone calls. 'You know I love to see my darling boy and his darling boy!'

He said bye quickly and hung up. He stared at the inert phone for a long time as if it was somehow implicated. If he'd asked for a laptop for himself, she would have said no. There would have been the insinuation he'd just use it for porn and video games and never even set up the video calls system. There would have been questions about how much and when and where from. But she said yes without any caveats because she was eager to see her grandson. Her grandson who she had never met, because he didn't exist.

*

'Huh.'

'What?'

'So, she's desperate to see this darling grandson of hers, a grandson who was missing for three weeks, yet she doesn't want to come visit him?'

I scratch my head. I'd not given it much thought, but when I do a pulse of pain strikes, like a firework going off in my brain. I wince and close my eyes, waiting for the sparkles to clear.

'You okay?'

'Yeah, yeah.' As the pain subsides, everything's clearer. 'She didn't come to visit because I didn't tell her.'

'Tell her what?'

'About Brodie going missing.'

'WHAT? WHY?!'

I sigh heavily. Again? She's really going to make me go over this again?

'Because. He did not. Actually. Exist.' It takes everything I have not to scream it in her face.

Jules's face is white. Her lips are tight, like she's holding in a scream of her own. Her eyes are sad and angry and penetrating. She wants something from me and I can't give it to her, because I don't know what it is. I reach for something, anything.

*

The crash of the *Blight Brigade* theme tune brought him back to himself. Brodie leapt across to the TV to change the channel.

'Don't you like *Blight Brigade*?'

Brodie shook his head.

'Why not?'

He shrugged.

Rob went over to the DVD cabinet. At the bottom were some old videos, recorded off the telly many years ago. The labels bore Rob's large childhood handwriting in wobbly purple felt-tip. GALAxY SkwAd.

He crossed back to the TV, pulled the SCART leads out of the back and linked up the old video player. Slipping the video into the machine, he pressed play and joined Brodie on the sofa. He fast forwarded some ancient adverts for dubious weeing dolls that probably wouldn't be allowed these days. And then it started. *Galaxy Squad*.

But as the programme wound on, Rob noticed things he never saw as a kid. Like the fact that although Detective Noxter had a big, green, bobbly alien head, his neck was pink and human. And Chief Yodpod, who looked like a large blue latex toad, never left his desk. The two human cops, who Rob had always thought the coolest guys ever, were actually kinda corny. They had fake tans and even faker white teeth and their acting was wooden. Feeling deflated, Rob reached for the remote. And caught sight of Brodie.

Transfixed. The kid couldn't take his eyes off Detective Noxter and as one of the humans clapped the lumpy old alien heartily on the back, a smile twitched at the corner of Brodie's mouth.

I knew he'd like Galaxy Squad *more.*

Smiling smugly, Rob went to make breakfast.

*

Jules's head is in her hands. She might be crying, although if she is, she's doing it silently, without moving. I think about touching her shoulder, but I'm scared. I thought that was a nice story, a good one, and this is how she's reacted? Although my judgement has been a little off lately, I'll admit that.

21

On the bus into town, Rob found he kept thinking about work. With the Empornium, he had only thought about work in an abstract way, like when he realised he couldn't eat his boiled egg because it too closely resembled the love egg in the returns bin, or when he was paying his gas bill and the operator's voice was the same as the person who rang and asked if they stocked nipple clamps suitable for someone with a nickel allergy.

Credit Co was different. He saw spreadsheets in his sleep and had to begin mentally preparing for team meetings several days in advance to ensure he didn't fall asleep or swear or cry.

Got two mouths to feed now. Better get back to it.

At least thinking about work was better than thinking about Brodie. Brodie was there, by Rob's side. Flesh and blood. If he moved his elbow, he'd touch him, his son. Instead, Rob kept his arms clamped to his sides.

Stop it, stop it, stop it. This isn't real. You've just been hit by a car and are lying in your hospital bed in a coma.

At least that made some weird sort of sense. A made-up boy being found by the police? Where was the sense in that?

Brodie hadn't objected when Rob took the window seat, which was strange, too. He seemed content looking at the other passengers. Rob watched the scenery slide past the window. It looked like the bus route to town. The school and the post office and the library and the church. None of it looked like a coma hallucination.

He looked at Brodie for about the millionth time that week. Reached out and gently poked his face. Brodie turned quickly in surprise and fixed him with that confused black-eyed stare. *He feels real. Even being stared at by him feels real, like he's thinking what an embarrassing dork I am.* Brodie smiled shyly and went back to examining the overhead signage depicting the bus route. Shaking his head, Rob rang the bell. *Only one way to find out if this is real or not.*

He got off the bus with Brodie trailing him like a faithful dog. Waited for the old woman behind him to lug her tartan shopping trolley off the bus and wheel it away up the path to the nearby maisonettes. Waited for the bus to pull away. The whole time, Brodie watched him curiously.

He looked away from the kid's face and told himself none of this was real. The cracked paving slab, the peeling paint on the bus shelter, the graffiti on the timetable saying 'Jodie will sit on yor face for 10p.' All of it was an elaborate construct in his fevered brain, like in a sci-fi film.

He stepped up to the kerb. It was still early and they'd got off just before the main stop. The road wasn't particularly busy.

There hadn't been a single vehicle on the road since the bus left, but Rob knew that sooner or later some rich twat in a people carrier would come speeding round the corner, and then he'd have his chance.

The sun blazed and he could see himself reflected in the windows of the house across the street, and Brodie behind him, like a snapshot of the past. And then he heard it, an engine revving. He squinted into the distance, and saw a small car with chrome alloys and a spoiler roaring up to the bend. *Perfect. A boy racer. Probably on his mobile phone or eating fried chicken or something.* Rob's foot left the kerb.

And then the strangest thing happened. A small hand snaked round his wrist, and a shrill voice yelled: 'No, Dad! No!' and he was pulled back with such incredible force, he smacked down arse first onto the pavement.

The boy racer slowed down and laughed at Rob sitting by the side of the road.

'No, Dad,' Brodie repeated softly, squeezing Rob's upper arm for emphasis. Rob got to his feet, rubbing his backside.

'All right,' he said, 'all right.' He pointed in the direction they were heading and let Brodie lead the way.

'I think I cracked my bum bone,' he told Brodie as the kid trotted along in front of him. Brodie looked over his shoulder and rolled his eyes.

Surely my arse would not hurt this much in a hallucination.

He continued weighing up the possibilities as they headed into the computer shop.

The shop was vast and chilly and all the staff were young, enthusiastic and impeccably turned out. Rob wandered down the mice aisle in the direction of laptops. Brodie scuffed his feet along behind.

'Pick your feet up, will you?' said Rob. He was just about to add that he didn't buy his shoes so Brodie could scuff straight through the sole when he realised he didn't buy them at all. Mum bought them about twenty years ago and they were probably actually on a landfill site somewhere.

Being ridiculous again. It's not those actual shoes. Just coincidence. They're black lace-up school shoes, every kid has some.

'We should get you some new shoes after this.'

Brodie nodded.

'And clothes, too.' *More money. And the kid's not even mine. Wonder if this is how Gordon felt all the time?*

'Excuse me, can this one do video calls?'

The assistant had a long fringe half-hiding dark, heavily lashed eyes. He could have been the brother of the department store assistant who sold Rob his awful green suit. Perhaps it was him. Perhaps he had a second job.

'Actually sir, most of these machines would be more than capable of coping with any of your video calling needs. But this one would be an exceptionally good choice, because...'

Rob let the lad reel off his whole sales spiel because he seemed the sort who'd get a kick out of that shit. Then Rob held out his card and said: 'If we can get it in chrome with a webcam thrown in, it's sol—'

'Young man, you can't do that!'

Rob turned. Another sales assistant was standing over Brodie with her hands on her hips. Brodie seemed oblivious to her presence. He'd got a dongle from somewhere and plugged it into the back of one of the display models and was typing feverishly. Rob couldn't see the screen from this angle. He could only see the sales assistant's expression – open-mouthed and flushed.

'You can't use a display model to... I mean, they don't have all the software for... How are you doing that?!'

Rob left his own sales guy standing with the chip and pin machine in hand and hurried over to his not-son.

Brodie's small white hand flashed to the power button and he hung his head.

'Sorry.'

Rob glimpsed colours and shapes on the monitor before the screen went black, but nothing that made any sense.

'What were you doing?'

Brodie shrugged. 'Trying to make a video call. I miss Grandma.'

Rob studied him, hunting for that tell, that indicator of a lie. 'You miss Grandma, huh?'

Brodie nodded.

It didn't seem like a lie. But it had to be. *You don't have a grandma in Malta. You just don't. Who the hell are you?* 'We'll get this set up as soon as we get home and give her a call, okay?'

Brodie nodded again, still looking ashamed. Rob steered him back over to their purchase and completed the transaction.

Next they went to the department store to pick up clothes and shoes. Brodie didn't make a beeline for the most expensive stuff, or the toy aisle, like Rob would have. He just quietly selected a range of suitable clothes and some shoes and trainers. His taste was uncanny. He chose exactly what Rob would have chosen at that age, only a little cheaper. Rob was the one who picked out the more expensive trainers, the ones with the red LEDs in the soles that flashed with every step. He knew as he picked them up he wasn't really buying them for Brodie. They were for eight-year-old Rob, who hadn't been allowed them because they were expensive and frivolous.

Rob started to feel horribly giddy and sick as they shopped. He put it down to the change in temperature. The department store was baking compared to the air-conditioned cool of the computer shop. Then he saw the lad who was here when he'd come suit shopping with Mum, so he was forced to concede that there were just a lot of floppy-haired, self-assured teenagers working in shops these days. The slick, good-looking kid in his slick, good-looking suit. He'd got his suit jacket buttoned up and a thick silk tie practically up to his chin. He was flirting with a girl and her mother, showing them a range of expensive fountain pens. He didn't look even slightly too warm.

Rob was relieved to get the bus home, even though they still hadn't got everything they needed. Brodie didn't have his own bed, or toothbrush, or anything.

*

Jules is definitely crying now. Her eyes are red, fat tears pouring from them, splashing into her lap. Her nostrils glisten and her mouth is contorted with misery. Between that and the greyish-purple cast to her teeth from the wine, she looks pretty scary.

'Oh, Rob,' she says, between sobs, 'it's like you really think all of this means something! Like it proves your story. But it doesn't, it doesn't.' She dissolves into her sadness, her voice lost in the sniffles, the gulps, the racking cries.

Maybe she's right. Maybe it's all in my head and all the things I thought meant something don't mean anything. Maybe I'm the kind of tinfoil-hat conspiracy theorist I used to think was a lunatic.

*

Rob buzzed into the flat easily as usual, hiking up the stairs with Brodie at his heels, dragging his shopping bags against the concrete steps with a hissing sound. At least he hoped it was the bags hissing and not Brodie reverting to his natural reptilian state. As he knocked at the door he scrutinised Brodie for signs of scales or sideways eyelids. Brodie was just studying the department store receipts, oblivious.

Eventually Tenike opened the door. She looked at Brodie oddly, then up at Rob, then back at Brodie. Rob's heart pounded. He could see it in her face, the confusion. She was going to ask him who Brodie was, he knew it, he just knew it.

'Dad's cooking. Dunno if there's enough for you... two.'

It was still there, that weird little buzz of interference between her acceptance of the situation and what her expression said about it. Whatever her actual feelings, Tenike turned on her heel and disappeared back into the flat, leaving the door wide open.

Rob crouched in the hall to greet Queenie without even really thinking about it. It was only when he stood up to shake the moulted hair from his fingertips that he realised Brodie was still standing rigidly in the doorway.

'It's all right,' he said. 'She's okay. Louise is the iffy one but she's gone to Malta with Mum. Grandma. Mum.' Queenie sniffed Rob's finger, then sneezed explosively, coating his hand in thick yellow mucus. 'You're not allergic are you?' Rob asked, wiping the cat snot on his trousers.

Brodie shook his head, cautiously stepping inside. Rob shut the door behind him.

'Bummer?' He shrugged out of his coat, hung it up and reached for Brodie's. He hadn't even noticed Bummer had coat hooks before now. He usually threw his coat over the back of the sofa. Queenie had put him into a different mode of thinking, like he was at his mum's house.

Brodie crouched very slowly, one hand stretched out towards Queenie. She snuffled a snot-bubble wetly in and out of one nostril, and then leaned forward to lick tentatively at his fingertips. A second sneeze racked her body, but she leaned delicately away from Brodie for this one. When she turned back, it was like her sense of smell had returned. She sniffed hurriedly, urgently along his fingers, up his hand, straining her neck to continue sniffing up his outstretched arm. She stopped suddenly and sniffed the air, as if for comparison. Her gummy blue eyes widened and she spun and sprinted through the hall and across the kitchen lino, paws losing traction on the slick surface, scrabbling.

'What did you do to that ruddy cat?!' Bummer shouted from the kitchen, his words carried on the smell of onions and burning.

'I dunno.' Rob shrugged. He was starting to give up on the whole thing. If God, or his delusional brain, or whatever, wanted him to have a kid, then maybe he should just have one, even if it was a cat-frightening lizard boy. He didn't really know why he'd gone to Bummer's. He wanted his mum, but Bummer was the closest thing he had now.

He considered telling Bummer everything. How close he'd come to being hit by a car, how he didn't remember Brodie, or Karen, and was worried that he was going crazy, really crazy. He was poised in the kitchen doorway ready to spill his guts and then he saw Bummer and Tenike cooking together. Passing spices to one another, tasting, making faces, adding more, rock-paper-scissoring for who would do the dishes when they'd finished.

He rolled up his sleeves instead.

'What are you making?'

22

She has herself back under control again now. She's taken a sheaf of tissues from her bag, and she dabs her eyes and blows her nose, noisily. Tucks the damp ball of tissue into her sleeve like she knows she's going to need it again later.

'Maybe you should,' she says with a small smile, 'maybe you should just accept he's your son, and we can get on with our lives. Work through this, together.'

The pain is back, low-level but insistent, like a chopstick tapping against the soft folds of my brain.

*

'Cabbage, Cabbage?'

Oh Mum, nearly thirty years of the same joke and it's still not funny.

'Funny, Mum.'

He hadn't held to his promise. He'd made Brodie wait until the following lunchtime, so Mum had time to prepare for the video call. She hated not having time to prepare.

Rob could practically smell the roast through the laptop screen. He looked down at the microwave 'roast' in his lap. Brodie was picking the burnt bits off the crust of gravy in his own compartmented meal. Even last night's home-made curry with Bummer was better.

'And Cabbage for Little Cabbage?' She held the ladle up in front of the webcam, dripping hot green water dangerously close to the laptop.

'Mum, you probably shouldn't...'

Gordon and Mum looked ravenous. They usually ate their Sunday dinner at one o'clock on the dot. Rob preferred it around three, so he could legitimately sleep the afternoon away when he'd finished. Now, for time difference reasons, Mum and Gordon were having it late and Rob and Brodie were having it early.

Everybody loses.

It was the weirdest Sunday dinner ever, but Brodie didn't seem to notice. He just smiled and nodded like this crazed imaginary tea party was how he spent every weekend.

Mum and Gordon looked different already. Tanned, relaxed. Mum had her sleeves rolled up and colour in her cheeks. She'd dyed her hair back to its rich chestnut hue. She hadn't looked that way since Rob was eight years old.

'Doesn't say much, yours,' said Gordon from behind his perpetual newspaper. 'Something wrong with him?'

'Some people don't articulate their every thought, Gordon,' Rob replied testily. He looked over at Brodie. The kid was shovelling discs of carrot down his neck like there was a world shortage.

'Got a good appetite,' said Mum appreciatively. 'Not like you when you were little. So many things he wouldn't eat,' she told Gordon's paper fondly. 'Anything green. Anything squishy. Anything round.' She giggled at the memory. 'You showed that boy a lime sorbet and he'd have the screaming ab-dabs!'

'Should've made him stay at the table till he'd eaten it.'

Suppose you'd've locked me in a cupboard with nothing but mushy peas and steamed Brussels sprouts till I got used to it, wouldn't you, Gordon?

Rob mopped gravy from his plastic tray with the last roast potato, sucking it off the fork as noisily as possible. He leaned back in his chair, smacking his lips and rubbing his belly.

'Nice.'

'Grandma,' a small voice piped up, 'any dessert?'

Rob stared at Brodie, astonished, but Brodie just licked his fork and rested it neatly across the exact centre of his tray. Mum cleared her table as if nothing was amiss. As if they had been doing this every weekend since she moved to Malta. Gordon let out a belch that made the laptop speakers crackle, but didn't offer any further comment.

'How's work?' Mum called from off-screen, no doubt in the kitchen depositing the plates in the sink. The ritual was so well established in Rob's mind, he didn't need to be there to see it. 'Victor doing all right?'

'Work's fine,' said Rob, wondering if it could really have been so long since he last spoke to his mother. 'Bummer's a bit crap actually—'

'We don't use words like that in this house, Robert.'

'Shop got shut down.'

'Oh, that's sad.' If he strained his ears, he could hear her stirring the dolly mixtures and dried fruit into a big bowl of cream. Mixed-up Fool, she called it. Rob smiled at the memory. Looked like sick, but had so much sugar in it; it was his favourite childhood dessert. 'How are the children?'

'The children are—' He stopped. What was it Jacob had said? 'We know he isn't real, Uncle Rob.' That was it, wasn't it? 'The kids are great!'

*

'Since when do we have family meetings?' asked Tenike, picking at her butterfly chicken.

'And since when are you family?' asked Chloe, stirring her vodka and lime with a plastic stick.

'I'm more family than he is.' Rob indicated Roderick with a jerk of his chin and then felt bad when Roderick looked guilty. 'Look, look, forget it, this is really important.'

'Where's Daddy?' asked Jacob, shuffling in his seat. They were in the same pub, in the same family room as before.

'He's taken Brodie to the play area.'

Jacob and Joel exchanged a glance that was part jealousy, part something else. *Dunno, suspicion? Concern?*

'Look—' Rob quickly checked the doorway to the play area before continuing. 'I don't know how much time we've got for this, so button it and listen.'

They were all listening now, leaning forward in anticipation. All except Tenike. She was making the most of her meal, dipping chips in the mayonnaise pot and sucking them joyously.

'Tenike, pack that in. You remember last time we were all here?'

Neil nodded. Chloe didn't respond. She was looking at him like he'd lost his mind. Roderick looked too unsure of himself to say anything without permission.

'We weren't here,' Joel pointed out. 'Mummy doesn't like us coming out with you.'

"Specially since you posted me through the school window,' Jacob added helpfully.

'Yes, right, great, you two just remember that time instead then, at the school, right? You all remember what we talked about here and at the school?'

'What are we, your biographers? I try not to listen to your babble.' Chloe rolled her eyes and looked like she might get out of her seat.

'Wait, wait, hear me out.' Rob realised he was sweating and breathless. 'We talked about Brodie, remember? And how I'd have to pretend he was kidnapped?' He tugged at the collar of his polo shirt. It felt uncomfortably tight. Picking up Neil's shandy, he rolled the cool glass across his forehead, eyes squeezed shut, trying to press the throbbing out of his temples. It was becoming his signature move. He felt like he did at the Fun Run and the department store, but this time there was no reason for it.

No physical reason, anyway.

The coolness of the water did nothing for him this time, even though he tried it a little longer. When he opened his eyes, they were all staring at him. They all looked shocked. No one spoke for an age, then Tenike blurted: 'Of course we remember, you loony!' just as Chloe said: 'You need psychiatric help, you realise that?' Both stopped and regarded each other strangely.

'I need psychiatric help because we did discuss that, or because we didn't?'

Lynda Clark

Bummer's kids and Roderick were all studying each other very warily now. And then, after the silence, it hit like a tidal wave.

'Made up? You think we made up your son's kidnapping!'

'I knew something was up – he shouldn't be here, should he? I helped you PhotoMorph the picture!'

'What? We talked about the appeal! Credit Co organised an appeal for Brodie, don't you remember?'

'What are you all arguing about?'

The silence descended again.

Bummer was behind them, holding Brodie's hand. Brodie looked around at everyone, that look that was now so familiar, those huge, sad black eyes. No one else at the table offered an answer. Roderick gouged his fingernail into a beer mat, not meeting Chloe's eyes. Chloe stared incredulously at her boyfriend. Tenike and the twins gawped at Neil like he'd grown a second head. None of them agreed. None of them fully remembered. But they knew something was up. They knew there was something wrong.

'Nothing,' said Rob, smiling at Brodie and patting the stool next to him. 'We're all just being stupid.'

The roar of children thrashing about in the ball pit gushed out of the open playroom door, engulfing the silence at the table. Rob looked past Bummer and Brodie to the brightly coloured balls, spilling out of the pit, turning and rolling and mixing like a kaleidoscope. For a moment that was all there was, just noise and colour, and he couldn't make any sense of it. For some reason he remembered the laptop screen in the computer shop, dancing with images he couldn't comprehend, images Brodie had summoned somehow. The coloured balls in the pit and spheres on the laptop screen. Yes. They were spheres, like a—

Brodie scraped his chair closer to the table and Rob turned to look at him. The kid stared up at him, wet-eyed, on the constant verge of a flinch.

'You have fun in there?'

Brodie nodded. Guiltily, grudgingly, conversation resumed, but there was an edge to it, like everyone was just saying nonsense words to fill the space because they couldn't find the words they'd really like to say. Rob wanted to scream.

*

She's looking at me differently now, differently again to all the looks she's given me through the course of the evening. Who knew those hazel eyes could hold so many looks?

'I always thought that if something like this happened, I'd be the ideal person to tell.' She massages her eyes, drags her hands down her face. 'Like I'd be down with whatever you told me. Secret society of vampires? Sure. Fairies at the bottom of the garden? Of course. Alien hiding in the wardrobe? Why not? I used to get so annoyed by all the parents, all the best friends, all the significant others in films who didn't believe their loved ones when they poured out their heart about the vampires or the fairies or the aliens.' She sighs. 'But you know what? It's hard. I want to think you're not just crazy, that what you're telling me adds up to something, but it's hard.'

'I don't know that it adds up to something myself,' I say, realising this is true. 'I just wanted to tell you.'

'Lucky me.'

*

Brodie 'returning' to school was another source of stress for Rob. He chewed on his nails as they walked briskly to the school gates, Brodie trotting alongside with his blue rucksack and his flashing trainers. If the kids at Councillor Dupois were anything like Bummer's kids, they'd know Brodie had never been their classmate. Brodie didn't have a pretend big brother to look after him, so what would happen?

'Anyone starts on you, you kick them in the nads, okay?' said Rob, straightening Brodie's already straight shirt as the kid waited patiently to join his classmates in the playground.

Brodie nodded, his large dark eyes swooping between the groups playing football on the grass and the ones making up dance routines by the school building. He titled his head, turned slowly to Rob and said: 'What are nads?'

Rob choked down a sob. The kid didn't even know what nads were. How could he possibly survive in there? Rob wanted to clutch Brodie to his chest and tell him they were going to forget about school and learn everything on the internet at home, but the kid had already given him a tentative wave and was taking his first faltering steps into the playground.

All around him far larger children raced around, pushing and shoving and yelling. Rob stood on tiptoe to watch his fake son's slow progress towards the school building. He was like an NPC in an escort mission, stopping every few steps to look around him, always in danger of straying into the path of a football or a running child. Rob checked his watch. Surely they had to blow the whistle soon? Brodie would be safe in the classroom with a teacher to protect him. He looked so tiny, too small to— Kids were pointing. Two, three of them, two girls and a boy, they were all pointing at Brodie. Rob was frozen to the spot. All around kids were laughing, screaming, shouting and yet he still heard the words, they still cut through everything like a loud fart at a cocktail party.

'OI, GINGE!'

Involuntarily, Rob's hands balled into fists. The words 'It's AUBURN!' bubbled in his throat, but before they could escape, two familiar children came running across the playing field. Joel and Jacob. One looped an arm across Brodie's shoulders, just like Bummer used to do for Rob, and the other gave the gingerphobe a firm shove in the chest, and a look that dared them to say it again.

To Rob's relief, the whistle finally blew and they all lined up in their form groups. Joel and Jacob may have known Brodie wasn't real, but they were still Bummer's kids, and that meant they knew he was family regardless. Brodie didn't have a fake brother to take care of him, he had two.

*

The first thing Rob did when he returned to his desk after the school run was add two new photos. One of Brodie and Bummer playing together, Bummer cradling Brodie in the crook of his arms, spinning him. Their faces were blurred but filled with light and motion and happiness. The other picture was just a headshot of Brodie, frowning into the camera lens. Rob put it next to the PhotoMorphed picture and compared them closely. They looked the same, pretty much. The eyes were maybe a little darker, but that could just be the exposure. Brodie looked just like the PhotoMorphed picture, only... real.

Rob was leaning over his desk, nose millimetres from the two photos, when Jules took a seat next to him. He almost headbutted the pinboard in his haste to sit back down and look normal.

She smiled.

'It's okay. After everything you've been through, you're allowed to be weird.'

'I'm not sure I *have* been through anything,' he said quietly.

'Since when were you so noble?' she asked with a laugh.

'Oh.' He looked at her, and made a decision. 'It's not that. Look, do you want to come and hang out with me and Brodie tonight?'

She looked at her lap, smiling. Probably looking for a way to gently extricate herself from the situation without hurting the Potential Mental Breakdown's feelings.

'I'd love to,' she said softly.

'You don't have to,' he assured her. Part of him hoped she'd take up the offer to back out. Then he wouldn't actually have to go through with what he was considering. A mad idea teetering on an already swaying pyramid of insane lies and poorly conceived decisions.

'You trying to make me beg to hang out with you and your kid?'

'No!'

'Then let's just leave it at yes, okay?' She swivelled towards her desk and unlocked her screen with two touches of the keyboard. He followed suit and, for what felt like the first time in weeks, slowly exhaled.

23

'Pizza?' asked Rob, peering into the freezer cabinet.

'Okay.' Brodie smiled and leaned into the cold depths. 'What about southern fried chicken? You like that almost as much as curry.'

A long sentence for Brodie. And true. Rob had never told the kid that, but it was true. Rob put down the double deep pepperoni he was holding and looked at his pseudo-son.

'You're looking at me funny,' Brodie put the chicken in their shopping basket, 'but it's okay, the school counsellor explained.'

'Your school has a counsellor?'

Brodie smiled again. 'Yes, silly.' He picked up curly fries and garlic bread and then led the way to the dairy aisle. 'It's called PTSD, she said.' He stood on tiptoe to reach a three-flavour dip selection. Rob got it down for him absent-mindedly. 'Thanks. You got so stressed when I was gone, it's messed up your brain, so you don't remember me properly. But you will.'

Rob was aware he'd frozen in both senses of the word,

motionless and so cold his nipples were like thimbles under his shirt. He was aware his mouth was open in a gormless query, but he couldn't find the strength to close it. Eventually, Brodie patted his hand and skipped off to the checkout.

When Rob caught up to him, the kid was in the queue behind a fat-bottomed woman, making eyes at the confectionery lining the conveyor belt. Rob reached for a packet of boiled sweets just to try to get those huge dark eyes to move, to blink. *To look more human.* Brodie smiled up at him as he dropped the sweets into the basket.

'Thanks, Dad.' And there it was again, that feeling like a punch to the stomach only in his heart, and as sweet as it was horrible.

Rob didn't say anything. He just ruffled the kid's hair and vowed to never forget that he made the kid up, even if that feeling in his heart never went away.

The woman turned from loading her shopping onto the conveyor and looked at Brodie. She stared into the dark eyes for a long while, and just when Rob thought she was going to remark on how weird they were, she smiled and said to Rob: 'He looks just like you.'

'Yeah,' Rob tasted bile and swallowed quickly, 'he does.'

*

He put the garlic bread in the oven and set the timer, wondering what Brodie was doing.

Probably something creepy and unkidlike.

Sure enough, Brodie was sitting on the bed fiddling with one of Rob's transforming action figures. He moved each piece carefully, scrutinising its bearings and the space it fitted into, sliding and clicking each piece as slowly as possible so he could take it all in. When he realised Rob was watching him, he feebly moved the semi-transformed jet in a swooping motion, following its arc with seed-black eyes.

'So,' said Rob, clasping his hands behind his back and suddenly understanding why Gordon always spoke so awkwardly to him. 'You okay about meeting Jules?'

Brodie nodded. He nodded or shook his head to pretty much everything Rob said to him.

You too hot? Too cold? Bloodsucking shapeshifter pretending to be a small boy? What answer would that get? Probably just that slight variation on that stare. That special, tiny difference, where by clenching his lower eye muscles he somehow managed to convey that whatever Rob had just said to him was the rambling of a king-sized dick.

Sighing, Rob turned to go.

'Dad?'

Another sucker punch to the heart.

'Yes, Brodie?'

And there was just the tiniest quirk to his eyebrow, just the merest hint of a smile as he said: 'Is she going to be my new mum?'

*

Jules throws back her head and laughs at that. It's a genuine laugh, although the worry quickly returns to her face as soon as it's done.

*

Rob paced around and checked his watch for about the fortieth time. The only sound was Brodie chewing curly fries. Rob went over to the stereo, thinking about putting some music on, something to create a little ambience. *That'd look bloody weird. A guy sitting at home alone with his kid listening to R 'n' B.* He shook his head, trying to clear it. Everything was going to look weird when he spilled his guts to Jules.

The knock at the door made him jump out of his skin. He suddenly felt like he might puke, or shit, or puke and shit. Brodie threw him one of his looks and got up to open the door. Jules stood outside, changing her look of surprise to one of delight in a flash.

'Hello,' said Brodie, offering his hand. She gave Rob a look that said: 'This little gentleman is *your* kid?' Rob shrugged and wiped at the hot, prickly sweat breaking out on his neck.

'Hello, you must be Brodie.'

'And you must be Jules. Dad tells me you might be my new mum.'

'Jesus, Brodie! I did not say that!' Then, to Jules: 'I didn't say that!'

Brodie turned to him, the picture of innocence, and said: 'But you always say that avoiding answering a question means yes.'

When? When have I ever said that in front of him? I haven't. I'm sure I haven't.

Jules chuckled softly to herself, enjoying his discomfort.

She'll laugh on the other side of her face when she knows the truth. Laugh, or have me committed, could go either way.

'You, PlayStation, now!'

'But I—'

'Now!'

Shoulders drooping, Brodie headed for the TV and dutifully began unwinding cables and sorting through game boxes.

'Interesting parenting technique.' Jules laughed.

'About that,' Rob said, voice dropping to a whisper. 'Would you join me in the kitchen, I want to tell you something.' Louder he said: 'Let's choose a bottle of wine!'

'Your kitchen is in your front room. Stop acting like you're in a sitcom! Three feet away from him speaking in a stage whisper! What the hell is wrong with you?'

Rob resisted an urge to stuff a tea towel in her mouth and drag her into the bedroom, where he could tell her everything unfettered by interruptions. He breathed out slowly and spread his hands.

'This is very important and I don't want Brodie to hear, so please...'

He led her into the bathroom and shut the door. *Maybe this is weirder than the tea towel idea. Maybe I should have gone with that.*

'Shit, Rob, you're scaring me. You're a nice guy, but if you propose to me, I'm going to kick you in the nuts and run away.'

'I'm not going to propose! Christ! You're full of yourself, aren't you?'

'Fine,' she said with a laugh, 'out with it then.'

PART TWO

NOW & FOREVER

24

'Well. Can't say you weren't thorough.'

He holds his breath. She's still wrestling with it, he can see that, but she looks more like the Jules he knows than the angry, anguished creature he's glimpsed throughout the telling.

Please, you have to believe me, please!

The words are already forming when she suddenly says: 'All right.'

'No, pl— What?'

'I don't believe you. But I'm going to try.'

'What?' His voice cracks, throat dry and burning from speaking for so long.

'I know something's going on. With you, with Brodie. Something's off, I can feel that. And I don't think he's some kind of alien plant or whatever you seem to think, but...'

She pauses and he imagines a drum roll in spite of himself.

'I'll try to help you find out what the deal is with y— with him.'

He ignores the momentary lapse and pulls her into a hug,

squeezing her tight as if he can absorb her level-headedness, her sanity, and make it part of himself, restore his own mind.

'Can I have some water?'

They both jump and spin round, but Brodie's raising his voice from the bedroom. Rob crosses to the door and sticks his head in and there's Brodie holding out his glass. The kid doesn't seem to have been paying attention to them at all.

*

After Brodie's had his water, they wait until he's dozy with exhaustion and Rob puts him to bed. Even with sleep dragging at his eyes, Brodie begs Rob to leave the door open 'to let the light in'. It's a little strange. The dark's never bothered him before. But if these last few weeks have taught Rob anything, it's that a child's behaviour is totally unpredictable. Particularly if the child is impossible. Rob uses an old dictionary as a doorstop, and then returns to Jules. He settles on the sofa beside her, thinking surely she must stay the night now, even if she sleeps on the camp bed and he sleeps on the sofa. Just having her under the same roof, that will be enough.

'Don't get me wrong,' says Rob, 'I'm glad you want to help, but... why?'

Jules pulls her feet up onto the sofa. One of her knees brushes Rob's leg.

'There are some things I'd like to investigate,' she says, holding up one hand and ticking them off on her fingers. 'It's been bugging me for ages that your dead wife would lumber her child with a name like Brodie.'

'You can't let that lie, can you? It's a brilliant name. It's the sort of name a successful soap actor would have, or a child star who went on to discover a cure for cancer!'

'Please! Only a dumb, weird bloke would think that!' She holds up a finger in his face as he protests. 'Anyway, if there's paperwork for Brodie, there's surely paperwork for Karen? The wife you... made up as well? Maybe if we can find out more about her, we can find out more about him.' He nods, knowing it will be futile, but glad, so glad he brought her in on this. 'Secondly, grief makes people do weird things, but I don't think it makes them bone everything within knobbing distance, and, SSSSSHHHH! And thirdly, the whole not having his own bedroom or toothbrush thing. I mean, I know you're weird but...' She sighs deeply, like admitting this costs her. 'I don't think you're so weird that you'd raise a kid in a one-bedroom flat and make him use your toothbrush.'

He can't argue with that.

'So what do I do?' he says weakly. She's silent for a long time.

It's really late. So late it's early. The coffee is gone and they've finished the wine and the cans of beer Rob dug out from the back of the fridge. They had the telly on for low background noise, but now it's off air. Rob didn't even realise some channels still did that. He thought in today's twenty-four-hour culture, all the channels just kept on going, right through the night. It had been a comforting thought, somehow.

Now there is nothing left. No drink, no sound, no conversation, no answers. They have run out of words. He looks at Jules. She's studying her hands, examining the curled fingers and the bitten nails. Her eyes are heavy, like it wouldn't take much for her to fall into a deep sleep. He thinks about kissing her. After all, there are no words left, so one of them may as well do something. He tilts his head and leans forward a little, wondering if it's actually a good idea, or if it's just exhaustion and booze making him think it is, like when him and Bummer invented stair-surfing and it was wicked until he broke his wrist.

She suddenly sits up and opens her eyes fully and, without even noticing that he's poised for a snog, says: 'What you need to do is make everything as normal as possible.'

She's done it. She's found more words and now they're on her lips where a kiss should be. She's already got her phone out of her bag and is hunting through the contacts for a taxi number. He sits back and sighs and says: 'What do you mean?'

'I mean sort the kid's room out, go to work, get on with your life.'

'Just... be a father to a kid I made up?'

'For now. Yes.'

*

They haven't really spoken since the night of all the wine, have been communicating primarily by text and Instant Messenger, perfunctory exchanges about things like what's on the canteen menu and how they should go and buy some odds and sods for Brodie. It turns out Jules has a car. Rob doesn't know why this surprises him. There's no reason she shouldn't have a car. She just didn't strike him as the driving type. She looks like she'd be more at home on a piebald horse or a tandem bike with flowers in the basket.

It's a small city-car thing and therefore a bit of a squeeze for the three of them. No doubt the drive back will be even worse when they're loaded down with Scandinavian tat, but it beats walking.

As they pull into one of the only free spaces in the car park, a couple are so busy arguing, the bloke nearly pushes his trolley of flat-packed furniture and extendable lampshades into the front of Jules's car. She honks the horn. He turns to look at her, apparently shocked that she's dared to interrupt his intended path. Rob considers rolling down the window and calling him a pissant, seeing if the guy will really kick off. Fortunately the bloke is distracted by his significant other launching his car keys into the wild blue yonder with an overarm throw worthy of a Russian shot-putter.

'This place does funny things to people,' says Jules, shaking her head as the man runs off in search of his keys, cheap purchases forgotten. 'Let's not stay too long.'

She seems oddly faux bright, like a travel agent trying to convince a client to travel to a war zone. Maybe it was the almost-kiss. Maybe it was the deluge of Rob's crazy. Either way, she seems to be staving something off with throwaway humour and polite helpfulness, so she doesn't have to take any responsibility when the bombs start to fall.

*

Everything here has a name. Not proper names like Chair or Sofa. Not even aspirational names like the Firestorm Corner Unit or the Gunmetal Vacuum Cleaner. People names. Rob passes an office chair called Steve, a desk called Clark and its matching filing cabinet, Carolyn. Bradley the shoe rack. Glenda the storage unit. Anthony the milk frother.

'Can we find the thing called Robert?' he asks, leaning down to check the label on a particularly sexy computer table. *Dammit.*

It's called Victor.

'Do you think there'll be anything called Brodie?' asks Brodie.

'No,' says Jules. She realises she's answered too quickly and adds: 'Who would want a piece of crappy furniture named after them anyw— Oh, I'm the multicoloured faux fur throw – score!' She disappears for a moment to fetch a trolley. While she's away, Rob spots a small plastic bin called Robert and hurries past it, feigning interest in a kid's torch someone's dumped in the middle of the officeware display.

Jules reappears with the trolley. It's large enough to fit a three-piece suite, but at the moment just contains the Julia throw. Rob adds the torch, just because it's in his hand.

'So, Brodie, what kind of stuff do you want?'

Brodie shrugs and reaches for Rob's hand. Rob takes it, still cautious even now that it might tighten like the tendrils of a strangling vine and crush all the bones in his hand. He knows that's silly science-fiction stuff, but it's always lurking at the back of his mind.

Brodie stares around at everything, looking suddenly sad.

This is someone's kid, Rob reminds himself, *even if he's not mine, he's someone's*. Brodie does that sometimes. Conveys such a sense of loss and loneliness, Rob wants to make him feel loved, no matter the cost to his own heart or bank balance. Rob and Jules exchange a look.

'What about a bed like a spaceship?'

And he runs towards the kids' area, dragging Brodie and ignoring the tutting of other shoppers as he crosses their lanes.

Brilliant bed. Brodie's maybe a little old for it, but Christ, I'd sleep in that and I'm a grown-up.

Allegedly.

The bed has a silver frame, long scaffold pipes for legs, a desk underneath and a curved, futuristic pod on top to put the mattress in. Rob lifts Brodie up into the pod so he can get a feel for it. The sign says for display purposes only, but if it's a bed, it must be useable, right? Brodie smiles as he stares up at the shining dome over his head. Rob is already thinking about how they could buy glow-in-the-dark star stickers and fill the ceiling with them.

Brodie's expression becomes thoughtful and then angry. A war is clearly raging inside him and Rob worries what will happen when it breaks out. He reaches up and tries to take Brodie out of the bed, but he's gripping the sides of the pod, eyes fixed and staring at the ceiling, tears running down his cheeks.

'Sir, I'm going to have to ask you to remove your son,' says a sales assistant with a bright orange uniform and a big nose. 'That Kevin unit is for display purposes only.'

'I'm trying to get him down,' says Rob through gritted teeth.

Rob gets a chest of drawers from the other side of the display scene, drags it over to the bedside and stands on it to get a better angle for grabbing Brodie.

'Sir, that Shirley unit is also for display purposes—' drones the assistant.

'Look, just fuck off, will you?' snaps Rob. He manages to prise Brodie's shaking fingers from the edge of the bed and bundles him into his arms. As he steps down from the unit,

Jules comes running over, her trolley overflowing with *Blight Brigade* duvet covers, pillowcases and rugs.

'Look!' She holds up a duvet cover with a picture of the main character, Alfred, as both himself and Breakstuff, one of his lumbering alien forms.

Brodie hides his face in Rob's chest and sobs, 'I hate *Blight Brigade*! I hate Alfred. I hate what he does!'

Jules lets the cover fall back into the trolley. She takes a step forward as if she means to touch Brodie, to comfort him somehow, but thinks better of it. The shop assistant stands open-mouthed, taking in the whole scene.

'Oh, piss off, gormy conk,' says Jules.

*

Rob expects people to stare as Brodie screams and cries, but no one bats an eyelid. Inconsolable children are part of the backdrop here. Rob wishes Jules was with them. She's stayed behind to buy the things they needed most, no doubt hoping that when she returns the tantrum will have passed. As they approach Jules's bug of a car, the front of Rob's t-shirt wet with Brodie's tears, Rob spots a figure, lurking. He's big and broad, and he's pushing a trolley containing pot plants and a trellis, but he still looks completely out of place here.

Bellamy.

'Everything okay?' he asks as Rob juggles Brodie and Jules's car keys.

Brodie's sobs are so huge, Rob fears the kid's in danger of choking on them.

Is that possible? Would I be arrested for manslaughter?

'He's a little upset.'

How do parents do this? What else do I say?

'I can see that.'

Bellamy looks at Rob for a long time. Rob has to keep looking away as he fumbles with the car door and struggles to insert Brodie into the back seat, as the kid clings and struggles and cries. He's like a starfish, spreadeagled to prevent Rob lowering him into the car, hands suddenly seeming to have suction cups with incredible grip.

'May I?' asks Bellamy.

Rob isn't sure what he's asking, but shrugs and stops struggling with his starfish son, for a moment anyway.

'Hey now,' says Bellamy, and to Rob's surprise, Brodie pauses in his wailing to look up at the craggy-faced cop. 'Is that any way to carry on?'

They hold each other's gaze for a moment, and then Brodie seems to agree that it isn't and drops his head onto Rob's chest. He's still sniffling and quivering, but the worst of it is over. Rob expects Bellamy to say something further, to give him some fatherly wisdom about halting a tantrum or soothing an anguished child, but he just smiles almost... apologetically and moves off down the car park pushing his trolley. Jules arrives then, with just the multicoloured Julia blanket, a matching quilt and a few other essentials. Bellamy's still slowly trundling his trolley away, presumably to wherever he's parked. He looks delighted by Jules's appearance and throws the three of them a salute.

Weird.

'Who was that?' she asks.

'Policeman.'

'What did he want?' She holds the quilt up to Brodie for his approval and just gets a sleepy nod. No alien-enslaving child prodigies in sight.

'I don't know.' Rob looks at Brodie's closed, twitching eyelids and wishes that was him passed out in the back of the car, safe and dreaming, crisis averted.

25

When they get back to the flat, Rob puts Brodie in his bed. He isn't about to go fannying about with a flat-packed child's bed at this time in the evening. Jules makes hot chocolates while he tucks Brodie in. She bought the Anthony milk frother and wants to try it out.

'So,' she says, holding a mug out to him, handle-first, 'that was bloody weird.'

'Yeah,' says Rob.

'You look pensive.'

'I don't know what that means.'

She laughs, so he smiles like he's joking. He really doesn't know what pensive means.

'What next?'

'I was going to ask you that.' He takes a sip of hot chocolate. It's frothy, no denying that. Anthony's done his job.

'We need to sit down,' she says, 'and forget about all this for a moment.'

He stares at her, confused.

'I mean it,' her voice is earnest, 'I'm worried about you. You've always got a weird pinched look these days, and you rub your temples all the time – you're going to give yourself an aneurism.'

'So what do we do to forget everything?'

She smiles.

*

He's never completed *Hunter Vs XenoBot* before, but with Jules shooting and commentating, the hours of sketchy gameplay and glitchy, granulated blood-splatter fly by. By the time the credits roll, they've finished the hot chocolate and the cheap boxed wine Jules picked up at the shop and the weird foreign liqueur Rob found in a cupboard.

Jules half-dozes on the sofa. Rob wonders if they'll ever be together. He wonders if he even wants that. As long as she's his friend, after everything, that's what matters. He wonders if she's starting to believe him, or if she's just hanging out with him because she's worried about his health. She yips in her sleep, waking herself up. Grins in embarrassment and automatically reaches for her phone. He wonders, if he'd intercepted it, if he'd deleted the taxi number from her contacts and denied all knowledge, if that would be enough to make her stay.

*

The very next day Rob uses the screens Jules bought to create a partition wall in his room. Slits the plastic on the mattress with a Stanley knife like he's cutting a butterfly free of a chrysalis. Old Rob would have just stuck the knife in the corner and dragged it to the bottom, consequences be damned. New Rob is wondering if he should have bought a mattress saver.

Brodie seems very resistant to the idea of his own room. He says he likes that Rob sleeps right near him.

'I'll still be right here, mate, just on the other side of this,' Rob says, wobbling the screen to emphasise how thin it is. 'Just gives us both a bit more privacy, is all.'

Brodie stares at the screen like Rob is bricking up his only exit. His eyes do that weird thing where they seem to grow darker, almost all pupil, and then they fill with tears and Rob has an overwhelming urge to do anything, anything to prevent those tears from spilling.

He looks around the room frantically for Optibot. Optibot is usually a good distraction. He can't see the damn robot anywhere, but for some reason his gaze snags on the torch because it looks like one he had as a kid – chunky red plastic with yellow buttons and blue trim. He's reminded of something Gordon used to do to entertain him when he was about Brodie's age. Pretty much the only game in Gordon's repertoire that didn't involve sitting still and being quiet.

Rob stands the torch on the floor on Brodie's side of the screens, pointing its bright bulb towards the ceiling. He gives Brodie a squeeze and points to the screen to make sure he's watching, then steps behind it.

He waves and is rewarded with a delighted giggle as Brodie sees his silhouette. He makes a bird flutter across the screen and then a rabbit, snuffling its nose and twitching its ears. He does a swan and an old man's head and a Native American with a feathered headdress. He tries to remember more stuff Gordon used to do, but he realises it's harder than it looks.

He gives up trying to make a panda's face and does a dance instead. His silhouette must look pretty dorky, because Brodie whoops and cries with laughter. Rob keeps on dancing until he's sweaty and laugh-crying, too.

*

Rob isn't sure what to expect when he knocks on Bummer's door. No one had answered Bummer's buzzer, so Rob had resorted to pressing all of them until the door clicked open. The Empornium was all boarded up. Someone had spray-painted 'Good riddance to bad rubbish' on the shutters. They were pretty handy with a spray can for old codgers, Poo Witch's lot. The handwriting was all slopey and elegant, like it was poetry in an old book, not a slogan daubed on a sex shop.

Brodie is beside him in the corridor, shuffling his feet and holding Rob's hand. Brodie scuffs his feet everywhere to make the lights in his shoes flicker. Rob wants to point out that this is wearing the soles down very quickly, but he doesn't feel he can, because he knows he would have done the exact same thing if Mum had been able to afford them for him.

He knocks again on Bummer's door and thinks he can hear movement inside.

'Did you hear that?' he asks Brodie.

Brodie shrugs, still mesmerised by the shoe lights. Rob doesn't think he's really listening, so he's surprised when Brodie leans down to the letter box and yells: 'Uncle Bummer!'

'Don't call him that!' says Rob, panic-stricken. 'Call him Uncle Vic.'

'You call him Bummer,' Brodie points out.

'That's because I'm a grown-up.'

Rob regrets the words as soon as they're out of his mouth. *What a cockish thing to say. I used to hate it when Mum and Gordon said that to me. It's meaningless.*

'Sorry, Brodie,' he says. 'What I mean is, some people might—'

The door swings open slowly like something from a horror movie. Bummer's just behind the door with a blanket round his shoulders. It's dark in the flat and his face is ghostly white. He's unshaven and the smell of unwashed skin comes off him in waves. He looks like he should have cartoon stink lines drawn in the air around him.

'Uh, can we come in?'

Bummer shuffles backward to allow them inside. Rob steps over the threshold and immediately slips on a crumpled beer can. He sidesteps, trying to regain his balance, and trips over a pile of takeaway boxes. They fly everywhere as his foot connects, trailing semi-rotten leftovers across the carpet.

'Christ, mate,' says Rob softly.

'It smells,' says Brodie, wrinkling his nose.

Rob puts a finger to his lips, then turns to Bummer.

'What happened? Where are the kids?'

Bummer flops onto the sofa. There's a crunchy sound. He reaches underneath himself, pulls out a half-eaten bag of tortilla chips and drops it on the floor. Some of the chips spill out, but he doesn't seem to notice.

'Haven't got any food in,' he says into his chest, 'so they're all staying with their mums for the foreseeable.'

Rob feels like he's in one of those films where the main bloke gets to see how badly off all his friends would be if he'd topped himself or never been born, or something. Only it's real and he isn't dead and he should do something, he should be there for Bummer, but he doesn't know how. He can't stop Poo Witch. He can't get the Empornium back for Bummer. He doesn't even know if he can help get the kids back.

While Rob's been pondering all this, Brodie's been talking quietly to Bummer. Rob has missed what they've been saying, but Bummer suddenly nods, gets up and shambles off to his bedroom. Brodie gets up, too, only he heads for the bathroom.

'What are you doing?' asks Rob.

Brodie sits on the edge of the bath and turns the tap on. He tests the water temperature with his fingertips, then puts the plug in. He casts around for a minute before spotting the bubble bath and putting a hefty glug under the running water.

'Running a bath for Uncle B— Uncle Vic.'

'Just call him Bummer. He shouldn't get called Uncle anything. It sounds weird.'

'I like Uncle Bummer.'

'If a lady with a clipboard, or a man, it could be a man – if anyone with a clipboard comes round, you must never, never say that to them.'

*

While Bummer bathes, Rob and Brodie discuss what they're going to do next. Rob finds it very strange, talking to Brodie like he's a person. Part of Rob still fears that he's actually gone completely off his rocker and is really sitting in a padded cell, swaying, with drool trickling down his chin as he imagines this alternative life with a made-up son.

'I want to help Bummer,' says Brodie, those large dark eyes shining with hope and conviction.

'Me, too, mate,' says Rob. 'But I don't think there's much we can do. The Poo Witch has closed down his shop. He doesn't have much chance in court.'

'So?'

'So if he loses in court, he won't have a job. And if he doesn't have a job, he'll lose his flat and then his kids definitely won't be able to visit, because he'll probably be sleeping on the sofa at our house.'

'So he'll find another job,' says Brodie firmly. 'His kids are what makes him happy.'

'He doesn't do well "Working for the Man". That's why he set up his own shop.'

Rob has a flashback to his mum in the kitchen with Bummer's mum. Hushed tones about Vic always coming back from lunch break at Newridge's with leaves in his hair and now the boss's daughter's up the duff and it looks like he won't be finishing work experience at the garage either thanks to that prank with the soup and the air horn.

'So he can do it again. Only selling other stuff. Stuff people actually need and want.'

'I think a lot of them did need and want… okay, sure. When he gets back, we'll try and think of something.'

Brodie tidies up while Rob sits and thinks about Bummer. He can't be as stupid as he looks. He set up his own business when he was eighteen and he pulled all those women. None of them stayed, but that wasn't really down to him. He just had a habit of picking women who weren't right for him. Chloe's mum just saw him as a bit of rough, someone to piss her dad off.

Tenike's mum saw him as a drunken mistake. Joel and Jacob's mum thought she could change him. Neil's mum thought he would stay twenty-one and slim and slick for ever. He would have stayed with any of them if they'd let him. And been willing to have kids in double figures.

Rob knows that part of it is just that Bummer likes surrounding himself with people. He'd always said he wanted loads of kids. He just hadn't met the woman prepared to pop that many out for him. So he'd ended up going about it a different way. But really, he'd got the life he always wanted. Rob never realised that until now. Stupid, fat, lazy Bummer, who appeared to just bumble through life drinking and eating crisps, had actually achieved everything he ever wanted. Until Poo Witch came along.

'Will you be all right here?' he asks Brodie, suddenly. 'There's someone I have to go and see.'

26

He's not entirely sure what makes him ring Chloe, she just seems like the right person to call. She's sensible and sober and if he tries to throttle Poo Witch, she'll stop him and she'll probably get him off for attempted murder, too.

'Rob?' she answers her phone, surprise and worry in her voice. 'Is Dad okay?'

'Yeah. No. He will be.'

'Have you been drinking? Where's Dad?'

'At home. I'm on my way to have it out with Poo Witch. Need you to be my legal representative, or whatever.'

She breathes out slowly and he thinks she's going to tell him to stop being an idiot and go home, but eventually she says: 'I'll get Roddy to drive me. Don't go in until I get there.'

Rob paces up and down the dark street, worried he looks like a rapist. He still can't quite believe Heather gave him Poo Witch's address so easily. He texted her and she sent it straight back, with a little x at the bottom that Rob told himself she must put on all her messages.

It's starting to get cold. The wind whips a chocolate wrapper out of a nearby bin and swirls it along the street. It's a pretty decent area round here. The chocolate bar was fair trade for starters. The tall, narrow town houses are all crammed together, but well kept and each with its own long skinny garden. Somewhere a fox yowls. It makes the hairs on Rob's neck prickle. Strangely, he thinks of Brodie and how he shouldn't have left him with Bummer like that. As if a fox was going to break into the house and murder them both or something.

Stranger things have happened.

A car approaches and Rob is glad to see it's Chloe and Roderick. They pull up under a streetlight and come over.

'Remind me why we're doing this?' asks Roderick. He's wearing jogging bottoms and a loose t-shirt that could be his pyjamas. His hair is mussed and he's wearing glasses. He stifles a yawn.

'Let's just get it over with,' says Chloe, hugging herself against the chill breeze. 'This cold is making me need a wee. Which house is it?'

Rob checks the text message again and points.

Unlike all the other houses on the street, this one has a porch. Trust Poo Witch to try to get one up on the neighbours. With Chloe and Roderick flanking him like bodyguards, Rob takes a deep breath and knocks at the door. He isn't sure why he's so terrified.

I mean, I've got no idea what I'm going to say, or how any of this is going to help Bummer, but it's not as if she's going to come running out in a kabuki mask and chop my dick off with a samurai sword, is it?

Rob is just about to knock again when the porch light turns on.

Great, now you've thought it, that's exactly what's going to happen. Good one Rob.

Kabuki-sword-wielding Poo Witch would probably be preferable to the sight that greets him instead.

'Heather?!'

She's wearing a sheer negligee.

'Oh, err, Rob, right, you've got people with you, okay, I just thought...' As she babbles she tries ineffectually to cover herself up. Roderick and Chloe politely study the pavement and the neighbour's flower beds. Rob wrenches his eyes up to Heather's face. She's wearing thick, shiny lilac eyeshadow, heavy eyeliner and lots of mascara. Her lips are bright red, clashing with the vivid orange of her face. She looks like a little girl trying on Mummy's make-up for the first time.

'Look, there's obviously been some kind of misunderstanding,' says Rob gently, 'so we'll just get going.'

'Heather!' a shrill voice calls from inside.

'Yes, Auntie?'

'Who's there?'

The voice is familiar. Rob's testicles climb higher into his body in response.

'No one, Auntie, I thought I heard a fox, that's all. I'm coming back inside now.'

'I might've known!'

This is said with such unbridled disgust that any doubts Rob may have had about the speaker's identity are dispelled. He stops in the middle of the garden path, but doesn't turn round, not yet.

Why didn't Heather mention who her auntie was? Why

did she not think that would be relevant? He's treated to a flashback of Heather sticking little heart-shaped gems into her nail varnish and wiggling her fingers at him, giggling her head off. She thought those nail stickers were the greatest thing ever.

'I'm calling the police!' Poo Witch yells from the doorway

That gets Chloe's attention. Previously she was hurrying back to the car, chuntering to herself about getting drawn into Rob's perverse activities. Now she's starting towards Poo Witch with a face like thunder, back straight, strides purposeful.

'On what grounds?' she asks, her voice quiet as a knife sliding from a sheath.

'Trespassing.'

'I was just leaving!' says Rob, exasperated. He should have known coming here was stupid and pointless. He's just going to make things worse for Bummer. The last thing he wanted.

'He's no longer on your property,' says Chloe archly as Rob reaches the car. Roderick is sitting with his hands ready on the steering wheel like a getaway driver. Rob hopes it doesn't come to that. He turns back to watch the exchange, scared, but unable to look away.

'Well, my CCTV camera has all the evidence I need.' Poo Witch points at the little grey box on the side of the house.

'...admissible in court,' Chloe is saying, arms folded across her chest. 'In fact, Mr Buckland could sue YOU for recording him without consent.'

'Who are you, his lawyer?'

'Exactly.'

Poo Witch looks shocked at that. If there's one thing that impresses her, it's people with status. Professionals. Her mouth goes into a little round O and she looks even more like a Deluxe

Debbie than the Birthday Every Day refund woman who started all this. Chloe takes the opportunity to forge ahead.

'So, we can either have this conversation out here on the street, or we can go inside and discuss matters like civilised people.'

She's got Poo Witch there. The old cow can't bear the intimation that her behaviour might be anything less than civilised. Heather's watching all this with her hands behind her back and her eyes on the floor, like she's hoping Poo Witch won't notice she's got her bits on show.

'Very well,' says Poo Witch, giving a brusque little nod, 'but HE stays in the car.'

'She means you.' Rob winks at Roderick but stays put in the back seat. Anything could happen in there. Heather could try to sit on his knee, or offer him a drink that accidentally gets splashed onto his crotch in an effort to get him to remove his trousers.

They wait in silence for a while. It's cold without the engine running. At least Rob has a jacket. Roderick is sitting with his hands in his armpits in an effort to keep warm. Their breath steams up the windscreen.

'She can't really be talking to her.' Roderick yawns. 'Who sorts out legal stuff at ten o'clock at night?'

'Yeah.' Rob grins sheepishly, pushing away images of the three of them spilling drinks on each other.

Bloody Empornium.

Fifteen minutes of shivering silence pass before Chloe comes racing out of the house. She dives into the passenger seat and crouches over the dashboard like someone might take a pop at her with a pistol.

'Go go go go go go!' she pants at Roderick.

He fumbles with the car keys and stalls a couple of times.

'What did you do?' Rob watches Poo Witch's front door, expecting her to come swooping out at any second, screeching to high heaven, but nothing happens. He watches out of the back window all the way down the street, but the door stays shut.

Chloe's doubled over, laughing hysterically, tears running down her cheeks, her face bright red.

'I peed in her teapot!' she manages between sobs of laughter. 'I peed in her little flowery teapot!'

Rob and Roderick exchange a look.

'And you thought you were going out with a posh bird.'

*

It turns out that once Chloe realised she wasn't speaking to a rational person who could be bargained with, but a cantankerous old bat with an enflamed sense of moral outrage, she tried to make her excuses to leave. Only Poo Witch was enjoying her captive audience and wanted to keep ranting on about how awful today's morally bereft society in general and Chloe's father in particular actually were. Heather had been sent to bed, so when Poo Witch forgot to bring out the biscuits and had to go back to the kitchen, Chloe took her opportunity, sneaked the teapot to the downstairs toilet, peed, returned the pot to its tray and legged it.

When they get back to Bummer's Chloe comes up with Rob to see her dad, wanting to tell him the teapot story. Rob thinks she's always been like her mum and is enjoying this opportunity to share a bit of Bummer-like behaviour. Maybe there's a little bit of glossing over the fact that the last chance to save the Empornium has been lost, too. Focusing on the weird to forget the crushing despair of reality.

Rob worries about how she'll react to the flat, to the detritus of Bummer's crumbling life. Kids shouldn't have to see their parents' failings, shouldn't have to realise that a life of ease in sunny Malta is more important to them than seeing their son on a regular basis. He wonders about warning her, explaining how hard Bummer's taken the court case and how it will get better, it honestly will. He takes too long trying to make the 'honestly' sound convincing in his head and Chloe bounds past him filled with post-prank enthusiasm and opens the door before he can say anything.

Rob has seen so much weirdness of late, and yet it just keeps getting weirder. Bummer's sitting on the sofa, wrapped in a towel, writing feverishly in a notebook. The worst of the takeaway debris has been removed, and the air is thick with the false cleanliness of air freshener. Brodie's standing on a pouffe, carefully combing Bummer's hair. He looks up with a smile as they enter.

'Chloe!' he exclaims. 'Just the person!'

Chloe stutters, lost for words for once. She's probably never seen Bummer with a parting before either. Brodie continues, unfazed: 'Your dad's thought of a business proposal, but he'll need to obtain some legal permissions. Perhaps you could go over it with him.'

Chloe looks at Rob. Rob shrugs.

'Uh, yeah. Okay, yeah sure.'

*

A couple of nights later Brodie has his first nightmare, apparently triggered by sleeping in his own bed, alone, for the first time. The night of the tea-pee incident, Brodie fell asleep on the sofa with Bummer after getting Chloe up to speed on the new business. The night after that, Joel and Jacob came over for a sleepover, which was really an excuse for Bummer and Rob to get rat-arsed like old times while the kids played video games.

Nothing seems amiss when Rob puts Brodie to bed. He turns those big dark eyes on again, of course, but Rob is used to that now, and he's fairly certain the bed argument is over. He's won. They turn on Optibot's night light mode and Rob tells Brodie that if he gets scared, Optibot will have his back. Brodie nods and shuffles down into the bed, allowing himself to be tucked in.

So the scream is totally unexpected. It slaps Rob in the ear, jolting him awake. For a moment he doesn't know where he is or what's happening, so deep is his fear. He looks at the clock and it's 3.33am, which freaks him out, even though there's no reason it should.

And then he becomes aware of a softer sound, Brodie's gentle sobs and sniffs. Breathing out slowly, relieved that he isn't under siege from gun-toting zombie robbers after all, Rob gets out of bed and steps round the screen.

Brodie is curled up in a ball under his blankets, shaking and crying. When Rob sits down on the edge of the bed, he shrieks, trying to make himself smaller.

'Hey, mate, it's okay, it's me,' says Rob, gently patting the quivering duvet lump.

At that, Brodie throws off the covers and leaps into Rob's lap, almost knocking him off the end of the bed. He cries and cries, tears soaking into Rob's t-shirt until it's saturated again, sopping wet against his chest.

*Can you dehydrate yourself from crying? Must be possible.
Better get him to drink plenty of water or something, once
he's calmed down.*

After a while, though, the crying subsides. Brodie ends up
just sniffing and breathing deeply, the sniffs and the breaths
locked in a bitter battle to be the first one out of his body.
Eventually, those noises dissipate, too, and Rob wonders if he
can get up yet. He's starting to need a wee.

'There was a man,' says Brodie, very, very faintly. So faintly
that Rob wonders if he imagined it, if the soft exhalations
of Brodie's breathing just formed themselves into phantom
words in his ears. So he waits a moment and then lifts Brodie
closer and says: 'What, mate?'

And Brodie repeats, still quiet, but as clear as a cry ringing
out in a church: 'There was a man.'

'Do you mean...' *Think carefully before saying this,
Robert. Think about what you're actually saying when you
say this.* 'Do you mean the man who took you away?'

Brodie doesn't say anything, just keeps looking down and
off to the side, like he expects his kidnapper to come crawling
out from under the bed.

'He wanted to take me away,' he affirms.

Rob coughs. There's a lump in his throat and no matter
how much he swallows, it won't go down. It's like a bubble
trapped in his oesophagus, rising up into his mouth, where
it'll burst and he'll drown. He squeezes Brodie tight, so
tight that the kid squeaks and wriggles until he slackens his
grip a little.

'No, that wasn't real, mate. That was just a bad dream, a
horrible bad dream.'

Brodie seems to accept that, nods and looks a tiny bit less fragile. Rob wishes someone would offer him some reassuring words.

*

No one does.

27

Bummer is at his kitchen table, writing. Rob doesn't think he's ever seen Bummer write anything in all the time he's known him. Draw, yes, mainly cocks spurting jizz and steaming piles of shit with flies circling them, but writing, never. He has surprisingly neat, even handwriting, but it looks like it takes real effort. It's obvious he's concentrating hard on the pen, as if he's moving it with telekinesis rather than his hand.

Brodie is round the corner in the front room, grudgingly learning the dance moves to Tenike's favourite pop video.

Rob puts his concerns about Brodie's broken sleep and his uncanny twerking ability to one side for the moment and looks at the pieces of paper spread out in front of Bummer. They are labelled with headings like: 'STUFF I'M GOOD AT' and 'THINGS I HATE'. This second list includes: 'those spiders with tiny bodies and gangly legs' and 'men with long fingernails'.

Rob surreptitiously checks his own nails.

Bitten down to the quick.

'What's all this?' he asks.

'Brainstorming,' says Bummer, most of his focus still on moving his pen.

'For what?'

'New business.'

'Mate, that's great!' Rob suddenly feels like his heart's been pumped full of helium. He claps Bummer on the shoulder enthusiastically and it's only then he notices the other changes in his friend. Clean-shaven, multiple chins allowed to roam free for once. A clean t-shirt and jeans, his hair brushed, washed and parted, only he must have done it himself this time.

'Chloe and Paul think we can get them to throw the case out if I show I'm changing the use of the premises.'

Rob smiles, aware it's not one of his best. Bummer puts his pen down, gathers all his papers together into a sheaf and slips them into a manila folder.

'What's with you, anyway?' he asks, laying the folder down and turning to face Rob with serious eyes. 'You seem all... sad.'

Rob resists a powerful urge to ask Bummer to hold him and tell him everything will be all right. Instead he shrugs, inwardly cursing his lip for quivering.

'Kidder!' Bummer leaps to his feet and pulls Rob into a hug, his concern evident in his voice. 'Whatever it is, we'll sort it out.'

Close enough.

Rob lets the hug go on as long as Bummer will allow, inhaling that familiar smell, like a Greggs hosed down with citrus shower gel.

He's a fucking star, that Bummer.

Later, when they're done hugging and are back to watching the kids play their video game, Rob tries to remind Bummer about Brodie. Not in the subtle ways he used when Bellamy first dropped Brodie on him. Overt. Right out there. It makes no difference.

Every time he starts, Bummer forgets what they're talking about. It's like it's too much information for his brain to hold. And not in a klutzy, classic Bummer kind of way, either.

'So... sorry, mate, what were talking about?'

Rob sighs deeply and gives it one last try.

'I'm worried for Brodie.'

'You're worried for Brodie,' Bummer repeats mechanically, eyes locked on Rob's as if that'll help him keep a grip on what's being said.

'Because he isn't my son, so he must be someone else's.'

'Because he isn't...' and there it is again, a strange something in Bummer's eyes, definable only by its absence, like a lost internet connection.

'Sorry, mate, what were we talking about?'

'Brodie's been having nightmares.' Rob's voice is leaden, falling out of his mouth like pennyweights. 'What should I do?'

'Aww, no worries with that, mate.' Bummer grins. 'Jacob used to wake up screaming, but I set him right. We'll come up with something.'

Queenie passes with a mouse clamped in her toothless mouth, dangling limply as she drools onto its fur.

'Eww!' Tenike yells, pausing their dance game. 'Queenie, gross! Drop it!'

Queenie obligingly spits the mouse onto the carpet, blinking.

Brodie crouches next to the mouse. Tentatively he touches it. Rob holds his breath, watching. He's not sure why. As Brodie's fingertip comes into contact with the mouse, it convulses. Queenie's unable to bear this tantalising movement and slaps at it with her paw. Brodie pushes her aside and Tenike hurries forward to pick her up before she can do any more damage.

Brodie touches the mouse again, but it's different now, stiff and dead. Whatever mousey essence it once contained is gone. Rob half-expects Brodie's finger to glow and the mouse to come leaping to life and run in circles round the kitchen. It doesn't. Brodie strokes it thoughtfully.

'Its fur is soft,' he reports. Then: 'Can we bury it?' as if Rob would have just put it in the bin otherwise.

I'm not Gordon.

*

They invent all kinds of late-evening activities to occupy Brodie's mind so he's full of happy thoughts when he goes to bed. Bedtime stories. Shadow plays. Hot milky drinks and card games. It works for a while. Everything gets better.

Rob goes back to work and things are almost back to normal, although on dress-down Fridays some people still wear the Bring Back Brodie t-shirts and look at him meaningfully. It's not so bad, though, because Jules is a mate again. Sort of. It feels a bit like an act now and sometimes he catches her looking at the Brodie photos with a strange expression, but he has someone to eat lunch with again, so it's definitely better.

Bummer gives up fighting Poo Witch. He rips down the Empornium sign and puts up one that says Waifs and Strays After School Club. He sells off all the inflatable people and whips and chains to some guy down the market. He stocks up on soft bright furniture and wipe-clean floor tiles. Rob gets to help with setting things up and is surprised by how much he loves it.

'I'm not sure I'm cut out for this,' says Newbie, on his hands and knees, banging the click-together laminate pieces into place like a difficult jigsaw puzzle.

'Sure you are,' says Bummer. 'Tell the kids about Drag, they'll love that.'

'Drag?' Rob asks. He's cleaning the dead flies out of the window. Always with the dead flies.

That's favouritism for you. He gets nice shiny new floors and I get dirty disease-ridden old flies. Won't complain, though, 'cos Bummer's worth it.

'Paul's imaginary dragon,' says Bummer, shooting a wink at Newbie. Rob expects him to grin at some shared secret joke, but he just looks uncomfortable and concentrates hard on getting the floor straight.

'Hey, I had imaginary stuff first,' says Rob petulantly. Bummer looks at him oddly and Jules hurries over and says: 'Me and Brodie need clean water, but the bucket's too heavy. Would you mind, Rob?'

Rob doesn't mind, even when he's so blatantly being manoeuvred out of conflict. He hauls the bucket across to the toilet, slopping dirty suds over the sides. He empties it into the toilet bowl, then forces the rim of the bucket under the tap. The bucket's too big to fit in the sink, so he has to hold it at an awkward angle to keep the water from gushing straight back out.

He hears Jules round the corner, sweeping and talking to Brodie. Brodie's voice is so muted, he can only hear the general shape of it moving up and down, can't make out any distinct words. Jules's voice is quiet but clear.

'What do you mean?' A pause and a gentle ripple of sound

from Brodie. 'So there's more than one man?' Another ripple, shorter this time, definitely an affirmative noise. 'What do you mean, "like you"?' There's no Brodie noise in response to that, just the shushing sound of Jules's broom moving back and forth. 'How are the men "like you"?' she presses, but Brodie isn't giving anything else up. Rob suddenly wants to see Brodie's face, to try to discern from his expression what's going on behind those large black eyes.

The bucket is full, too full, and red-hot bleachy water splashes his hand. The water burns and the bleach stings, but neither sensation really means anything.

*

They wander through the arboretum, Rob and Jules trailing slowly behind while Brodie skips off ahead, investigating trees and rocks, the terror of bedtime temporarily forgotten. Rob glances out across the lake. The sun ripples on the surface and he's momentarily dazzled by the glare.

It seems like for ever ago since they were last here, but it's only a couple of months. The tree branches are heavy with blossom now, and the moorhens are fully grown, the babies indistinguishable from their parents. And the aviaries are full.

During the summer months, the aviaries house parrots, budgies, parakeets, brightly coloured finches and, down on the ground, a couple of tortoises and quails. Rob doesn't know where they all go during the rest of the year. Maybe they die and the council just buy new ones each year.

He's woken from his reverie by Jules linking her arm through his. She does stuff like that now. He kind of likes it, but it also feels a bit like a liberty, 'cos he never asked her out, or said she was his girlfriend or anything. If he'd have done that to some woman without permission she'd have acted like he was scum. Jules says that's the patriarchy for you, and he feels like she's maybe making fun of him a little, and he's not sure exactly how. At least she's back to doing that now rather than treating him like an unexploded bomb.

'You know how I said I always wanted to be in on a secret world and shit?' says Jules, her words brushing his earlobe.

He nods, watching Brodie scamper to the edge of the lake, trying to tempt the moorhens towards him with an outstretched twig. They flee into the water with a splash and frantic flapping of wings.

'Well, I'm in over my head and I want it to stop.'

He turns to look at her and then steers her away from the lakeside, veering towards the aviaries. Suddenly it's very important to him to see lots of pretty little birds. A bit of beauty and light and colour in the world.

'What are you saying?' he asks, glancing back to make sure Brodie has seen where they're headed. He has. He drops his twig into the water and follows them at a run.

'I'm not saying I believe you. I'm still not saying that, because it would be crazy because Brodie has a birth certificate and a guitar teacher and all that jazz, but...' Rob watches the birds flit from perch to perch. Jules continues. 'I emailed your mum – don't get mad, don't get mad – and I asked for some photos of you as a kid, and she mailed them to me because she couldn't figure out attachments and...' *They have simple little lives, the birds. Someone puts food in their little troughs and water in their little trays and they flutter back and forth and fuck and lay eggs.*

'Well, it *is* kind of weird how Brodie was found in the exact same outfit you wore as a kid, I can't deny that. Especially because I did some digging and they don't even make that tank top any more. I mean, what eight-year-old even wears a tank top these days?' *And maybe at the end of the season they drop dead from battering themselves against the mesh one too many times and a man comes and sweeps them up and throws their tiny bodies into the furnace and heads out to the pet shop to put in his order for next year, but at least they don't have to deal with this kind of shit.* 'And anyway, Brodie says that men have come here from another world to try and take him away. He says they left him here by mistake and now they want to take him back. And although it can't be true...'

'It's nightmares,' he says, switching his attention to the tortoise, languidly eating lettuce in the woodchip at the bottom and getting his shell shat on. 'Everyone has nightmares.'

Maybe the tortoise is the same tortoise every year. Maybe he witnesses the bird massacre, the burning of the bodies, season after season. Maybe he sees it going on, over and over, but what can he do? He's only a tortoise.

'But—'

Just sit there chomping on your lettuce, mate, and don't worry about it. There's nothing you can do.

'Everyone has nightmares,' he says again, firmer this time, to her or to himself he's not sure.

'You said you made this boy up, and he says men are trying to take him to another planet and you don't think that might... mean something?'

'YOU DON'T BELIEVE ME ANYWAY SO WHAT DOES IT MATTER?!'

And Rob knows his voice is too loud and his face is too red and spittle's flying from his mouth and he's waving his arms like a crazy person, but he's just had it. At the edges of his vision he sees shadowy figures and shapes sort of like circuit boards, only now they look more like planetary diagrams. It's like his brain is shorting out, throwing out random arm twitches and facial contortions and images in a final surge, just before total

shutdown.

28

Mr Buckland, I think it's time you and we had a little chat.

The voice is soft and gentle as branded toilet paper. Rob's eyelids flicker, but he's not able to open them, not just yet. For now he's trapped in the darkness of his own head.

'Who are you?' he says and is surprised to find his voice works fine, loud and clear.

You can call us Mr Anderson.

With great effort, Rob manages to open his eyes. He immediately wishes he hadn't. He's lying in bed and there's a creature standing at his feet. A seven-foot-tall, grey creature, wearing, of all things, a skinny-fit suit, a white shirt and a tie. Its long neck sticks up and out of the shirt at an angle, like a boomerang, and doesn't look thick enough to support its large, strange head. It looks how bank managers would appear if they'd evolved from sharks rather than apes. There's something of the hammerhead about its ugly grey face and wide-set eyes, but it has no discernible mouth or nose.

'Mr Anderson,' says Rob weakly, raising his head for a

moment, then letting it drop back to the pillow. He tries to lift his arms, his torso, but it's like there's a great weight pressing down on him, invisible straps fastening him to the bed. He's stuck.

We can only apologise for the inconvenience we have caused you. This matter is most, most unusual. It has never happened before in our entire history.

The thing's voice, wherever it's coming from, is very soothing and Rob doesn't feel afraid, even though he knows he probably should be. He keeps thinking back to the day he went to the computer shop with Brodie and became convinced he was actually in a coma. This is like the absolute opposite of that. For all its strangeness, everything in the room is totally real. Hyper-real. If he could lift his arm and pinch the creature, he's absolutely certain it would flinch away and rub its wrinkled grey flesh with its three-fingered hand.

Of course we would, says Mr Anderson, a trifle wearily, *it would hurt. Now, will you listen? We'll try to be brief, we are not sure all this is good for you.*

Rob succeeds in raising his head and looking alert.

Our planet is struggling. A few thousand years further along than yours. Severe overcrowding, limited resources, widespread famine. He spreads his arms and spherical shapes appear above the bed, moving slowly like the ones Brodie pulled up on the demo laptop in the computer shop. Rob finally recognises it as a solar system.

We are far more technologically advanced than you, so we could have come scooting over in our ships, enslaved you all and taken over. But we are not barbarians. We considered coming peacefully, requesting asylum, but looking like this, he waves a hand towards his modern-art features, *and knowing how your lot feel about asylum seekers, we devised another way.*

We saw an opportunity in the way you people behave towards children and we took it. We saw that sometimes, humans take children from their parents, children who do not belong to them. He sounds genuinely shocked by this, although there is no movement in his face. *And we also saw how relieved parents were to have their children returned to them. And we also saw...* He pauses and when he speaks again, there is an unbearable sadness in his voice *...that sometimes there is no child to return.*

Rob waits. It seems that the creature is trying to compose himself, even though externally he's still an ugly impassive fish.

We thought there would be no harm in providing our own children with a future. A future with surrogate parents who are guaranteed to love them, parents who will be so grateful to see them return they will not question their child's initial lack of... 'normal' behaviour. And after enough time has passed, our children are no longer ours, they are yours.

Rob wants to cry. The creature's voice echoes inside his head, filled with decades of sadness and loss and regret. Rob's mouth is dry and itchy and his eyes are tingly, but he won't cry. He can't.

Mistakes happen from time to time, of course. Mr Anderson seems to have forgotten Rob's presence. His voice is distant and thoughtful. *We have our limits. Sometimes the real child is not unrecoverable as we suspected. On other occasions the parents are not so happy to see their child returned to them. This is because they are not the parents of a kidnapped child. They are the murderers of their own flesh and blood.* His voice takes on a different timbre, tight, strained. Rob feels rage building within him. He wants to tear down the walls, set the world on fire. But the feelings are not his. *Those instances are rectified quickly. Our children are returned to us and the parents' memories are erased, or...* He pauses again and this one has an atmosphere to it, like the sky before a thunderstorm. *...left intact if that is a more... appropriate course of action.*

'Memories erased?' says Rob, finally starting to feel afraid, finally struggling against his invisible bonds. 'Is that what you're going to do to me?'

Mr Anderson's eyes move at that. They swivel and scan Rob like searchlights, but they are not devoid of kindness.

It is what we intend to do, Mr Buckland. But our child is resisting. This has never happened to us before. He is not your child. You did not really lose a child at all, you just told some strange and vivid lies and a coordinator who was not properly attending to their duties... There is no reason for him to be with you. And yet, he will not return to us, he will not let your memories and those of your friends and family be set to rights.

'So why are you here?'

Mr Anderson steps close to the bed and lays a hand on top of Rob's. It's cool and the skin feels strange, but it isn't wholly unpleasant. Rob isn't about to go skipping off through the buttercups holding hands with this guy, but he won't recoil in horror either.

To appeal to you as a parent. Mr Anderson's eyes are large and blue and they look a little frightening, but only because they are the eyes of an innocent baby in the face of a prehistoric sea beast. *Please talk to our child on our behalf and tell him he must allow us to take him back where he belongs.*

'And if you take him back? What then?'

He would not bond again with a different human, and you have shown yourself to be... unsuitable. So he will be reunited with his biological family. Earth is no longer a fitting environment for him. But you can rest assured, he will be loved.

Mr Anderson clasps his hands over his chest for a moment, presumably where his heart is, although not necessarily.

Please, Mr Buckland. Think about what we have said.

He backs slowly away from the bed. The room darkens and Rob's eyes grow heavy.

*

'...did he take?' a big burly guy is asking Jules. He's crouching in front of Rob looking concerned. He has a tattoo on his arm that says 'We Are Distorted' in shaky blue lettering.

'Nothing, he didn't take—' Jules is saying and then she realises Rob is trying to sit up, looking at her.

'I'm fine,' Rob says. His back hurts and his hand smells. He landed on a fallen tree branch, right in the lumbar region, and put his hand in dog shit as he was trying to sit up. *What kind of arsehole doesn't clean up after their dog in a kids' park?*

'You sure?' the big guy asks, mobile phone in hand. 'I can call an ambulance if you like.'

'No, really, I'm fine, thank you.' Rob continues blurting reassurances as the man helps him to his feet and Jules does her best to clean the shit off his hand with a wet wipe.

'Probably best if you go to the public toilets,' Jules says, 'get it cleaned off properly. Don't want you getting worms as well!'

Rob looks round to thank the burly man again but he's already some way across the arboretum, striding off into the shade of the trees, and Rob feels weird about shouting after a stranger. Jules's words suddenly register with him and he turns back to her.

'As well as what?'

'Whatever you've got. Rob, you didn't see yourself. Your eyes were rolled back in your head, you were drooling – I think you should get yourself checked out.'

He suddenly realises she's looking at him oddly. Like she's re-evaluating him again. Moving him out of one category in her head and into another.

'I'm not crazy!' he finds himself blurting, which is possibly the worst thing he could've said.

'I don't think you are,' she says soothingly, just like she'd say to a crazy person, 'I just think you ought to get checked out. Maybe get Brodie checked over, too.'

'Right,' says Rob. 'I'm going to settle this right now. Brodie!'

Brodie is over by the aviaries, staring at the tortoise. He's crouching close to the mesh, trying to push a dandelion leaf through a gap for the scaly old reptile. The birds suddenly freak out as one, all launching into the air and making tight circles of their cages, shrieking and cawing. Bird shit spatters the tortoise's shell like white paint, but if it feels it, it doesn't react.

Brodie leans back, looking hurt. The tortoise stretches out its neck, trying to eat the tantalising leaf poking through the bars, but it's just out of reach.

Rob lays a hand on Brodie's shoulder and pulls him upright, away from the cages. He knows this probably isn't the time or place, but he has to prove a point to Jules.

'The men in your dreams, is one of them called Mr Anderson?'

Brodie's face whitens and his lip trembles and Rob expects another tantrum like the one in the shop, but it doesn't happen. Brodie just clenches his small fists very tight and nods once.

*

'That is MENTAL.' Bummer sits back in his chair and spreads his hands wide as if there's nothing more to say.

'It isn't,' says Neil, 'something's not right.'

'I'm not real,' says Brodie simply.

'You are real,' Rob says quickly. 'You're just not... entirely... human.' He wants to take it back as soon as he's said it, but Brodie just looks faintly proud. As much as he ever looks anything.

'That is so cool,' says Tenike, grinning at Brodie. 'I'm going to tell everyone!'

Rob flicks her nose, making her squeal. 'You are not. I don't want any more police or psychiatrists or anything sniffing around.'

They are all round the table again at the pub, just like before, only this time Jules is there, too. She's sitting on the edge, sipping a rum and Coke like she's not sure whether she wants to be part of this or not.

'Let's just say for argument's sake,' says Chloe, laying her hands on the table and regarding them all seriously, 'that you haven't been sniffing glue and everything you say is as it seems.'

'But—' Bummer starts incredulously, but Chloe waves him quiet.

'In that scenario, someone is trying to take away a child who is, to all intents and purposes, your son. Don't you think you should do something about that?'

They talk it round in circles until Rob is dizzy. Something seems to have changed. Since Brodie acknowledged his status as an alien, Bummer is able to follow, able to remember that they made him up, although it doesn't make him any less confused. Eventually they reach the point where they've repeated everything enough times to be tired of it. They drain their glasses and head home.

29

The sound fills Rob with terror. It's sort of the sound of a squeegee mop being pulled out of its bucket, if that squeegee mop was also capable of manipulating time and space. He's lying on his side, facing the screen that separates his bed from Brodie's. A bright, white light illuminates the screen, like when he was shining the torch, only it's coming from everywhere.

Rob feels he can't breathe, and yet the sound closest to him is his own mad panting.

Shapes appear behind the screen, two tall, skinny silhouettes with large heads, just popping into being with that inter-dimensional squeegee noise. Rob wants to move, wants to do something, but he's frozen to the bed with fear. His heart hammers in his chest and he knows now, knows for sure how the mouse must've felt when Queenie caught it.

Like I may as well just die.

But then, another sound, thin, but growing stronger and firmer all the time.

'No. No, I won't. NO. DADDY!'

And each cry is a like a shot of adrenalin to the heart, each refusal provides the kick up the arse Rob needs to get to his feet and wrench the screen to the floor.

And just like that, it's dark and it's quiet, and Rob is already wondering if it's just a bad dream.

If it is, Brodie had the same bad dream, because he's curled up on top of the covers, crying, and his wrists have livid red marks that might have been made by hands, if the hands were huge and had fewer fingers than usual. Rob picks up his phone, and as he cradles Brodie in his arms, he's making the call.

*

Before they know it, it's all agreed. A mad plan for a mad situation.

Rob and Jules will take Brodie to the coast. Bummer will stay at Rob's with all the others, even Roderick. Joel will act as a decoy in Brodie's bed and the others will lie in wait. If and when Mr Anderson comes back, they'll all leap out with tennis rackets and cricket bats and beat the living shit out of the kiddy-snatching alien bastard.

'Don't hurt him too bad,' says Brodie.

'But what's to say he's going to come this weekend?' Rob points out, even though he's the one who came up with this, the one who suddenly felt that it was imperative they get away. 'What if he doesn't turn up? We can't go on the run for ever!'

'You wouldn't have to go to school,' Tenike tells Brodie with a grin.

'You wouldn't have got us all together at this hour over

nothing,' Jules says, looking from Rob to Brodie and back again. Her gaze lingers on Brodie's bruises. 'They must have really scared you this time?'

They both nod.

'Then you have to realise this, Mr Anderson... He's not going to let you just keep Brodie.'

Rob has two horrible feelings, like toothache only in his brain and the pit of his stomach, throbbing away, nagging. Part of it relates to Jules. How she's gone from not believing him to accepting everything and how she took in Brodie's bruises with a curt nod and won't meet Rob's eyes any more. And part of it, the larger part, that's making him nauseous with worry, is about the plan. There's something they're forgetting, something huge, something important, something obvious, but he just can't see what it is. Maybe Mr Anderson's done some kind of mind control on them all to stop them thwarting his plans.

'If Detective Bellamy calls round,' he tells Bummer, suddenly sure that it will happen, that Bellamy knows something somehow, 'don't tell him where we are.'

Maybe that was it.

*

Jules heads home to get all her camping gear together. Apparently she was well into it when she was at uni and still has a really good tent and everything. Rob has to resist a strong urge to video call his mum.

Should probably let her see her grandson one last time.

No.

That's the wrong way to think. It's just a nice little holiday with Jules. Not the last anything.

And yet the thoughts persist. He should take Brodie round the After School Club – one final look before it opens and gets wrecked by hordes of kids. He should cook a roast dinner, a proper one, one last, delicious meal. They should have a kickaround in the park, eat ice cream, buy a dog with one floppy ear and teach it to cock its leg on command. All the things he intended on doing if he ever had a son—

Stop that! It's not the way to be thinking. Nothing is over. That fishy bastard isn't getting his hands on Brodie and that's all there is to it.

*

Rob realises when Brodie tugs his sleeve to indicate their stop that he should be savouring every moment rather than wasting time worrying about the flaw in his plan. Soaking up all the Brodie-ness while he still can.

Right, that's it. That's the last thought like that, you bastard, or me and you are going to have words. End of.

'Everything okay, Dad?' Brodie asks as he struggles to detach a trolley from the trolley line.

'Yes.' Rob smiles, genuinely, glad the voices have finally been silenced. 'Let's find lots of nice things that'll cook on a camping stove.'

Everything in the supermarket has been moved, and Rob stumbles around, hanging onto the wonky trolley, trying to orient himself. Brodie runs off ahead and disappears into the dairy aisle.

Rob walks as briskly as he can with the trolley dragging at

his arms like a fat kid in a sweetshop. He apologises profusely to the teenage lad he sends careening into the garlic bread and chilled pies. The lad complains down his mobile phone that 'some dickhead gave me a proper bailing' or some such unintelligible rubbish. He doesn't look at Rob or acknowledge him or his apology. Rob starts wishing he'd hit the lad harder. Flipped him right over onto the chiller cabinet so it rocked on its base and tumbled over, burying him in a mound of ready meals and cold meat.

He rounds the corner preparing to tell Brodie about the mardy little git, only Brodie isn't there. Rob rounds the next corner, into the egg aisle. There's nearly a catastrophe when the trolley lurches towards the stacked cardboard cartons. He manages to right it, even though he's not looking, not paying the slightest bit of attention to the stupid bloody bollocking eggs.

'Brodie!' he calls out, abandoning the trolley and taking off with long strides, down one aisle and up the next. It's not busy at this hour; finding a small boy should be easy.

'Brodie!' He's really shouting now, and the few people there are staring, but fuck them, and a woman in a staff uniform comes over and asks if he needs a message going over the PA system, but he waves her away.

What good's an announcement if the kid's in space?

For a moment there's a strong image of Brodie trapped in a transporter pod, drifting endlessly through a sea of stars, clawing at the sides, unable to get out. Rob shakes the image away forcefully and hurries on.

Suddenly, there's a tiny voice and it sounds embarrassed.

'Dad?' Brodie steps out from behind a shelf full of cakes.

'I was looking for those biscuits you like with the M&M's in,' he says, almost reproachfully, almost as if his behaviour was perfectly normal and Rob is the one acting out. Rob considers yelling at him for running off, but instead he crouches down and crushes Brodie into a hug.

'Dad?' Brodie squirms. 'Dad, are you crying?'

'No.' Rob sniffs. 'Hold still and let me hug you.'

*

They spend far too much money on a ton of unsuitable food, but Rob doesn't care. Maybe there *is* a way to cook frozen mini pizzas on a camping stove. They get back to the flat and everyone is there, sitting on the stairs with a pile of bags and rucksacks.

Jules stands up and hugs them both, although he can't help noticing she hugs Brodie tighter and for longer. Still, that sets everyone off and soon Rob is fielding hugs left, right and centre, from Bummer and Tenike and even Roderick. Rob wants to trap the moment in a bubble of glass and keep it on the mantelpiece like one of Mum's dustcatcher ornaments. Only he doesn't have a mantelpiece, or glass-blowing skills, or the ability to manipulate matter and the flow of time. But it's a nice thought.

When they've squeezed everything into the rucksacks, they sit around in the front room and the atmosphere is thick with tension and the unsaid.

'Better all get an hour or so's sleep then,' says Rob tentatively, hoping someone will disagree.

'Why not just go now?' asks Jules. 'That is – if you don't mind?' She looks to Bummer and he looks to Joel and Jacob.

'Can we play on the PlayStation, Uncle Rob?' asks Joel.

'Knock yourselves out.'

'We don't mind,' Jacob answers for both of them, already rooting behind the sofa for Rob's collection of games.

Bummer's the only one who comes to see them off. The kids are either too tired or can't be trusted not to make a God-awful din at an inappropriate hour. It's cold outside and Rob's arms prickle with goosebumps. He opens the back door of the car and reaches in for the thick tartan blanket he knows Jules keeps in there.

Bummer has picked Brodie up and is holding him close, whispering in his ear. Brodie is crying and smiling, hugging Bummer and telling him he loves him. Rob stands shivering, waiting for them to be done, then bundles Brodie in the blanket and tucks him into the back seat. He approaches Bummer, hand outstretched. It feels like the final time they'll ever see each other. He knows it isn't, but that's how it feels. He's determined not to cry. Bummer looks all red-eyed and sniffly, the big soft shit. He grasps Rob round the wrist and pulls him into a tight hug. It's like being smothered by a bear in a greasy vest. They pull apart at last and Rob can't meet Bummer's eyes.

'See ya then, mate,' he says to a crisp packet lying at the kerbside.

'Yeah, see ya, mate,' Bummer parrots back at him.

Rob gets into the passenger seat and finds he still can't look at Bummer, not even to wave goodbye. He fiddles around with his seatbelt and then leans across to check Brodie's, waving without looking. As Jules revs the engine and they pull away, he hears Brodie laughing, and waving, waving, waving out of the back window. He knows Bummer's running along behind the car, waving until his little chunky legs can't keep up any more and he has to stop, but Rob doesn't turn round. He can't.

*

Rob isn't aware of having fallen asleep until he awakes with a jolt. For a moment he's panicked.

What if they've taken Brodie while I was sleeping? A quick glance in the back shows that this is just the paranoia creeping in again. He rubs his face. He's drooled onto the collar of his jacket. His chin is sticky with saliva. He wipes it away and looks over at Jules.

'Aren't you just the little angel when you sleep?'

'Fuck off.'

She makes a small noise that could be amusement or derision and turns her attention back to the road. The headlights cut a path for them along dim country lanes. Occasionally something small and furry scurries into the undergrowth at the side of the road. Once, a pair of yellow eyes throw back the glow of the headlights. Rob shivers and rubs his arms to warm them.

'Why don't you drive for a bit?' Jules asks. 'I'm knackered.'

'Can't drive.'

'Useless munter.'

They continue in silence for a while, the little car eating up the miles between them and—

'Where is it we're going?'

'Seaside.'

'Right. But you're not just driving randomly. You must have somewhere specific in mind.'

'Yeah. Actually, I'm taking us where my parents always took me when I was little. It's beautiful.'

Rob watches the shadows of passing trees dapple her face. *Yes, it is.* He doesn't say it aloud and before he can, she tells him: 'Anyway, it's not far now. Why don't you go back to sleep? I'll wake you when we get there.'

He wants to stay awake, chat to her the rest of the way, but his eyes are so heavy. He fights it as long as he can, but eventually his chin drops forward onto his chest and sleep bundles him away in a deep black sack. His last thought as he slips into its warm soft folds is:

Jules won't let them take him. She's tough.

30

'All right sleepy drawers, you don't want to miss this.'

He doesn't know how long they've been stationary. He thought the car coming to a stop would wake him, but obviously not. Jules has the window rolled down, but even the cold air licking at his face wasn't enough to rouse him. He must have been a long way off.

Brodie is outside, clutching a cup of soup, still warm and steaming from the flask. He's staring off into the distance. Rob follows his gaze. He suddenly understands why Gordon and Mum get all misty-eyed about sunrises.

Jules has parked them on top of a hill, overlooking the deserted beach below. The sun is creeping up above the ocean, throwing out colours that have no business occurring in nature – violent reds, luminous pinks, oranges on the very edge of vision. It looks like an explosion in a Japanese animation – colours vivid, shapes and motions realistic, but not quite real, the knowledge of the artist's brushstrokes ever-present.

They watch it until it's completely risen and then it's just a glowing ball in the sky, nothing special at all, and Rob feels like he's been conned. Brodie and Jules don't look as if they feel that way, though. They're smiling at each other as if they just shared the secrets of the universe. Rob wonders if maybe Mr Anderson got it wrong. Maybe Rob is the alien changeling, the pod person. He doesn't seem to have the proper human credentials, that's for sure.

'What shall we do now?' asks Rob, getting out of the car and stretching his legs. They feel a good few inches too short.

'Well, Brodie and I,' says Jules, going round to the boot and opening it, 'are going to pitch the tent and get a few hours of sleep. You can do what you like.' There's only a tiny bit of admonishment in her voice – most of it is tease. He hopes. He yawns and stretches.

Hope they don't sleep for too long. Don't know what I'll do out here on my own. Wish I'd brought some music.

'Might go for a walk then,' he says, wondering what the hell people do in places without pubs or offies or takeaways. He swings his arms aimlessly for a moment, then realises that if he doesn't go now, he'll probably be expected to help put the tent up. He ruffles Brodie's hair and receives a tight hug in response.

'Help Jules with the tent, mate,' he says, plunging his hands into his pockets and striding off down a sandy track. Despite his desire to soak up all the Brodie, he just can't right now. It hurts too much. He needs a moment to think.

Perhaps the sea air will do him good. Not that it smells particularly good. Beneath the salt freshness there's the tang of dead fish, rotting seaweed and crabs decomposing in their shells. As Rob reaches the beach itself, there are the sploshes of tiny living crabs plopping into rock pools at his approach, gulls cawing angrily overhead and in the background, the constant, insistent gushing of the sea. It should be soothing, comforting, but to Rob it's intrusive. He hikes up a sand dune, longing for the smells of the city – hot tarmac and exhaust fumes. He misses Bummer already and the sounds of home – the washing machine trying to get curry out of the bed sheets, the water boiler clanking, the man in the flat above coughing and hacking with his emphysema.

None of this—

Shit!

He catches his foot in a knotty thicket of grass and plunges forward, arms flailing. Somehow he regains his balance.

That's it now. Eyes on the ground at all times. No more looking at scenery. Only sea and more sea anyway.

A gull flies up and scares the shit out of him. It's huge and makes the same amount of noise you'd expect from a walrus defending its territory. He stands still for a moment to catch his breath from the fright, trying to get his bearings. He can see the beach stretching out behind him, but not the pathway leading back to the campsite car park. He decides to head up a slight incline, thinking that the brow of a large dune might help him spot a landmark.

At the top of the dune, all he can see is yet more beach. He's also now a bit sketchy about what direction he actually came from. He thinks about lying down in the sand, sucking his thumb and waiting for Jules and Brodie to come and find him. He realises that that's stupid and pathetic and he can't be that far from a road because they drove in on one, but all he wants right now is electricity and a packet of crisps.

He half-falls down a little dune and forces himself up the next one, cursing under his breath. A couple of hummocks later and there's a small pier with a little lock-up on it. The lock-up's shutters are down but there's light coming through underneath. He raps hard on the shutter, hurting his knuckles.

'Not open,' a voice barks from inside the lock-up. 'Come back in two hours!'

Rob pauses. He's about to knock again when he has a thought. If this person is loony enough to come to work two hours before opening time, particularly when their place of work is a shed on a beach, then they are definitely loony enough to have a shotgun or a toothy dog.

At least they'll be able to have a breakfast that isn't M&M's biscuits and soggy pizzas imbued with camping stove fumes.

Rob limps back towards the car park, his homing instincts reawakened by the possibility of properly cooked food.

*

When he gets back, Jules and Brodie are snoring away in the tent like it's a king-sized feather bed rather than a polythene hellcase. Rob gets a few winks in the back of the car, waiting for them to wake up.

When they are up, there's an odd atmosphere. Rob senses there may have been a conversation while he was away, and that Brodie didn't think too much of it. Jules seems to be trying to make amends somehow, mostly to Brodie, but a little to Rob as well.

Despite all that, the day passes surprisingly quickly and well. They return to the lock-up to find a stout old woman selling bacon and sausage butties cooked on a griddle and ice creams from a chest freezer. After a sarnie and a cornet each, they go for a walk.

Brodie finds a trickling little stream running down to the sea, cutting a natural channel through the sand. It looks so much like something sea sprites would play in, Rob nearly shouts in delight at seeing something move between the nearby rocks. Brodie goes to investigate and finds the ever-present tiny translucent crabs rather than the anticipated water fairies. It takes a long time for them to convince him that the crabs are happier where they are than they would be in a jam jar in the tent.

'Why don't we go and buy a spade instead?' asks Rob. 'Do some digging?'

'Yeah, we could build a sandcastle,' Jules agrees, but Brodie looks at them like they're the ones from another planet and goes searching for belemnites instead.

First steps towards finding that dragon skeleton.

Rob pictures the museum scene again and smiles. Perhaps Jules is right. Perhaps they can make it. He adds her into the fantasy, wearing a wide-brimmed hat for some reason, applauding Brodie as he steps up to the podium to make his presentation.

Perhaps he's not me at all.

When Brodie's filled his pockets with ancient squid bones, they head back to the car and Jules drives them to a little village where the average age is ninety-five and everyone looks wealthy and disapproving. They buy fish and chips and eat them in the car, laughing at all the interchangeable elderly folk passing by.

The village has a picturesque estuary complete with a

Victorian pier, so they walk along it, skimming stones until an angry old man tells them that they'll kill the ducks. Rob isn't a duck expert or anything, but he's pretty sure most ducks don't go in the sea.

Maybe all the sea ducks were skimmed to death.

After that they find a tea shop and eat cakes and then Rob suggests a pub but Brodie's tired and wants to go back to the tent. It's only about seven o'clock.

'Why don't we find an offie?' suggests Jules. 'We can put the world to rights while Brodie sleeps.' Rob half-hopes that 'putting the world to rights' is code for 'naked action' but with Jules you can never be sure, so he just nods and smiles.

They spend ages looking for an off-licence. It turns out the post office is the only place in the village that sells alcohol and that's shut.

'But,' says the kindly gentleman they asked, 'there's always Auld Joss.'

'Sorry?' says Rob, glad that they've found the only friendly villager but now wondering if his niceness is linked to being simple.

'Lives at t'other end of the village, in the old fisherman's cottage.' The man has big, wide baby-blue eyes. Rob feels unnerved by this, even though he knows it's irrational. Lots of people have blue eyes. Heather has blue eyes, and Bellamy. It doesn't mean anything. 'He makes moonshine,' the man finishes, having rattled on for a while about Auld Joss while Rob was distracted. The blue-eyed man taps the side of his nose at them conspiratorially, grins and strides away, glancing over his shoulder every now and then to see them standing perplexed.

'Do we bother with Joss's moonshine?' Rob asks Jules.

'What's moonshine?' Brodie pipes up.

'Adult drink. How tired are you?'

'Awake enough to get adult drink!' Brodie grins.

'Okay then.'

They walk back along the pier, joking about Joss living in the abandoned shack they saw on the drive up. As they get closer to the road, they spot something on the grass verge, half-buried in knotweed and dusted with sand blown up from the beach in bad weather. A wooden sign, words and an arrow branded into it: 'Fisherman's Cottage, 300 yards'.

'No way,' says Jules.

The cottage is perched on the narrowest part of the estuary and a low, rotting footbridge stretches out across the brackish water like a fireman's blanket outside a burning house. You'd only use it if your life absolutely depended on it. Rob says as much to Jules, but she has a twinkle in her eye, the kind that usually leads to a formal warning and a black mark against her name at work.

'It's not so much the bridge,' says Rob, 'but the house itself. Look at it.'

Dirty net curtains dangle limply from a bent curtain rail in the one good window. The other downstairs window is broken, jagged teeth of glass leering out of the frame. The upstairs windows are boarded. A bottle of milk is out on the step, curdling in the dying sun. Next to the step there's a plant pot, holding the browned, crispy corpses of several primulas.

'I mean, think about the kind of guy who would live somewhere like that.' Rob bats away an image of a bloke with no teeth, staring milky eyes and a hook for a hand. He suppresses a shudder. And gives Brodie's hand a squeeze, suddenly noticing that the hot little mitt has snaked into his own.

'Let's forget the moondust,' says Brodie.

Rob agrees, not bothering to correct him.

'Oh, you pair of wimps. I'll be back in a sec!' Jules bounds off, skipping across the creaking bridge in light, loping strides, skidding to a stop outside the house. She takes a moment to move the milk into the shade, although it must be too far gone by now. Turns and waves to them. Rob grips Brodie tightly, as if somehow that can protect Jules from the hook-wielding psycho. They both wave back, transfixed with mute terror. She knocks on the door and it falls open at her touch. It's like watching a horror film as she cranes her head inside.

Rob wants to shout: 'For God's sake don't go in, you idiot!' just like he would at the TV, but it feels like a cold, fat toad has taken up residence in his throat, and he just has to keep swallowing in an effort to dislodge it. He glances down at Brodie. The kid's eyes are saucers filled with fear.

In slow motion and a thousand miles away, Jules disappears inside the house.

Rob can't breathe. The toad has exhaled and blocked his windpipe. He waits, sure he's going to die from lack of oxygen, until suddenly his body lurches, dislodging the obstruction, and he takes a deep gasping breath.

'She's taking ages, Dad,' says Brodie, worry in his voice.

Rob shakes his head dismissively, sure it's just that their perception is off, thrown off-kilter by adrenalin and fear. He checks his mobile phone, stands and watches the numbers dissolve into one another as one, two, three minutes pass.

Thinks about calling her, but there's no reception here, and even if there was, what if her jaunty ringtone just alerted the killer to their presence?

'Okay,' he says, rolling his shoulders, jogging his head from side to side like a prizefighter limbering up, 'I'm going in. You coming?' Brodie nods and together they sprint across the bridge, leaping the broken plank at the end.

Rob tiptoes to the doorstep, motioning for Brodie to get behind him. Pokes his head inside. The hallway is dim, the air warm and stale. Either side of the door are bulging black bin liners, filled to the brim with old newspapers and magazines.

'Jules,' Rob hisses in a hoarse whisper. He takes a step inside. The hall floorboards creak and he freezes, biting his tongue. He looks right, then left. To his left there's the sound of movement.

'Jules,' he repeats, praying that it's her and not the hook-killer of Fisherman's Cottage.

Jules bursts out of a side door at a run, a bottle gripped tightly in her fist.

Upstairs there's the creak of a door opening and footsteps moving towards the landing. Rob locks eyes with Jules and there's fear there now, overriding the mischief and sense of adventure. Rob turns, scoops Brodie up onto his back, and they're away, bounding over the bridge. It makes an ominous cracking sound, but it holds and they keep on running. They don't stop until they're back at the car, even though a lot of the villagers are staring at them like they're mad.

When they're safely inside the car with the doors locked and the midges batting themselves hopefully against the rolled-up windows, their brush with death seems suddenly hilarious. By the time they're back at the campsite, ridiculous.

The house was probably abandoned, the 'moonshine' some squatter tramp's leftovers.

Rob eyes the bottle in Jules's lap. Is he that thirsty? Desperate enough for an alcohol buzz to drink a tramp's unmarked stash? There are no labels on the bottles. *They could contain anything.*

'They could be bottles of piss,' Rob notes out loud. Brodie elbows him in the ribs reproachfully.

'You said a bad word.'

'I thought you were tired.'

'I'm not now,' Brodie protests, 'the fisherman might come for me!' His eyelids are heavy. Rob can't tell if he's actually scared or just angling to stay up with the grown-ups.

'Well, why don't we put Optibot on Guardian mode?'

Brodie nods, so Rob heads out to the tent with him, tucks him into his sleeping bag and hands Optibot over. Brodie programs him in about three seconds. Rob smiles and ruffles the kid's hair.

'Me and Jules are just outside,' he tells him, 'give us a yell if you need us.'

Jules is sitting on the car bonnet when he gets back out. She's opened the bottle and her cheeks are flushed. Her woollen hat is pulled down well over her ears and her scarf is wound up tightly round her chin, so her blush is like a beacon in the dark.

'It's not piss,' she informs him, her voice shrill with excitement and intoxication, 'definitely not piss. Not sure what it is, but it's good!'

She holds the bottle out to him. He hesitates.

Can you get hepatitis from drinking out of a tramp's bottle? Remember the flat? You can always rely on beer.

Rob jerks and spins round.

'What?' asks Jules.

'Nothing.' He takes the bottle from her outstretched hand, but doesn't drink. He's already forgotten what spooked him so much, but he still can't bring himself to drink.

Jules tucks her elbows into her sides and flaps them, making accompanying squawking noises. If the burglary showed anything, it was that beer was the one thing he could rely on.

'All right, all right. If I die, I'm totally blaming you, you bastard.'

It doesn't exactly taste good, but it's identifiably some form of alcohol and that's good enough right now.

Rob cautiously puts his arm round Jules. She snuggles in tighter against him and snatches the bottle back for another swig. Rob smiles. Staying awake will be easy.

31

The siren pierces Rob's slumber like a stiletto blade. He doesn't remember falling asleep. His body's stiff and cold. He's just wearing his jumper and his underpants. The empty hooch bottle is half-buried in the grass. Everywhere is dark, except for the tent. At the tent there's a bright white light, so white he has to look away as spangling colours assault his brain. The siren goes on, Optibot's alarm, ear-piercing as ever, almost drowning out Brodie's own cries for help.

'Brodie!' Rob slithers off the car bonnet. Jules is alongside him, wrapped in a blanket, somehow still asleep. She's snoring softly – the moonshine must have been too much for her.

A small dark shape bursts out of the tent, on all fours at first, then scrambling upright. Rob holds out his arms, but Brodie doesn't run towards him; he veers off towards the beach without slowing down even slightly.

'Dad, help!' he screams over his shoulder, still running, disappearing into the dunes. 'Help me, Dad!'

Rob feels leaden and stupid – the moonshine has made

him an idiot. He can't process what's going on, what he needs to do. He blinks and tries again to look at the tent. The light is a little dimmer and he thinks he can make out two shapes standing either side of the tent's opening. Huge, monstrous shapes with big wide heads. He rubs his eyes and looks again; his ears pop. The tent is suddenly dark, there are no shapes and the air smells like burnt hair.

'DAD!' The cry is distant and desperate and heart-rending and it pushes Rob into action. He's suddenly running in the direction of Brodie's anguished voice, dragged along by instinct and fear. *What if I'm running the wrong way?*

The shout comes again and it's nearer, it's definitely nearer. He stumbles and swears, picking himself up as quickly as his wrenched ankle can manage. Sand and gravel are stuck to the grazes on his knees, but he doesn't stop to brush them down, just lurches forward, towards the yelling, towards Brodie, towards his son.

The light flares up again, that awful, terrible, beautiful light, and Brodie screams louder, his voice cracking with fear and exhaustion.

'I'm almost there,' Rob pants as loudly as he can, his eyes tight shut against the light, seeing only the black redness of his own eyelids, following Brodie by sound alone.

And then he's there, by the sea, able to open his eyes, and there are two of them holding Brodie and the nearest one looks almost sad.

That's far enough Mr Buckland, says Mr Anderson's voice in that weird mouthless way of his. Maybe it's not Mr Anderson. Maybe they all just sound that way. *It's time to let go.* He holds Brodie tightly, pulling him in close, tenderly, firm yet gentle.

'NO!' Rob shouts, surprised at the strength in his own voice. 'No, he's my son and you can't have him!'

'Daddy!' Brodie sobs and strains against Mr Anderson's grip, his small white hand stretching out, reaching desperately for Rob. Rob reaches out and takes it. He's surprised Mr Anderson doesn't try to stop him.

He's not your son, Mr Anderson says softly, lowering those huge baby-blue eyes. *If he is anyone's son he is ours.*

'He is,' says Rob, and suddenly he's fighting back tears. 'He is my son, and you can't take him from me.' He squeezes Brodie's fingers and his next words are a plea, not a demand: 'You can't take him.'

We must, says Anderson, and now he takes a few steps backward, pulling Brodie with him into the lapping water's edge. Rob follows stupidly, still clinging to Brodie's fingers like they're his anchor to the world. The water makes him gasp, it's so cold, surging around his feet and ankles. Anderson looks to his colleague. The colleague nods and fiddles with a device in its large strange hand. *This was a mistake. It must be corrected.*

'It mustn't.' Rob suddenly realises he's ready to beg. 'I won't tell anyone, I'll go along with it, no one need ever know.'

He will know, says Anderson, indicating Brodie with a nod of his head, *and that could prove dangerous, for him and for you.*

And then it happens. Fast and slow at the same time. Anderson gives Rob's wrist one swift, firm jerk and suddenly he can't hold on any more. They take two steps backward, starting to shimmer and glow, Brodie cradled limply between them. There's a rushing sound, like blood pumping into his ear canals unbearably fast and hard, or the sea crashing over his head.

We're truly sorry, says Anderson. He doesn't raise his voice but the words still come crystal clear into Rob's head, despite the swirling noise all around them. *The only condolence we can offer is no one will remember him at all.*

'I will!' screams Rob, suddenly furious, outraged that this stupid ugly shark-faced bastard has the nerve not only to steal his son away, but to claim that none of it will mean anything if he does. 'Everyone else might forget, but I'll remember him! I'll remember and I'll come for him. I'll come for you, Brodie, wherever they take you, I'll come for you.'

You won't.

Brodie is crying and straining, straining towards him. Rob strains, too, stretching his fingers, willing them to be longer, to be stronger, to pull Brodie back to him. A rush of air swirls the sea water, flinging it into his face, stinging his eyes, getting into his open mouth, but he ignores it, continues to reach, to stretch, he can make it, he knows it, he has to. He wades out further and further, up to his thighs, up to his waist, up to his neck, the coldness of the water making it harder and harder to breathe, to move. It's like the room with Mr Anderson, like his arms and legs are trapped by bonds he can't see, much less break. Lights dance on the surface of the rippling water. Waves rise up, splashing his face, pushing him back towards the beach. A strange feeling comes over him, a melancholic sense of nostalgia and love that might be his, or Brodie's or Anderson's or the whole world's and then the light flares a final time, magnesium bright and he is lost in it.

*

Okay. Don't panic. You've just gone blind. Not a big deal.

His hands go to his face to check whether his eyes are open or not.

They're shut, you bellend. Come on now. Open them and think.

The opening them bit's not too bad. Kind of like peeling two strips of Velcro from the surface of each eyeball, but doable. The thinking bit's harder. Nothing makes sense. The tent doesn't make sense.

I may be pretty fucked up right now, but I'm pretty sure I don't live in a tent. Reasonably sure of that.

His phone is flashing – a voicemail. He reaches for it, presses it to his ear and his finger knows which buttons to press even if he doesn't. The voice is familiar, though he can't place it yet.

'Kidder? Bellamy rang. He was worried about... I told him where you were, I'm sorry... Not the campsite, just the village... But still... I'm sorry.'

The guy does sound sorry, really sorry and sad and hesitant and afraid. Rob supposes he should ring him back at some point to reassure him that everything's okay, nobody's hurt. Well, maybe he's hurt a little.

Slowly, painfully, he sits up. Fire explodes down his spine, in his knees and his right ankle, as if that one small movement has awoken his entire body. His grunt of discomfort must've been pretty loud, because the shape in the sleeping bag next to him stirs.

I hope that's a woman.

He realises he fears not that it's a man, but that it's something else. What else he can't imagine.

She moves and lifts her head, her eyes squinting, tiny raw holes in her face.

'Oh,' says Rob, 'It's you.' He doesn't say her name because he can't remember it. He knows she's a woman from work, though.

'Did we...' she asks, sitting up slowly and looking around the tent. Her movement dislodges an empty bottle and it clinks against her discarded shoes. 'What's that?' she asks.

He's still thinking about the other question and says: 'I don't know. Maybe. My head hurts.'

'It doesn't even have a label,' she croaks, holding up the bottle for him to see. 'We could have been drinking fucking turps. That's how my throat feels, at least.'

Slowly they come round and awkwardly they pack up the tent and he knows that probably neither of them should be driving, but the thought of sitting around here trying to make conversation with some woman he hardly knows is just unbearable. She's just about to get in the car, Jane or Jewel or whatever, when she stops and says: 'Whose is that?'

There's a child's torch lying in the back seat, one of the chunky bright red ones with big yellow buttons and a sturdy blue plastic trim. Rob frowns and picks it up. For a moment, a memory drifts towards him, an image of his hands and a smaller pair both making animal shapes in the torch's bright beam, a child's light laughter, so infectious it brings a smile to his lips even now.

'I think...' he says, narrowing his eyes and thinking so hard, it's like fingernails digging into his brain, retrieving the information is actually painful. 'I think I used to have a son.'

'Oh—' She stops and he realises she's looking at him differently now, like maybe he's not just some dickhead who takes women to the coast and gets them drunk on meths. He notices, too, that she doesn't question his haziness, his uncertainty at what should surely be an absolute, so maybe she has that weird feeling, too. 'What happened to him?'

'I...' He thinks harder, and the pain in his head gets worse and spreads to his chest and his stomach, until he feels like he's going to puke and he knows that the only thing that will bring relief is to stop, to stop thinking about him, about the boy, but he can't. And it all floods in on him, like a crashing wave, all of it, the sex shop and the made-up boy and how aliens made him real and then they took him back. And it all seems mad, so mad and he can scarcely believe it himself even though he knows it to be true, so how could he expect her to believe it, his friend, this Jules, this wonderful woman who stuck with him through all of it even though she thought he was losing his grip on reality, how could he put her through all that again? He shrugs and opens the car door. 'I don't really want to talk about it.' She's nodding gently and maybe she remembers their friendship even if she's forgotten everything else. Maybe that's a good thing. Something passes between them, some kind of shared feeling, and even if it isn't a memory of their experiences, it's warm and it feels good. She slides into the driving seat but she doesn't start the car, just keeps looking at him, expectant. She needs to know more before she can draw a line under this and take them back to their lives.

Anything he says about the kid will sound like a lie, because so much of it was, and the only parts that weren't don't make any sense. And he's done with lying, he's done with kidding himself that a made-up life is somehow better than a real one, but he has to tell one more, a final white lie to keep them both safe. He thinks he'll get away with this one, as long as it really is the last.

'Perhaps I'll tell you about him some time.'

Bookclub and writers' circle notes for
Beyond Kidding can be found at
www.fairlightbooks.com

ABOUT THE AUTHOR

Lynda Clark graduated from Nottingham Trent University with a BA in English Literature and an MA in Creative Writing. She has completed a PhD in Creative and Critical Writing. In 2015 she won the BBC Award at the WriterSlam, and the Canada and Europe region Commonwealth Short Story Prize in 2017.

Lynda previously worked as a writer and producer for a videogame company where she created in-game dialogue and marketing copy. She was also a bookseller at Waterstones Nottingham and will shortly be joining the University of Dundee as a Research Fellow in Narrative and Play.

Beyond Kidding is Lynda's debut novel.

FAIRLIGHT BOOKS

LOU GILMOND

The Tale of Senyor Rodriguez

A dead man's house. A dead man's clothes.
And a dead man's wine cellar...

It's 1960s Mallorca. Thomas Sebastian, an English conman, is hiding out in the house of the late Senyor Rodriguez – carousing, partying, and falling in love with his beautiful but impossibly young neighbour, Isabella Ferretti.

As the boundary between lies and reality blurs, Thomas' fiction spirals out of control in ways that are quite unexpected.

'A gripping, atmospheric novel, with a brilliant twist.'
—G.D.Sanders, author of *The Taken Girls*

NIAL GIACOMELLI

The Therapist

*'I am levitating above the curvature of the earth.
Weightless, unencumbered. Flung like a comet out of
the atmosphere and into some great beyond.'*

In this bittersweet and hauntingly surreal tale, a couple finds
the distance between them mirrored in a strange epidemic
sweeping the globe. Little by little, each victim becomes
transparent, their heart beating behind a visible rib cage, an
intricate network of nerves left hanging in mid-air. Finally, the
victims disappear entirely, never to be seen again.

'I dreamt we were at sea,' she says.

*'If the population of the world had vanished while I was
reading Nial Giacomelli's beautifully observed novella, I'm
not sure I would have noticed. It's that good.'*
—Christopher Stanley, author of *The Forest is Hungry*

SOPHIE VAN LLEWYN

Bottled Goods

*Longlisted for The Women's Prize for Fiction 2019,
The Republic of Consciousness Prize 2019 and
The People's Book Prize 2018*

When Alina's brother-in-law defects to the West, she and her husband become persons of interest to the secret services and both of their careers come grinding to a halt.

As the strain takes its toll on their marriage, Alina turns to her aunt for help – the wife of a communist leader and a secret practitioner of the old folk ways.

Set in 1970s communist Romania, this novella-in-flash draws upon magic realism to weave a captivating tale of everyday troubles.

*'Sophie van Llewyn's stunning debut novella
shows us there is no dystopian fiction as
frightening as that which draws on history.'*
—Christina Dalcher, author of *VOX*

*'Sophie van Llewyn has brought light into an
era which cast a long shadow.'*
—Joanna Campbell, author of
Tying Down the Lion